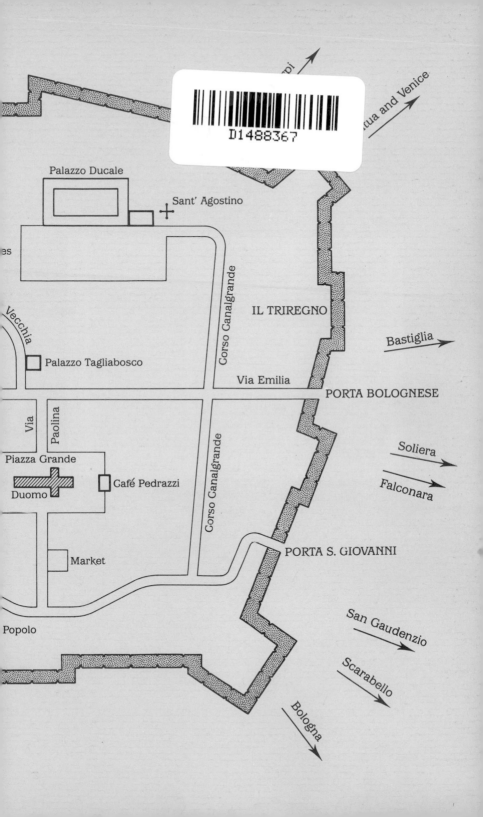

The Strangers' Gallery

The Strangers' Gallery

by
Jonathan Keates

Hamish Hamilton · London

HAMISH HAMILTON LTD

Penguin Books Ltd, 27 Wrights Lane, London W8 5TZ (Publishing & Editorial)
and Harmondsworth, Middlesex, England (Distribution & Warehouse)
Viking Penguin Inc., 40 West 23rd Street, New York, New York 10010, U.S.A.
Penguin Books Australia Ltd, Ringwood, Victoria, Australia
Penguin Books Canada Ltd, 2801 John Street, Markham, Ontario, Canada L3R 1B4
Penguin Books (N.Z.) Ltd, 182–190 Wairau Road, Auckland 10, New Zealand

First published in Great Britain 1987 by
Hamish Hamilton Ltd

British Library Cataloguing in Publication Data

Keates, Jonathan
    The Strangers' gallery.
    I. Title
    823'.914[F]   PR6061.E25

    ISBN 0-241-12335-6

Photoset in Linotron Times by
Rowland Phototypesetting Ltd
Bury St Edmunds, Suffolk
Printed and bound in Great Britain by
Butler and Tanner Ltd, Frome and London

To Gianni Guidetti

I

THERE IS THE country of curves, the country of heights and depths, the country of profusion and the country of desolation, but this of Villafranca is the country of straight lines. Imagine a broad, flat plain, its western distances bounded by the bluish-grey bar of the Apennines, and everywhere else towards Ferrara, Bologna or Mantua stretching away in a limitless regularity, a mirror of the infinite world. Put upon this blank a grid of ditches and channels, each with its level bank, striping the yellow and green fields. Add to this the ranks of lacy poplars, the grizzled brick bell towers of the churches, and the absolute roads laid point to point across the landscape like pieces of tape, with a rationality born less of benevolence than of despair. Here and there, gently intrusive to the design, stand the farms and country houses, in parks of beech, chestnut and elm, with big colonnaded barns, discreet chapels and mounded ice-houses in the grounds. In winter freezing fogs steal up off the river, and the orchards and vineyards glisten with damp. Summer makes the towns and villages of the unshaded plain turn colour in the heat, as an ochreous patina of dust spreads over everything. Yet neither these violent transformations nor the tyranny of unbending lines become monotonous. In this workaday country, without pose or suavity, the traveller reckons with the sublime commonplace, a directness in lights, shapes and colours which lingers naggingly in the mind's eye.

It hardly seemed thus to the young man who rode his horse

along the road from Rubiera to Villafranca one spring afternoon in 1847. The labouring folk and people in carriages who passed might have seen that both he and his mount were still fresh, and that the ride was ambling rather than exercise. His hands lay slackly with the reins on the saddlebow; now and then he turned to glance at the fields, or swung round to watch a yoke of oxen go by, or the lumbering diligence with its clutter of bags on the roof. There was no animation in his pale, fair features as he watched. Those who looked at him once, and looked again, might have noticed the overwhelming boredom of demeanour which a vague smile thinly concealed. His gaze was inspired less by interest itself than by the need of some interest to experience. His face, long and thin like that of his own horse, was clouded with touches of impatience and satiety.

At that moment it could not have mattered less to him to know where he was. The duchy of Villafranca, with its dependent municipalities of Reggio, Carpi and Massa, its sovereign highness Carlo Francesco IV, and all the customary furniture of Austrian auxiliaries, police spies, passport inspections, taxes at the city gates and a rash of rescripts, *attenzioni* and *avvertenze*, was at present nothing more substantial in the mind of this boy than if it had been Spitzbergen or Kamchatka. The sense of a charmless mediocrity in everything about him united with his loneliness to exacerbate the feeling that he was an alien, almost though not wholly without friends in a country whose rhetoric of association defied him to master it. Perhaps his was not a smile, only a tightening grimace as he felt his nineteen years and choked back a rancid self-pity at the contemplation of the fate which placed him here. He could not feel homesick, since he had never possessed what is ordinarily thought of as a home, yet he imagined a dozen places where he could have been happier.

The boy turned the sharp corner of a side road running down towards a big, yellow house islanded in its shrubby park. The sweep gates were open, and he wondered what would happen if, with a sudden perversity, he were to canter up the drive and announce himself. What would happen, he thought sardonically, is that they would shrug, in their dreadful, eloquent, resigned way, and ask the maid to bring me a dish of *minestra*. A surge of ennui engulfed him as he sat up in the saddle looking blankly at the house. Its shutters were all drawn to. It was still March. Of course there would be nobody there.

Just then his ear caught the sound of a carriage. Down the inexorable highroad came a light britzka, which pulled up suddenly as it drew abreast of him. Though the whole equipage, from the fetlocks of the horses to the fringes of the hammercloth, was grey with dust, there was an air of listless, over-exercised grandeur about it, matched in the face of the woman who now leaned from the window and beckoned to the boy to come near. The wisdom of her eyes both gave and received emphasis within a singularly plain countenance. He raised his hat and looked away, bewildered.

'Where, good God, are we?' she murmured, as if talking to herself. Then to him she said: 'Villafranca? Is it far?'

He looked at the coachman and then furtively at her. Noticing this she said: 'Antonio is deaf, and in any case says that he does not understand you people here in Emilia. We have come from Milan.'

'I am English, signora . . .' the boy began.

'Then do you even know where we are?'

'Yes, you are less than a league from Villafranca. Over there is the road, and there you can see . . . well, no, perhaps you can't . . . the cathedral tower. It's quite famous, I'm told. There's a bucket on the top.'

When she laughed, he heard the different laughter of another woman inside the carriage.

'We shall enjoy this tower with the bucket, I expect.'

She sat back, and her companion now looked out at him.

She was almost still a girl, hardly older than he.

'Tell us,' asked she gravely, 'why they put the – this bucket there.'

As he told them the story, which he never had cause to tell anyone before, of how the Villafrancans in the struggles of Guelph and Ghibelline made war on Bologna which ended in the carrying off from the town of a single leather bucket, he found himself held beyond distraction by the features whose alertness he now seemed to control. There was, for example, that effect of lingering regret which a lightness of colour in the eyes invariably produces. The grey ribbon of the girl's bonnet threw the pallor of her complexion into melancholy relief. Despite these things her

3

address had an eagerness, an evident wish to engage, marked by barely perceptible movements of her mouth as she listened, and by the play of her fingers grasping the carriage door. Because she did not smile he was emboldened to go on, as if she expected to hear more, dropping the reins and waving his hands about in nervous enthusiasm.

'And that was all?'

'Yes, I think so. The tower is called the Ghirlandina, you know, because when the Jewish exiles from Seville came to Villafranca they said it reminded them of the Giralda in that city. So Giraldina, Ghirlandina, no?'

'Well, it is charming whatever the reason,' she said rather loftily, 'but that must have been because you told it all so prettily.'

For a moment they said nothing, the two of them, but stared at one another in silent appraisal. Then the older woman leaned forward and touched her companion's arm. Starting as if awoken, she called out loudly to the coachman 'O Antonio!', inclined her head towards the boy by way of thanks, and the britzka trundled off along the road.

He did not stay watching it for more than a moment. His first thought was to gallop forward like an outrider to conduct them into the city, and pulling up his horse he put him to a vigorous trot. Then, reflecting, he slowed to a walk when he had got himself to where he could keep the carriage always in view.

A curious excitement began stealthily to take the place of his residual gloom. Two ladies in a britzka, coming from Milan, had stopped to ask him the way, and he had retailed to them a trivial story of a tower and a bucket. Yet something in the encounter, he could scarcely say what, held out a promise to him, caused his firmer grip upon the reins and made him see in that picture of straight lines, of ordered poplars and mathematical fields, a complex life whose newness almost alarmed him.

Having crossed the river, the boy reined up beyond the bridge to watch with intense, gratified relief as the carriage bowled along the last stretch of road and up to the customs post at the Porta della Duchessa. He looked at the town, at Villafranca. He saw the delicate vertical of the tower of the Ghirlandina, the angular pediment of San Domenico, the sombre grey horizontal of the duke's palace and the tilt and fall of huddled roofs. The

4

strange, capricious flushes of light cast upon the place by the waning afternoon gave it a welcoming blandness which, to the boy's unbelieving gaze, was more in the nature of a threat. Thus the bastions projecting from its huge pinkish girdle of walls were like the tufted talons of a hawk's claw. Confused, he turned his head away.

Neither the bitterness of former sensations nor his present embarrassment of pleasure disturbed him now. What moved, what stirred, was a recollection of the girl's solemn face looking out at him from the carriage window, and the feeling that the town, feared until this moment, offered him, however un-accountably, the same kind of certainty. He looked again at Villafranca, affronting him with a suddenly achieved beauty. He wanted to run from it headlong.

'Deuce take it!' he cried and, pulling his horse's head up, he rode down towards the city.

 2

EDWARD WAS SEVEN years old when he last saw England. At nineteen he could remember nothing of it, though his memory of everything else he had ever experienced was amazingly precise. Yet he knew himself to be English. It was not simply that he was reminded of the fact on those occasions when a familiarity with alien scenes lulled him into complacency, but that the sight of his own countrymen made him realize with embarrassment that he could not pass for anything else. He spoke Italian, German and French without an accent, and his parents' unwillingness to pass through any city without impressing a knowledge of their presence upon the dukes and princes of the locality meant that his manners, since he had been able to walk, were polished almost to extinction. A dispassionate survey of his own image in the looking glass, however, brought such sophistications to nothing. In the perpetual unruliness of his reddish brown hair and the way whereby his long legs and arms seemed to defy the ingenuity of even the most skilful tailor, there was something which stamped him for what he was.

And not by these tokens alone. Neither rebellious curls nor ill-fitting trousers offered the ultimate confirmation, tendered at last by that very glance returned to him from the mirror. Held within it, like the wing of an insect or the fragment of a leaf in a piece of amber, was an imperishable innocence. Through the lattices of his own detachment from the world Edward gazed eagerly out in search of whatever should invite him to engage.

6

The bitterness of solitude covered simple intentions towards truth and honesty, though it could never destroy them. And it was this part of him which had not grown old, a child's trusting openness, that joined him in some way to the English he had met about the world. He saw it concealed, as letters sewn into the lining of a coat, under that freeborn bluster with which they addressed themselves to the people at inns and frontier posts and gaming rooms. He found it hidden likewise behind that delusive glaze of reserve which gave Englishmen the fame of being cold and unsociable. Beneath the noise and rudeness, and the boorish reluctance to learn languages and customs which on numberless occasions ashamed him, lay a wild, unregenerate spontaneity of impulse, disdaining community or understanding.

His parents were singularly without this. At more indulgent moments Edward was ready to concede that he might only have failed to notice it, though as yet he was hardly convinced. Even in his father, whose valetudinarian crotchets had driven them abroad in the first place and kept them there ever since, but whom he had lately developed a certain disposition to pity, he deplored that eternal knowingness, that inability to betray surprise, that sense of tired familiarity with everything, the antidote to passion or enthusiasm.

In his mother the process was complete. Edward had long ago relinquished annoyance at her, and his keen acknowledgment of pain on first realizing she did not love him was brief enough. It was as if she had formed her opinion of her son on the vague displeasure of a first meeting and had never cared to change it since. Now and then she caught him looking at her with an enquiring scrutiny and angrily bade him stop staring so. It was because, he perceived, she was afraid he was ready to unmask her incomparable dishonesty. But so long as he was affable in company and knew how to dance and hand a lady to the carriage and make a leg at an archduchess she would not hate him. The one thing he had learned instinctively to suppress in her presence was the least sign of fervour or intensity. Any fallal of that kind she would never forgive.

At moments when he paused to wonder what he was doing in the world, he saw that, where other children grew up because of their parents, he had grown up in spite of his. He had never, in any case, been granted what might strictly be called a childhood.

The place of games and toys and easy pardon for misdemeanour was taken by the company of books and the handful of children like himself, with whom friendship was finally impossible because of their vagabond lives. The courage, meanwhile, of a succession of tutors was measured by their ability to accommodate his increasingly formidable wisdom.

Thus, like some lonely botanist glimpsed afar off among the fields at work with notebook and collecting bag, Edward had trailed about on the edges of the world for a dozen years, observing and committing to memory in the prescient expectation that such an archive would, at some moment yet unknown, prove useful to him. It was at least something to do.

Elegant nomads, the family had early evolved a seasonal rhythm of movement which only suffered the lightest of variations from year to year. After a spring at Paris, where his father had time to grow sickly and irritable, they set off to the baths of Ems, moving thence, in a weirdly crab-like fashion, to the loucher delights of Homburg and Baden and always contriving to finish the summer at Carlsbad, when the Wiese and the Sprudel were at their most brilliant. The autumn at Vienna was just long enough to convince them that they had better go south before the cold weather began, and the winters were passed most agreeably in Florence.

This year, however, their migration was alarmingly disturbed by the discovery that Mr Rivers, for so long ill in fancy, was now an invalid in earnest. The climate of Naples was prescribed for him, with the proviso that he should retire to Rome should the weather become too hot. It became suddenly unthinkable that Edward should go with them, and Lady Augusta opportunely recalled a standing invitation from her youngest sister, the Countess Castelvetro, whom she had neither seen nor thought of since her marriage six years previously. A letter was sent peremptorily announcing Edward's arrival, and he was sent off with a great deal of money and new clothes, accompanied by firm instructions that he was to stop at Villafranca until summoned.

Edward also, until this moment, had never considered his aunt. Her existence in one of those cities on the plains of the Po which are notoriously avoided by travellers held a quite legendary vagueness for him. He was not, perhaps, even now sure that she was altogether a real thing. Never before had he been so alien to his own life. The palace, with its dim, cavernous saloons and beeswax-scented corridors, embodied such unfamiliarity to perfection. He loafed, friendless and alone, through the earliest days in a blank, nerveless expectancy, occasionally touching some hard surface, the top of a table in pietra dura, the pedestal of a marble vase or the alabaster coping of a balustrade, to see if its reality gave way beneath the impressure of his fingers. In Florence, a place clutched at by that part of his memory with any apparent truth remaining in it, the servants at the villino had always smiled. In the Palazzo Castelvetro they preserved a frozen respect, as if they had been their own studied images.

Only at the coming on of dusk could Edward feel a recall of spirit. Then he would go up to his room and stand by the window, not looking out but listening. Sounds, sometimes together, sometimes one by one, began to rise from the city: the dry clatter made by the opening of shutters, the rolling of a cart in the street below, a voice in a lane beyond, calling a name, and the muffled, toneless clank of church bells.

This evening, listening once more, he remembered the two women he had met upon the road not an hour or so before. Moving closer to the window, he walked out onto the balcony and stared along the Corso Canalchiaro, as though he should see the britzka, yellow, dusty, coming again towards him. Then he shrugged and went downstairs to wait for his aunt.

He sat down on one of the spiky gilt chairs in the hall, suddenly regretting that he hadn't put a book into the pocket of his dress coat. Reading, for Edward, was not merely an opiate to solitude, but a way of avoiding the need to talk to others. As the faces of servants removing dishes from the dining room brightened through the shadows like those overpainted figures which re-appear on old canvases, he shrank back a little in returning their civil bows. When the Countess at last came down, it was like a rescue.

Her air of bewildered grandeur, the assumption of a role she could not altogether carry off, had still not quite ceased to embarrass him.

'Dear me,' she exclaimed, 'how handsome you look, quite the *homme du monde*. You favour your grandfather, I think. Old Marchesa Loschi told me the other night that she thought you were *un vero gentleman inglese*.'

Edward smiled weakly. There was a discomforting flirtatious-
ness in his aunt's praise of him.

'Is it next week that my uncle comes back?' he said.

'Or the week after, I suppose,' she answered, sighing. 'He has
to go to Bologna on some business of the estates, I forget what.
Thus I'm the more grateful that you're here, Ned. Now let us be
off, or we shall miss all the music. The Rangoni are noted for
their music, you know. They say that is why they are so poor –
and the oldest family in Villafranca too. But a great-grandfather
a century back used to take the theatre for private performances.
Though, between you and me, that wasn't the only reason.'

He gave her his arm, and the footman, who had been hovering
in the doorway with candles, lighted them out past the staircase.
As they went, Edward saw, hanging back in the darkness, the
gaunt, awkward figure of the house steward, Basevi. Something,
his drab clothes perhaps, the expression in his features almost of
hopelessness, made Edward give him a complicit nod of the
head.

'And what's more,' said the Countess, 'we shall see the
Marchesa Rangoni's famous granddaughter at last. She has
talked of nothing else all month. Everyone in Villafranca, *santo
Dio*, seems to have granddaughters, enough to make me feel
quite ancient.'

Edward looked sidelong at the Countess as they settled themselves behind the coachman, seeing a connexion between her
last remark and the distressed brilliance of her attire. In the
unseasonably warm evening she had ordered them to put down
the top of the carriage, and he dreaded the likelihood of her
remarking, as she had on several previous occasions, that people
who saw them together would take him for her lover. Very
conscious of his height and the length of his neck, he shrank
lower into the cushions.

She said nothing tonight as to lovers, seeming, indeed, more
inclined to that natural wistfulness of which her levity was but an
enforced covering. They drove on in silence towards the arcades
of the Via Emilia, when at length she said:–

'I'm sorry, Ned, that we can't amuse you more here. But I
expect you'll soon find yourself an object of curiosity among
people of your own age and that they will begin inviting you.'

'I've never really cared much for people of my own age,'

rejoined Edward manfully. 'But I always enjoy being with you, aunt.'

She gave a thin laugh. 'I suppose that's the truth. At any rate you are gallant. I like that. Your mother never said anything about it, though mothers don't often notice such things. You and I, Ned, *poveri noi*, are the only English in Villafranca. They pass through, but they none of them stop.'

He knew. He had seen them, scarlet and disputatious, on their way to Venice or Bologna.

'There's nobody else?'

'No. Only the two of us.'

In a country where horses are often put to merely as an excuse for not walking, they appeared to have gone inordinately far across the city. The houses grew more dingy, their fronts blotched with holes where the plaster had fallen away to show the raw brick beneath, and on several the shutters hung drunkenly off a single hinge. There were those sudden, swift smells of decay in the air which, in these towns of the plain, announce the gamy, fly-blown approach of summer. Turning from one of the lanes, they came out onto a broad piazza, shaped like an egg, its buildings so blank of windows and doors as to look as though they had turned their backs upon it. Utterly dark and empty, mottled here and there by tiny, pallid gleams of light, it was an immense drum of silence. Edward, half fearful, asked:–

'Where is this, aunt?'

'Ah, this,' she looked about her. 'A queer old place, no? This is the Piani d'Ungheria. Not at all fashionable, indeed, but since the Rangoni are what they are they may do as they please. A palace is where one's people have chosen to build it, even if it looks into the ghetto and stands in the Piani d'Ungheria.'

This, then, was the Piani d'Ungheria, a name he had once overheard and kept in his memory ever since, half disbelieving. The Plains of Hungary. He had imagined it as somehow it must be, Villafranca spilling out into a huge, rolling wold, where wild horse herds grazed, the winds moaned in the grasses, and troops of warriors pricked along the horizon of shaggy downland in ant-like lines. But never thus.

It would supply him with something to exercise his mind upon during the evening ahead. He had no great hopes of after-supper entertainments in Villafranca. The houses in which the Countess

11

had already introduced him were notable only for the slavishness with which each copied the other in their flourishes of hospitality. He steeled himself anew to hear the same talk about food and marriages and clothes, to answer the same questions as to his stay in Villafranca, and to be told how very well he spoke Italian, no but truly very well; it was a marvel, where had he learnt it, but it was excellent, and he an Englishman, while the starched folds of his neckcloth scratched his chin and the palms of his hands turned clammy. Music was the only mitigation.

As they went upstairs, the Countess took the opportunity to whisper:–

'They're a little fast, you see, the Rangoni. Not always quite the thing. They don't go to court more than once a year, and the Duke never asks them there – not since what happened in '31.'

A great many things had apparently taken place in 1831. People shuddered nostalgically as they mentioned it to Edward, then promptly refused to say anything further. He nodded sagely, so as to quell his aunt, who was threatening to embarrass him again. Soon he would hear her trying to use the lilting Emilian dialect, which makes every statement sound like a question, and see her acquaintances smile indulgently while they tried with lethal tact to edge her back towards pure Tuscan.

The music room, or at any rate that large room in which music was playing, was unwontedly dim and cool where he expected it to be hot, glaring and noisy. At some early moment of the last century it had been painted on two sides in grisaille to simulate the columns, frieze and cornice of a temple, and the prevailing sense of unworldly solemnity given by this decoration seemed to pervade the faces of the listeners to the concert. For they were, as Edward soon saw, most of them actually listening. At the far end a man and a woman accompanied by a piano were performing the duet from the prison scene of the *Due Foscari* of Verdi. The three musicians were all very young, and though, in his judgment, they lacked the force of a more seasoned talent, it was a performance which carried with it a certain sort of truth. Beyond them, which he had not at first noticed, two small doors, opening like cracks in the spectral illusion of a landscape with ruins which covered the wall, framed other motionless groups of the Marchesa's guests. The scene, wholly unguessed at, challenging his cynicism to deny its existence, disarmed him at once. He wanted to snap his fingers for it to disappear, for them all to be yawning and sweating under the wax-lights, to hear some dismal account of a foul Lambrusco at somebody's table or yet another joke about Metternich and the Papal amnesty. Left undefended by his own coldness, he started to feel afraid.

The sound of the distant gondoliers rose off the canal and Lucrezia and Jacopo sang of the hope which yet remained to them. The duet closed at a pitch of mournful serenity. Through the dry rattling of applause across the company, the Countess began walking down the room and greeting those she knew. Edward did not follow, but stood to one side of the doorway, hoping that nobody would speak to him. Shadowed against the grey wall, he could stay unremarked, nursing his strange fear. Faces, vague or preoccupied, slipped past him, once or twice he was acknowledged with a smile or a nod, a girl blushed when she mistook him for someone else, a young man he did not know gave him a good evening. He was glad that none of them paused. The music began again, and again the extraordinary stillness mantled the room. Everyone stood where they found them-selves, as in a children's game. Since music in Italy nearly always means vocal exhibition, he was surprised to see the accompanist of the two singers sitting down alone to the piano, and to recognize a series of improvisatory figures he had heard last in Carlsbad a year or more back.

'Do you know this piece? It's Weber's *Invitation to the Dance*, I think, but I can't be sure.'

Startled, he turned, seeing no one at first and conscious of the surrounding darkness. Then, close almost to the touch, he saw her, standing alone like himself, listening intently to the music, with the same slight parting of the lips and animated gravity of expression he had noticed that afternoon. He looked at her, incredulous of her presence, as if it were the fulfilment of everything in the room which most frightened him. When the waltz tune began, with its exhilarating sequence of bounding chords like somebody taking the stairs two at a time, he put his hands to his face to stop himself crying out aloud. Then swiftly she glanced at him, meeting his gaze as his arms dropped to his sides and his mouth fell open. He could no longer move. If he did so, something within him would break. The music's glassy, febrile textures seemed to protect him against any response to her invocation, and he longed for it not to end. When it did so, the two of them made no instinctive motion of applause, remaining as they had been, looking at one another in silence, until at last she said:–

'Does it distress you, this saying nothing?'

He tried to smile. 'It's you who won't speak.'

'Come, you know that's not true.' She looked cross. 'Are you always this dishonest with people? For that matter, were you telling the truth with your story to us this afternoon about the bucket on top of the church tower?'

Stung, he cried: 'How dare you doubt it?'

'I've every right to do so.'

'Forgive me, *signorina*, but what right have you to my honesty?'

'Oh, pooh, don't be so lofty with me! As for my silence . . .'

'For your silence, yes, I was afraid of it. Not because of you, but for myself.'

'Why?'

'Because people use it to hide things.'

'And when they are thinking?'

'That is all fiddlesticks, whoever thought in silence? And it was yours as well – or perhaps you'd simply have said that you were quiet because you were overcome by the power of the music, or something of that sort.'

She laughed, as if laughter were a concession of seriousness.

'Ah, perhaps. In any case I shouldn't care what they played as long as I heard music.'

'It's the first I have heard in Villafranca. To listen to, that is.'

'Your opera here is held to be as fine as ours at Milan. In fact I believe it is the only thing in which you can rival Milan,' she added with a certain impatience. Her directness, accompanied by an increasingly evident nervousness of manner as she closed and unclosed her fan and clenched her gloved fingers into a fist, confused him. He felt bound to answer her, resenting the impulse at the same time.

'It isn't my city, *signorina*. I'm only stopping here at my aunt's until they all go away for the summer. My uncle is Count Castelvetro. But only my aunt is here tonight. You'll meet her, I expect.'

'And your uncle, where is he?'

14

'Oh, he doesn't care for women's company, I believe. Some think him strange for that reason.'

'Why should they?' It was as if he had aimed the remark at her.

'There are men who don't. Do you, English boy, who talk such a deal about yourself?'

Nettled at the injustice, he sensed nevertheless that in some way she was relieving her own feelings by criticizing him. She must have caught something of his annoyance, for she instantly said:–

'You mustn't think I'm going to ask you to forgive me, for I'm not. I say what I think.'

When it suits you to do so, thought Edward resentfully. Just then the musicians began to reassemble, and he heard someone exclaim: 'Magnificent! They are going to do 'Suoni la tromba' and Arturo's scene with Elvira, from the *Puritani*. The Marchesa has asked for it particularly. The two basses are from Parma, really capital, she says.'

'Do you . . . I mean, do you like Bellini's music?' he asked tentatively, half knowing that he had betrayed himself, yet flinching when she said: 'That is not an answer to any of my questions.'

'Then you can take it as another part of my dishonesty,' rejoined Edward with a discomfited laugh. She drew away from him, her pale face moon-like against the shadow.

'Perhaps after all we had nothing to say to each other,' she said, and flung off down the room, never looking back.

Only for a moment did he think of following her, but a prevailing obstinacy made him stay close to the door in hopes of catching a glance from her as she left. The day seemed to have piled upon him huge burdens of superfluous emotion, which he could not find the spirit in himself to move. He was glad she had not seen the trembling of his lip or the tearful brilliance of his eyes. Or maybe she had guessed at it, even contrived to bring it there. He felt mean, like a whipped lurcher. Should he now go home, losing his way in the featureless alleys of the city, or stay dodging about in the shadows, listening to pieces of which ordinarily he was fond, but which here, in their nakedness of sentiment, made his efforts at composure ridiculous? The Countess, however, abruptly redeemed him from decision, coming and clutching his arm as though he would fly away.

15

'How *gênant* this music is! They'll keep on till morning, you know, and I'm sure,' she yawned, 'that we've missed the best of it. One only comes here to *farsi vivo* and hears a snatch or two, and then one goes. Unless one quite raves about music. And besides, it is so late.'

Edward felt too weak to protest. In the hall he shook the shawl over his aunt's thin shoulders and saw her looking down at her dress in disappointed vanity. The mixture of sympathy and contempt he felt towards her emboldened him against yielding, for the moment, to an access of wretchedness. It was not her fault that she was bored by music and disliked the Rangoni, though he wondered what the young woman of the britzka would have said as to her sincerity.

They crossed the Piani d'Ungheria, blacker and more hollow than before. Neither spoke until they were out and lumbering through the close midnight streets.

'The famous grandchild,' began the Countess, 'did you meet her? I did. A pert young miss, with the affectation of being twice her age, who arrived today from Pavia or somewhere, with her guardian, a Signora Lupo, a banker's widow of whom nobody seems to know anything. The Rangoni of course are too proud to say much. They think a mere association with them is enough. This Cristina Bentivoglio is an orphan.' Misinterpreting her nephew's astonishment, she went on: 'Yes, you are going to tell me that you met them on the road. I would have asked you why you hadn't said so earlier, but you're growing just like everyone else in Villafranca with your secrets.'

'I didn't know this afternoon that she was Marchesa Rangoni's granddaughter.'

'Would it have made any difference if you had?'

'I don't think so.'

When they came down beside the open space before the tower of the Ghirlandina, white and tilting into the night, Edward thought of the story of the bucket.

'Aunt,' said he, very seriously.

'Yes?'

'Do you have secrets?'

She answered – which was surprising – 'Some. Marchesa Rangoni asked whether you might not like to visit there soon. I remembered what you told me about not caring for people of

16

your own age, so I said that I didn't think you would.' He was silent. 'Or would you?' The carriage swung into the courtyard and they got down.

'We'll talk more of it in the morning,' she said, as the sleepy footman carried the candles before them into the house. 'But I expect you would like to go there.'

She offered him her cold cheek to kiss, as if he were to give her a benediction. As she turned to follow her maid, he asked:—

'Aunt, is there any particular reason why Signorina Bentivoglio should have come to Villafranca?'

'The Marchesa was going to tell me, but we were interrupted when they brought the cake round. Italian cakes are horrid, don't you think? Perhaps it is because she is fond of her poor aunt, like you. Good night.'

Edward did not go directly to bed. Once in his room, he sat down in the angular little armchair and started to read *The Vicar of Wakefield*. It was his favourite book, and he had read it a hundred times if he had read it once, but now the story of Moses and the gross of green spectacles and Mr Burchell who cried out 'Fudge!' to Lady Blarney and Miss Caroline Amelia Wilhelmina Skeggs could not divert him. Sighing, he put it down and went to open the window. The night air was still full of the moist warmth which had fallen upon the city during the afternoon, and an earth-smelling freshness of flowers and leaves, which he had not known in Villafranca before, came to him on the light gusts of wind that eddied the dust about in the streets below. He stood on the balcony as he had earlier done, but this time not listening.

Confusedly at first, he thought of the things which had happened to him that day. He thought of the shuttered house on the road, of Basevi's greasy coat, of 'Speranza dolce ancora' in the feigned temple of the Rangoni Palace, of his aunt's secrets, of Signora Lupo's sagging face, of the yellow britzka among the straight ridges of the fields, and of the city seen in the ingratiating clarity of late afternoon. And to all these, defining or explaining each, his imagination sought to add a remembrance of her as he had seen her first, alert at the carriage window, or when she had appeared from the profound shadows of the music room, or at the moment she had hurried away from him as though nursing some unaccountable offence. Their meeting tonight, freed at its

17

beginning from any bland sociability, was, he realized, a determined collision. He did not know why, any more than he knew the reason for her awakening within him a charge of feeling he scarcely knew himself to possess. His earliest mortification had yielded now to the anger in which he already heard himself remonstrating with her for daring to accuse him of her own faults. If this were so and the rage endured, then might she not burn with an answering fury, and the two of them run seeking one another up and down Villafranca like paladins in the field? Better this than never seeing her again.

He thought of her, Cristina Bentivoglio, an orphan, with her nervous fingers and the catch in her voice as he last heard her speak, in the tall drab-fronted palace across the Piani d'Ungheria. Once, when he was much younger, ten or twelve maybe, he had been taken for a picnic with some other children on the grassy slopes of a fortress beside a river. Inside the ruined walls, overgrown with houseleek and wallflowers, there was a keep with four towers and inside the towers, up and up, ran a ladder to each worm-eaten floor. Towards these he had wandered, accompanied by a friend, the shadow of whose insouciant bravery offered protection, and by a thin, severe girl who had made herself their companion. The stones were very hot in the sun, and at first they amused themselves by trying to catch the lizards which flickered across them. Then they went in under the towers and called out 'Aaoohh!' to hear the echo come back 'Aaoohh!' His friend had begun, quite fearlessly, to climb the ladders, and the two of them, Edward and the tall girl, stood silent below, hearing him call to them as he scrambled from floor to floor. Then, with a kind of glee, she had dared him to climb as well, and at first he had not dared, until she began to tease him with cowardice, and he knew that, though he could not, he must climb. So he began, his mouth dry with fear, feeling his boots scrabbling for a toe-hold and his wrists cracking as he grasped the splintery rungs of the ladder. He thought of himself falling, his body spinning backwards into a heap on the weed-grown floor of the tower. Then he felt his friend's hand clasp his own and hoist him up onto the wormy planks. They had stood there a moment, he breathless with his own realization of safety, his friend exhilarated by the daring which had brought him so high. When they got down again, slowly, carefully, the girl, he saw, waited to

18

taunt him. But his friend looked at her and she said nothing. And none of them said anything more, but went out, kicking desultorily at the grass and stones, to play with the others by the river.

Something in this evening vividly recalled the moment. It was as though this precious Cristina, with her hankering for some notional honesty and her consequent refusal to allow him any quarter, had defied his composure for the sake of what lay within him. Their encounter, however trivial and fretful, carried its own justification. Except that in Villafranca he confronted his challenger quite friendless and alone.

His hands pressed the smooth marble coping of the balcony. Remembering Basevi's glance of unchanged hopelessness, he said aloud, almost without knowing why: 'I hope experience does not make me hard,' and felt the first chill tremor of morning on him as the cocks crew and the palest finger of light came into the sky.

 3

THEREAFTER HE COULD think of no one else. An invisible presence in the shape of Cristina seemed to dominate his every action. Hers was the system, the rhetoric, the decree by which his slightest moments of existence were suddenly governed. Passion, which in his boyish way he had despised or wondered at in others, now ruled him, detaching him from instinctive life in its ruthless insistence on defining everything by reference to the lover's imagined will.

Yet, despite the Countess's hint as to another invitation for him to the Rangoni, nothing came. He might call and thank the Marchesa, but politeness would allow no distinction of Signorina Bentivoglio to be made, nor might she ask him. Youthful impatience, however, and a pardonable selfishness made Edward believe that he deserved better from Cristina than to become the slave of her recollected image. His daily ride was now given over for walks through the frowzy lanes beyond the cathedral as far as the mouth of the Piani d'Ungheria, where he stopped, fearful of crossing it and meeting anyone he knew and thus being thought a fool for staring across the empty immensity of the square towards the ugly red palace beyond. Once, in a clear silence of early afternoon, he heard somebody there playing the piano. Once he saw Signora Lupo's yellow carriage come out under the arch, and ran off directly.

Those two palaces, Rangoni and Castelvetro, placed at either end of the city, were for Edward the very types of danger and security. The one, tall and frowning as a fortress, its roofs clustered round a squat brick tower, menaced him with his own timidity as he stood looking into its strange windows, dented in the walls as if by the blows of a chisel. The other, lifeless unless informed by his own presence, he now greeted with a subdued relief as he caught sight of its rational lines of grey shutters at the bottom of the Corso Canalchiaro, and quickened his pace towards the gateway, with the Castelvetro *stemma* and coronet, into the courtyard.

In this courtyard there was one thing Edward specially loved, a positive badge of achieved safety. At the end farthest from the street, high in the pediment, was an oval medallion of stone, carrying the half-length relief of Evaristo Castelvetro, founder of the house, his head flounced in a great periwig, his hand grasping the baton he bore as field-marshal to the Emperor Leopold against the Turks, gazing from heavy-lidded eyes down a long, spoonlike face, oddly similar, Edward always thought, to his own, as if through some process of adoptive inheritance.

His solitude within the palace contrasted vividly with the furtive, shuddering loneliness of his watches on the Piani d'Ungheria. Here he liked to wander from room to room, his reflections brought to a kind of docility by the insipid existence he had so spurned before. He looked up at the paintings, *Achilles and Briseis*, *A Storm at Sea*, *The Fortress of Preveza*, *Lot and his Daughters*, which he liked because there was no tiresome connoisseur at his elbow to tell him how particularly bad they were, and liked them the more now for their comforting, unobtrusive mediocrity. He sat down on the fat little sofas and ungainly chairs, under the pale washes of fresco which seemed rather to heighten than to allay the tremendousness and distance from each other of the walls, ceiling and floor, hugging himself with pleasure in this effect of diminution, almost hearing his feelings reverberating, like the wings of birds, among the tall looking-glasses and the glimmering leaves of the chandelier.

Not that he thanked Cristina for this. His memory, painfully exact, fretted him with her incessantly. Thinking of what he had said made him in turn think of what he should say if he were ever to see her again, and of how she might answer him. He caught himself mimicking aloud her tones and inflexions of speech, and once, standing before the glass, he made a face at himself, half way between a pout and a glare, that was absurdly her own.

Now, when it rained and the water hissed and gurgled in the gutters and the light from the windows weakened into a cobwebby gloom, he was chafed with a hunger for distraction from her eternally present idea. He thought of seeking out his aunt, with whom on wet afternoons he always had tea – but what indeed could he tell her, supposing he were ready to confide in someone he did not trust? Going to his room, he took out a sheet of paper, preparing to write upon it all he then felt, as if this would purge him of feeling. Such a resource was useless. So was *The Vicar of Wakefield*. He went downstairs again and began wandering along the piano nobile, angrily bursting open each set of doors as he passed through gallery, ballroom and drawing room, and leaving them to swing wide.

At one corner of the house, on the south side looking into the garden, was a library – the Count's insofar as the Countess had her own shelves of Eugène Sue, Harrison Ainsworth and *The Book of Beauty*, and nobody else ever went there. Edward had only looked into it once or twice, and tiptoed quickly out again for fear of meeting his uncle. It was a broad, handsome room, with pillared window-bays between the shelves topped with their eminent busts in wigs and togas, with the dished equine noses and great heehawing chins of the face in the courtyard. In the nearest bay was a pair of brown globes like gigantic walnuts, and here and there lay those triangular foot-rests one meets with in Italian libraries, designed to take the chill of the marble from the reader's shoes.

With some boldness Edward now pushed open the doors, suspecting that his uncle might leap out at him from behind them. There was apparently no one there. The light fell in patches, and it was hard for him, going gingerly along the shelves, to see the gilt titles on the spines. In the lower stacks lay big brown folios, a couple of atlases, four tomes of the *Case Nobili Ed Illustri di Villafranca*, and catalogues of coins and medals. Above them, ranged in diminishing courses, ran sets of volumes, Giannone's Neapolitan History, Muratori's *Annals*, Tacitus, Boiardo, Filicaia and, on the highest shelves, a huddle of French novels. He pulled out a book and sneezed, breathing in the dust, acrid yet clean-smelling. Then he chanced on a row of English works, a

Chalmers's Poets, *Cecilia*, *The Romance of the Forest*, *Sir Charles Grandison* and *Kenilworth*. Taking down a number of *Bell's British Theatre*, he riffled among its frontispieces, thinking he should like to read a play lest a novel in the end made him too pensive.

The rain outside fell more heavily now, and the shadow lay thick around him. Edward meant to settle himself in the big window at the further end of the library, with *The Man of the World*, chosen only for the name of one of the characters, Sir Pertinax Macsycophant. There was a currule chair, with curving ebony arms, big enough for him to crook his knees over. He had just spread himself in it and opened the book when he distinctly heard somebody cough behind him. His uncle, good God? He turned to see, at a table in the alcove closest to the window, crouched behind a pile of books and portfolios, a man sitting watching him. It was the steward Basevi.

Edward stood up and remained for a while without saying anything, irked with embarrassment, half expecting Basevi to get up and leave at once. Indeed he did make a movement to raise himself, and in doing so knocked some of the books onto the floor as the skirt of his coat brushed against them. Edward did not stir to help him pick them up. When Basevi came in front of the table and knelt down, he paused to look up at Edward with knitted brows. Then Edward stooped to take up an armful of thick green volumes. As he put them on the table he caught again the smell of library dust and smiled.

'Thank you,' said Basevi. 'I didn't mean to distract you from your reading.' Edward wondered why that sounded odd. It must have been because he had not called him '*milordo*'.

'Oh, I wasn't reading really. I was just looking at the book in case I might want to.'

'Yes, that happens sometimes, I know. A sort of voluntary blindness, when your thoughts are where you want them to stay, but you're afraid lest they disturb you too much.'

'I suppose that never happens to you. Since . . . that is, you must be so used to reading.'

'And are you not?'

'Not to your sort of book.' The steward smiled but did not interrupt him. 'My tutors used to scold me when I only read Walter Scott. That was at Carlsbad. One of them even made me translate pieces of *Rob Roy* into Latin as an imposition. Then in Paris I used to read all the plays we ever saw, *Henri III et Sa Cour* and that sort of thing.'

'Do you like *The Bride of Lammermoor*?'

'That's capital!' cried Edward, laughing and surprised. 'Please, it's not that I find you funny, only . . .'

'Well?'

'It was . . . well, the idea of your enjoying Caleb's raid and Lady Ashton racing Lord A—'s carriage down the avenue.'

'Ah, but maybe you laughed at something else too,' Basevi gently insisted. 'At the notion of the person who keeps your uncle's accounts enjoying an English novel. Or because you were amused at that person enjoying your favourite book – if it is so. In the way of position and money I'm nothing: your uncle pays me with the rest of the household. So I imagine it is funny.'

Edward looked at Basevi, fearing lest an apology seemed condescending. The other in any case was not offended. He took his spectacles off the table and began wiping them with his handkerchief, saying very quietly:–

'When you picked up those books just now, did you see what they were?'

'Yes.'

'What?'

'Voltaire.'

'Exactly. Then will you honour me by keeping that a secret?'

'I don't understand.'

'It can't be of any importance to you, so there's no reason why you should know.'

'I once heard . . .' Edward began.

'You heard?' There was an extraordinary intentness to Basevi's glance as he continued abstractedly polishing a lens between thumb and forefinger.

'Something in Vienna, from a cousin of my mother's who knew a family in Hungary who . . .' Edward paused. The bundle of circumstances made it all sound ridiculous. 'It may be nonsense, but during the war with the French one of them was put in prison for being found to have read Voltaire. It was true. My cousin knew the family.'

Basevi nodded. 'Promise me, please,' he said earnestly, 'that you'll tell nobody.'

A silence fell between them. They could hear the rain tumbling onto the young leaves of the sycamores in the garden outside. Then Basevi suddenly gripped Edward's arm and began talking to him in a low, voluble murmur, as if there was barely enough time for him to speak. He talked of things that had happened a long time ago, of his family, of the arrival of Napoleon's armies which had driven the old Duke into exile, of how his father had gone to Milan to be a secretary to Eugène de Beauharnais, of Moscow and Leipzig and the Hundred Days and of the misery and emptiness which came so swiftly after them. He spoke of General Nugent's government, of Ciro Menotti and the events of 1831, of his brother Giacobbe who had been killed in the scuffles in the streets by the Porta San Biagio, and of his two cousins from Carpi who had been brought before the secret tribunal at Novellara and were now nobody knew where.

To Edward it seemed that while he listened he understood less and less. His state was a parallel one to that voluntary blindness in reading Basevi had mentioned earlier. He stared fixedly at the steward as he spoke, at the angular yellow face, with its incongruously full mouth and heavy folds of skin along the jaws, and the reddish marks given to the bridge of the nose by the wearing of spectacles. He did not care to note what was being said to him. He wanted to gain from this scrutiny a certain particular intimation. It was a hint of something he had felt before, by the shuttered house on the road, as he told the story of the tower to Cristina and Signora Lupo, when his aunt spoke of the Rangoni, when he first saw the Piani d'Ungheria, the sense of a barely suppressed wildness of impulse in him as in others, like a cry heard straining beneath the hand which stifles it. Yet in Villafranca? This man, he found himself thinking, to whom I do not listen while he speaks to me, is a foreigner. I am a *straniero*, a *forestiere*, with a passport and an accent and fair hair. But he is such a stranger as I never knew at Florence or Milan, because he is of this place, with a used, worn look in his clothes, with ink on his cuffs and smelling of coffee and tobacco, and he is saying what he means to say about the things which have happened here in Villafranca.

'Now,' said the steward, 'do you see why I asked you to say nothing? Especially when I have told you all this.' He shrugged hopelessly. 'But what can you know? Because you're an English

25

milordo, I suppose, and thus our affairs can't mean anything to you.'

Oh, can't they though, thought Edward. When Basevi asked him again if he understood, as if the elicited fact was much to him, he nodded, frowning, though his apprehensions had been of another kind entirely. The steward turned towards the window and looked down into the garden. The rain had slackened somewhat, and there was the pattering sound of water falling from the trees onto the mossy paths beneath. Basevi said:–

'Tell me one thing more. Why are you always standing at the end of the Via del Gallo, where it comes into the Piani d'Ungheria?'

'I only . . .' Edward began bashfully.

'I'm sorry, that was an impertinence, forgive me.'

'Of course,' said Edward, wishing he were able to tell him about Cristina, and almost thinking he might do so.

'My family is there, you see,' Basevi went on, 'behind the Palazzo Rangoni, in the ghetto.'

'They are Jews?'

'You can't have heard me when I told you so just now. Here in Villafranca there are laws against us: we pay different taxes, we may not serve in the army or study sciences at the university. There are a good many of us.' He laughed. 'There must be a hundred Basevi in Emilia, and many more Artom and Finzi and Treves from here to Venice. My younger brother plays the violin in the band at the theatre. He is Abramo and I am Daniele.'

He said this not coldly, or as if hurt at Edward's surprise, but with a detachment which suggested that he too was aware of the distance between them as sentient variations of the same life. Putting on his spectacles, he became the young steward once more. Edward, irked by the transformation, said:–

'When I go to the Piani d'Ungheria, and you are going to visit your family, that is, if we should leave the house together, will you walk with me – at any rate as far as the Via del Gallo?'

'Shall you only go so far? If you truly wish it I'd be honoured, but it must depend upon your wishes, I think.'

At that moment the doors of the library were flung open, and Berta, the Countess's maid, came hurrying down the room towards them.

'*Milordo*, they are searching the house for you, you must go at once to your aunt, she has guests this afternoon.'

'*Ah già!*' cried Basevi. 'It's her day for them.'

'I'll come at once,' Edward said, and, feeling the little book of plays still in his hand, scarcely remembered why he had taken it. As he moved to put it back in the bookcase, Basevi touched his arm. They watched Berta out of the room.

'Can I have your word that you'll say nothing to anyone of what I have told you?'

In truth Edward could not remember what he had been told. 'Do you imagine they'll ask me? As for Voltaire, the fault is my uncle's.'

'Ah, your uncle – he is another thing. But you promise?'

'I promise.'

Edward wandered away towards the Countess's little sitting room, pausing once to look down into the courtyard, its wet flagstones burnished by the feeblest glint of sunlight after the rain. The sound of bells crashing and moaning over the city enhanced his excitement. For the first time in his life he had been trusted with a private, familiar confidence, had been made to believe in the concomitant value of his own silence. The idea presented itself to him that a friendship between the two of them, him and Basevi, must have formed already, in that moment when he had seen him looking down from the stairs on the evening of the music party. If he did not question the steward's motive for confiding in him so readily, it was because he knew that he would trust Basevi as Basevi had trusted him, since there was no one else in Villafranca for either of them to trust. He remembered what the Countess had said about secrets and felt a freshly-acquired substance in possessing his own.

Countess Castelvetro always had tea brought to her in the sitting room at five o'clock in the afternoon, and it was customary for three or four of the ladies of Villafranca to assist on these occasions. He was not surprised, therefore, to find a small table spread with white cups, a plate of rusks, another of macaroons, and one of those sandy, and to him almost inedible, yellow Italian cakes. The room, divided by a folding screen of stamped leather, seemed as empty as the library had been. Edward sat down and busied himself with lighting the lamp under the tea urn. Then he filched a macaroon and began eating it. As he did so, he heard someone move from behind the screen. He got up, his mouth still full, as a woman came towards him. It was Signora Lupo.

4

'AND THAT WAS all?'
'That was all.'
'She said nothing more?'
'I'm quite sure of it. Then my aunt came in, and she would only talk to her for the rest of the afternoon – and the others of course – but not to me. She did not so much as nod at me when she left. I must say that I find her a little strange, your guardian.'
'That's like her. She says no more than she needs to. Yet you took her at her word and came to us. And you have gone on coming.'
'At her invitation.'
'It was not she who asked you. Don't feign surprise, you must have known.'
'Yes.'
'Ah, yes.'
They stood on the broad rampart walk which runs along the western side of the city wall from the Porta della Duchessa to the Sant'Agostino bastion. Though this is always in a state of pre-pared defence, with cannon and sentries, it was long ago per-ceived how it might be made a place for walking. The consort of one of the dukes planted sharp lines of lime trees along the straight, and set up, as though in mockery of her husband's soldierly earnestness, a belvedere tower, a domed kiosk with three terraces one above the other, which the Villafrancani, struck by its papal aspect, irreverently nicknamed Il Triregno. In

a city which so abominates walking, this is the only place where people promenade for fashion's sake, and in spring and summer and on the finer afternoons of autumn the crowds go backing and advancing like the tides before the little belvedere, its grey dome spotted yellow with moss. Edward had come here once or twice already with his aunt and thought nothing of it until this evening, when Cristina and her Rangoni cousins had called for him in the carriage and driven off as though it had all along been assumed that he would accompany them.

It was only because he could not bear not to be with Cristina that he went now. There was an airy condescension in the way they bowled up under his balcony as he sat reading, and in Massimo Rangoni's summons to him to come down, while Cristina, detached as always, sat gazing along the street. So he must have nothing better to do, so he must want for company, so he might amuse them for a while. He longed for the courage to refuse. He wished she hadn't been there.

They had divided soon enough, because the Rangoni wanted to follow their custom of moving about among the throngs to receive acknowledgment, in the manner of monarchs taking a salute, leaving Edward to walk slowly at Cristina's side as the shadows of the trees lengthened and the clustered leaves were still and blurred in the dusk.

'Which of my cousins do you like the best?' she asked, as if the answer were to have proved something and she were inexorably awaiting his judgment.

'Girls are always doing that, expecting us to declare a partiality so that they can pretend to feel cross when we don't praise them.'

'You're shrewd, aren't you?'

'You say that as if I'd no right to be. If you must know, I prefer Maria Clotilde, the one you all call Mariclò. Aldegonda is too much the fine lady.'

'And Massimo, do you think him good-looking?'

'Yes, I suppose so. He's vain, in a way which doesn't interest me. When we were at the Prignanis' ball the other night he told me he had spent two hours getting his hair cut. You think him handsome, presumably.'

'It's not something I consider.'

He felt galled by the briefest spurt of jealousy, but clenched his fists and went on:–

'Mariclò is so plain that one can't help feeling sorry for her. Therefore, you see, one likes her.'

'I don't see that at all, it sounds stupid.'

'I'm sorry. I meant . . .' Edward kicked at the gravel, ashamed. It reminded him of things she had said at the music party. Only now he felt more intensely the likelihood of losing her.

'I don't care for any in particular,' Cristina said. 'In fact I don't think I like them when they are together. Look at them grubbing for deference, that's so shabby, I think. Yet stupid people admire that sort of thing.' She turned to him with an odd fervour about her. He had never seen her so engaged. 'Do tell me that you don't admire it.'

'I have never thought to do so,' replied Edward. 'I hope I may always be judged for what's within me.'

'Then you can't like Mariclò for that. There must be something else.'

'Yes, there is. It's because she does not ask so many questions as you do. She accepts that things are so, that she will grow plainer as she grows older, that her destiny is to be an aunt to Aldegonda's children and always to sit at the edge of the drawing room in the most uncomfortable chairs and not be asked to evening parties except as companion to a pretty niece and recall the time she fell in love with the boy who flirted with her for a joke at a picnic. And Massimo will go on teasing her and calling her names when he is fifty. And she will endure it all because bitterness will have made her wise and patient.' Edward stopped, amazed at his own vehemence.

'She is fond of reading: that makes her different from the others,' said Cristina 'She borrows my French magazines and asks me what the difficult words mean. Do you know that her mother found her reading Dall'Ongaro's poems – goodness knows where she picked them up from – and threw them in the fire because he has the fame of being a republican. By the by, do I ask so many questions?'

'Everything between us is your question and my answer to it. Maybe you presume it's your right to know everything of me, yet you've told me nothing of yourself.'

That much was true. Though at their last meeting there had been the constraining presence of the Rangoni, crowding vociferously into the room and placing themselves together to attract his notice as if he were some painter to whom they intended sitting, he contrived, interstitially, to speak to Cristina. Now and then their voices fell to a mutual murmur while their conversation, dogged as a mole, worked its way under the noisy civilities of the others. They had been asked both to play a duet, largely, he supposed, so that the Rangoni could judge of his execution. They all played, even Massimo, and thus Edward was forced disappointedly to acknowledge that the music he had heard through an open window in the square might not have been Cristina's.

The instrument was opened and they sat down. Aldegonda, in the imperious fashion inherited from her mother, selected a hectic polonaise, whose black clumps of notes made the page look like a currant cake. It was obvious to Edward what was expected of him and he was glad that Cristina had chosen to play the upper part. Soon enough a complicity established itself between them, turning their performance into a dialogue. He felt Cristina sharing his contempt for the occasion, was amused by her interpolated trills and apoggiaturas, and caught the rising laughter in her eyes at one of the piece's more meretricious moments. Together they appeared to withdraw from the music itself, as though pulling away from the welcome of some dull island into the more simply hazardous world between the blank planes of sky and sea, thereby to lose themselves more freely with each other. From time to time, when their hands crossed, he held the soft weight of her wrist over his, and sensed, in a passage of scales, the cold smoothness of the edge of her little finger. These sudden touches, like vague intimations of a shared knowledge, were the first between them, yet they seemed to bring her no nearer.

Though Edward and Cristina played with as much taste as was needed to mitigate vulgarity, the Rangoni, satisfied that he would do, did not urge them to go on. The pair retreated thankfully to a terrace running along the back of the palace behind the tall, blind houses of the ghetto. Vague against the glass of the window, Signora Lupo watched them from within, a presiding ghost.

As they walked, Cristina incessantly questioned him on every point respecting his life. To many of the questions, he imagined, she must already have known the answers – why was he at Villafranca when his parents were at Rome? Where was his uncle Castelvetro? Why was he not at school in England? The redundancy of his ensuing replies gave him a curious and not altogether agreeable hint as to her overwhelming reasons for this strange, intense inquisition. It was not so much that she wanted to know for interest's sake as that she needed, for some motive he could not yet fathom, to seize upon him for herself, forcing Edward to re-create his life in a system of responses so that she could, in whatever way, make use of the image thus formed.

Edward's experience had naturally been less of women themselves than of their society. He was used to associating them with faint, unsolicited gestures of affection, given with a knowing pity and a sidelong glance in the direction of his mother. He liked old women, if they were amusing and told him stories, and liked also their smell, that peculiar savour of age, like something taken from a trunk. Girls he found capricious and incalculable, but young women were a sort of terra incognita, crammed with infinite possibilities.

Whether Cristina were either a woman or a girl it was hard to say. Edward supposed she wanted him to think that she had always been nineteen but might turn forty next birthday. To his perception her sad air of elderliness made her awkward and nervous where to others she was merely cold. The clarity with which he saw this was alarming. He must give her, he sensed increasingly, some sort of encouragement, as her self-conscious gravity started to drag upon her with the superfluous, fagging elegance of a ceremonial dress. Feeling this now, he looked full at her as they came up beside the porch of the Triregno. The scent of the limeflowers held a sticky, pungent sweetness. He was suddenly very happy and secure. Massimo and the girls, now crowding upon them, proposed that they at once go in and eat ices.

Inside the pavilion was a hall with a buffet at which girls in white aprons sold lemonade, barley water and coffee. It was rather a jolly affair, this Triregno, Edward thought, with its open arches making a little balcony, and a telescope to examine the view. Everyone took their glass of ice-cream and a beaker of water, and since there was nobody else there, they disposed themselves in a proprietary fashion around the balcony. How was Mariclò's ice-cream? It was good. Could Aldegonda try some? Yes, excellent, though she preferred her own. And Edward's? No, she thought she wouldn't try that, not caring for lemon. She was sure it must be good, it was always so here. Massimo, who never ate like a Christian, had finished already. What a savage! Hers, she must say again, was really good.

Massimo got up and began to fiddle with the end of the telescope, twirling it this way and that and making it squeak as he did so.

'Ouf! Listen!' he said, squeaking it again. 'There's a pretty noise for you. They say that old Duke Ferdinando used to spend hours looking through this thing. I wonder what at? Listen! That one was really tremendous!'

'Perhaps . . .' Edward began.

'Oh, stop it, Massimo, stop it at once!' cried Mariclò, truly angry. Pettishly her brother retorted: 'Very well, so I'll stop, there!' and walked away into the pavilion.

'Now, do you see, you've made him cross,' said Aldegonda. With an impatient gesture to Edward, Cristina got up quickly, half whispering: 'Come, let's walk a little,' and with the most natural assumption he took her arm and they went out onto the terrace.

'I wish . . .' he said, when he supposed they were a little out of earshot, then checked himself. Cristina laughed.

'Yes, I know what you wish, I do as well. That there were only the two of us, isn't that it? My cousins are quite dreadful, so *bornés*, so coarse.'

'If you must know, I thought that was rather engaging of Massimo.'

'You can hardly be serious.'

'He's barely older than me. I expect it was what I should have done.'

'Ah, I don't think so. You would have been apologetic in that dishonest way you have.'

Edward writhed under the stricture. 'And what would you have said to Mariclò? But then I don't imagine you have ever done anything so simple as making a telescope creak on a swivel.'

'My simplicity is of a different kind,' Cristina said, 'as you'll discover.'

She flung away and started to climb the steps to the higher

34

balconies of the belvedere. He noticed, as he followed her, the turn and slenderness of her ankles when she caught up the heavy skirts of her walking-dress. At the last step before the top she all but tripped, then steadied herself and stood looking down at him, a little breathless, her mouth open, as he reached her. There was room for the pair of them to walk abreast, and they moved slowly along the terrace together, feeling the pleasurable coolness of the air upon their faces.

'Yes, after all,' said Cristina, 'I do pity them. It's a kind of luxury for me to do so.'

'Why? Why now, suddenly?'

'Because, don't you see, they are jealous of me. In the end they're like all these Emilians, I suppose. They don't judge as we judge in Milan, by family and position, but by the things they possess. That, for them, is freedom.'

'Nobody in Italy is truly free,' said Edward, 'at least not here in Villafranca.'

She laughed sadly. 'Ah, you've seen that. But they must think so, of me I mean. Because I have five estates in the Lodi district, none of them mortgaged, and bonnets and dresses whenever I please, and can speak French without an accent, they think, poor creatures, that I am free.' She shivered. The noise of the people in the avenue below came up to them like the spilling of water over stones. 'I wish I were free, as you are. I wish I were you.'

Edward, who had never wanted to be anyone else, was silent, though Cristina seemed expecting him to answer her. At length she said: 'I'd like to be able to feel things as you do. Something more, at any rate, than a little scorn.'

'Has Signora Lupo taught you nothing?'

'It's not something one learns. She knows me too well, besides. But I might learn from you.'

It was something his aunt could have said, though given here with a sincerity of which she was incapable. In his embarrassment he found himself listening once more to the murmur on the rampart walk, a sustained, unvarying susurration. From where they now stood they could watch the customs officers slouching under the massive, cauliflower-like garlands of the gateway arch, with now and then a waft of their strong cigars rising on the air across the glimmer of lamplight. Beyond, the countryside, fleecy and blurred in the bluish light, spread out in its pattern of unyielding lines, as far as the one stark black line of mountains over which the sun sank. It seemed as though, when it had gone, everything else too would dissolve, fields, ditches, trees, barns and roads, having even now a filmy vagueness about them. Edward looked at Cristina, at those almost hidden movements in her face that he had noticed from the first, like the half-formed articulations of a suppressed language. Her glance called something out of the grey landscape. Gently he touched the edge of her hand with his own and was bravely not surprised that she withdrew it at once.

'Fancy if this tower were the tip of the earth,' he said, 'and we were both to fall from it into nothing, and fall and fall. Sometimes I am as unhappy as you.'

'I know. That's why, you see, I had to ask you those things, that day when you came to us, to make sure of you.'

'Why?'

'I must trust someone!' she exclaimed, as if that were a foregone conclusion. He thought of Basevi, who also trusted him.

'Sometimes, yes, I do envy my cousins,' she said swiftly, 'more than despising them. I never knew my father. And my mother – my mother died when I was three.'

'Then you never knew her. I, alas, know both my parents too well. You must simply promise to trust me.'

'In Villafranca there's nobody else – but I suspect you don't know half of what you ask.'

At that instant their attention was distracted by a movement upon the road, and the figures of two horsemen became visible, cantering steadily on among the scattered houses clustered in the shadow of the wall. They reined up with a suggestion of impatience at the customs barrier, as if their arrival was to have been taken for granted. Edward, watching them exchange words with the guard, noticed the deference of officers to riders as they waved them forward without the barest examination of their papers. He turned to look at Cristina watching them. She raised both her hands to her face with a quick indrawing of breath, and almost as soon recovered herself. When the two riders had passed under the gateway she muttered, shivering: 'How cold it has grown. We'll go down, no?'

He stood aside to let her pass, and turned once again to look at

36

the open countryside, now full of shadows. It was difficult indeed to imagine that the horsemen had passed across it, less so to believe that they had arisen from it, taking life only from its indistinctness, which had suffered them to appear and then closed back upon itself. In the crevice of the huge scarp of wall beetling below him hung a flowering bush of valerian. If he stretched a hand through the railing of the platform he could touch it, but he felt that if he did so it would crumble to powder. With it perhaps would go, though he could not understand why, the whole of Villafranca.

'You'll come home with us,' said Massimo, more as a statement of fact than as an invitation, while the carriage pulled out from the Piazza d'Armi into the Via della Gloria. Edward felt loftily independent in declining and hoped Cristina would notice. When he parted from them in front of the palace he saw in her expression a smiling complicity which nothing could afterwards efface.

He was inordinately pleased with himself. A quarter of an hour alone with her was something, but he had gained beyond his hopes. He took the stairs two at a time to his aunt's sitting room and, bouncing confidently in, found her waiting for him with the lamp hissing under the tea-urn.

'There were a whip and a pair of gloves thrown down on the stair when I came up,' he said. 'Has somebody left them behind?'

'It is your uncle who has returned, Ned.'

'He is here, then?'

'No,' answered the Countess forlornly. 'He went out at once to Baron Stappler's. Baron Stappler is an Austrian. One of the court chamberlains.' She pulled herself up in her chair, as if with supreme control, and turned at last towards him, her mouth tautly smiling. Picking up a book she said:—

'I forget where we got to yesterday. You read so well and I quite dote on Mrs Gore's novels, but my mind's on other things, I fear.'

'Would you rather I didn't read to you this evening, aunt?'

'No, it distracts me very agreeably, Ned dear. You enjoyed yourself on the rampart, I think.'

'Yes thank you, aunt.'

'And was Cristina Bentivoglio with you?'

'Yes, aunt.'

'The old Marchesa Rangoni came to me this afternoon – a rare thing, as she does not go much into society. She told me that you had made a good impression there.' The Countess gave a smothered laugh. 'Which, in view of the circumstances, was a pity. Still, such things are quite thrown away on pert Miss Cristina.'

'What circumstances?'

'Oh, for the present it is strictly *entre nous*. Even her cousins do not know, though I can hardly see why they shouldn't be told. They must suspect, as it has been on the *tapis* for a long while.'

Edward's mind misgave him. 'Please, what is it, aunt?'

'Ah, I thought that perhaps you had guessed,' answered the Countess compassionately. 'For myself I half supposed it before the Marchesa told me. Goodness knows why they chose to keep it silent until now. The poor child is engaged to be married, Edward. And to a man she has only ever seen once in her life before.'

5

THE CAFÉ BERTOCCHI, on the south side of the cathedral square, is a florid, handsome, self-consequent establishment, which pretends to something beyond what the capital city of a small duchy can embrace. Above the plush-covered benches of its hot little salons, the raffish panels of painted glass show muses, graces and cupids implausibly occupied in playing billiards, smoking cigars and pouring tea and the yards of gilded scrollwork around the expanses of mirror look as though they expected you to live up to them. There is always a good deal more effusiveness and gesticulation than is altogether necessary, and nobody arrives without someone there to greet him as though he were returned from a ten-year exile.

Thus the place is absolutely in favour throughout the opera season. The languid youth which hangs about theatrical green rooms, vaunts itself on gala nights in rainbow waistcoats and is quick to disparage enjoyment of the evening by telling you that the Persiani or the Brambilla is not at her best, spends long hours here laboriously picking each performance over, defending a *pianissimo* against an E *in alt* and claiming to remember Pasta. Notoriously uncharitable as the Villafrancan public may be, when it does approve its generosity takes the form of a torchlight procession from the theatre right across the town to the café, where the singers are treated on sweet wine and Bertocchi's famous cakes.

The waiters are young, handsome scallywags, much given to

39

mouthing at themselves in the mirrors as they pass to and fro, quizzing the women in the square, teasing the customers and resolutely implying that theirs is only a temporary servitude. Not so their counterparts at the Café Pedrazzi, over beyond the cathedral, all on the respectable side of fifty and full of the weary dignity essential to their calling. Moving gravely among the tables with their loaded trays, they carry the air of superannuated field-marshals, actors who have seen better days or figures chosen to represent the Doctors of the Church in a fresco painting.

There is, indeed, something positively religious about the Pedrazzi, which Villafranca cherishes in its quieter moods. The wine is generally accounted foul, the eatables are dusty, and everything takes so long to be brought that you have almost forgotten you ordered it, but the mere fact that these dispositions never change makes the establishment valued by those intent on other things than eating or drinking.

To this wonderful archive of secrets, confidences and confessions came Edward and Basevi, turning aside from the mounting heat of morning to take refuge in the Pedrazzi's musty shadows over a cup of indifferent coffee. Outside they could hear the clapping-to of shop shutters, the scraping and clattering of chairs and plates and the comfortable mutter of chat sustained by feeding, and the café was starting slowly to empty as the clients sloped away to lunch. Edward, who was not feeling hungry, went on talking to Basevi, who was, but who felt that today it mattered to be patient.

'If you like,' he said, 'we won't go as far as the Piani d'Ungheria. Unless you'd rather.'

'Thanks, I don't mind, truly,' Edward rejoined but, catching himself at the end of one of Basevi's fixed stares, said ruefully: 'Oh God, yes, of course I do. To see a stone of it would kill me.' He had never said anything like that before. He was so astonished at having been able to say it at all that he wondered briefly whether he were himself any more.

'What you mean,' said his friend, 'is that you'd rather not see it, so as to avoid having to know whether it would kill you or not. Who can say? Perhaps it might. You're in love.'

Edward reddened to the ears. They had spoken of Cristina's marriage, of the suddenness of his aunt's news of it, of the

40

mysterious vagueness and reticence of the Rangoni respecting it, but the one thing they had not touched upon was the exact nature of his own feelings. He peered into his coffee as though it held some sort of vatic answer. Then he looked at Basevi and said: 'Yes, I'm in love.' It was like acknowledging a sin. 'Oh, I wish you hadn't told me I was, I wish you'd let it go.'

'I'm sorry, I thought it might be easier if you admitted it.'

'Is it obvious?'

Basevi shook his head and laughed. 'You cannot stop thinking of her. She is with you every minute of every hour. You write letters to her which you never send and those you do are only half of what you might say if only you dared. The sheets on your bed are mapped with your passion for her. You mutter her name in your sleep.'

'Don't mock me, for God's sake, even if you don't understand it!' cried Edward as if he were betrayed.

'Listen, Edward, lovers always think as you do, that their desire is without example. Do you imagine I don't know what you're talking about, that I haven't made myself sore with longing for girls? That's why I recognized it.'

'I'd rather she recognized it.'

'You imagine she doesn't?'

'Ah, it's impossible to tell what she understands. She seems all the time to be wanting to speak with me, yet when we are together we say nothing of any consequence. She merely asks me questions.'

'She does that with everyone.'

'How do you know?'

Basevi laughed again. 'There, you see, you're jealous, so you must be in love. As to how I know, conceive for a moment. But you, Edward, can't need to hear these things, they are simply the tattle of grooms and chambermaids.'

'What, for heaven's sake?' cried Edward furiously.

'Oh, well. For example, that no one knows who her parents are, that she is perhaps only a Bentivoglio by adoption. I know that isn't true.'

Edward was on the point of asking him how when, looking up, he caught that singular expression he had learnt to recognize in Basevi's countenance which meant that he absolutely declined to

41

say anything more. It was not unfriendly, nor was it final: it simply declared that the occasion was inapposite.

'Coffee's cold and I've no cigars left,' said the steward, 'and it's time to put something under the teeth. You can't eat, I know. See me to the end of the square and go home and write a sonnet or whatever it is you do. This is my treat, by the way.' A tragic old waiter stalked grandly up to proffer the bill and when he had gone, Basevi, laying a hand on Edward's arm, said: 'I can't bear to see you like this. Don't let her break your heart, she has no business to be doing that.' They went out into the square. Basevi appraised him sharply. They walked on a little and then he said: 'Don't give her everything you have. Keep something back for yourself.'

'If that were possible!' Edward exclaimed, 'I don't know what's mine and what isn't. Anyway she isn't, she belongs to Tagliabosco or whatever his name is.'

'His name is Count Guido Tagliabosco. The name is comical, since he's as unlike a woodcutter as it's possible to be. He is some two or three years younger than I and rich – why, richer even than your uncle. Everyone here speaks well of his discretion and taste. They consult him, you know, on little matters of form, arrangement, that sort of thing. When he was barely into his teens women asked his advice about jewels and took him with them to match silks. I remember meeting him for the first time when I used to help my uncle, who has a curio shop in the Via Paolina. He used to bring the ladies in to look at the trinkets and pictures and old Venice glasses and odd pieces of jewellery, and my uncle once said banteringly to me in his presence, "the young count's got an eye, Daniele, an eye for fine work, which is more than you'll ever have if you live to be a thousand," and that was true, I suppose. He made bargains with us – my uncle used to say he'd be the ruin of him, his eye was that good – and took me once to the palace in the Contrada della Posta Vecchia to see all the things he had got together. His father went off to live in Bologna. They never cared for one another. The mother died when Guido was two days old. She was a Neapolitan, one of the old families, I forget which, but reputed a handsome woman, and they say he takes after her. God knows how she fetched up here. Anyway, he lives well and is clear of debt, I know for a fact, and the Duke allows him to travel a lot, so all our nobility are agog for hints on

what to wear and how to arrange their drawing rooms. Our
Petronius Arbiter, indeed.' Basevi paused, smiling at Edward,
then looked away and laughed. 'But you needn't worry yourself
with him, believe me. Oh no!'

'Is that all you're going to tell me?'

'Isn't it enough? You won't wait, will you? Yes, that's all I'll
tell you, though it's not all I know.'

Edward suddenly felt very cross with Basevi. They walked
across the square in silence. He would not be the first to
speak. As if sensing this, the steward stopped and, turning, said
quietly:–

'Perhaps I'll tell you one more thing after all. This arranged
match which you deem so barbarous isn't always such a bad
thing. Jews do it as well as Christians. I had a wife chosen for me,
in Carpi, and we shall get married in due time.'

'Yes, but do you love her?' rejoined Edward with an obstinate
directness which clearly struck Basevi.

'We love each other, but we aren't in love. Ride over to Carpi
with me one of these days and you'll see.'

There was the merest hint of roguishness in the invitation, as
though he were being tempted towards something not altogether
correct, which disarmed Edward, the more so because he knew it
was honestly given.

'Thanks, I'd like that. You won't tell anyone, will you?'

'About your going to Carpi? I shouldn't dream of it. We can
rendezvous outside the town if it embarrasses you to be seen
riding with me. I do ride rather well, you know. Like a gentleman. Your uncle taught me. He said it was something his steward
should know.'

'I didn't mean that. I don't mind if I am seen with you.
We are together now, after all. I mean about me and Cristina
Bentivoglio.'

'One secret the more won't kill me to keep.' Basevi shook him
by the hand, with a sort of awkward solemnity that was touching.
'On my honour. And courage, Edward: no one's worth hanging
yourself for.'

He watched Basevi cross the square and disappear down the
Via Fontanella. Left alone, he felt frightened. He seemed to
be standing beside the colossal uselessness of his passion for
Cristina, wondering what to do with it. Maybe he should go and

seek out Count Tagliabosco and dare him to fight. But ten to one Tagliabosco would be silky and effete, a little monkey with chocolate eyes and glacé gloves who would faint at the sight of a pistol, so what was the point?

More to the purpose, something needed to be done with Cristina – not as she was, but as she inhabited his desire for her. Not without a twinge of retrospective shame, Edward found himself remembering a time, impossibly distant though it now seemed, when his inchoate thoughts about girls had gathered a determined shape. It was at a house outside Paris to which his parents had taken him with them to stay. He had been put to sleep in a room opening off that of the youngest son of the family, a forward spotty boy of his own age who had decided, with the arbitrary positiveness of childhood, to make a confidant of Edward. Lying awake in the darkness with the door open, the two rattled on together, the boy talking most, Edward listening and shaping the rudiments of a desire from his friend's fabulous anecdotes of laundrymaids and kisses and erections and what he did when and what he would do if, in the truth-annihilating dark . . . Here now, however, was a truth he had never suspected it possible to encounter, and had no rhetoric to overcome.

A heavy, miasmal silence started to spread across the city. Not even a cat moved in the blank streets. Scared by the moment's vacancy and by the dreadful echo of his own boots on the paving stones as he began to walk, Edward felt the square defying him to cross it. Wide-eyed, he looked about. The houses, above their arcades, were a strange scabbed brown colour, like lengths of blood-clotted bandage. Below, on the pillars of the arches, was the habitual archaeology of ducal proclamations, one law pasted onto another, a sight so common everywhere else in Italy that Edward had grown insensibly to ignore it. Now the presence of these frowning notices, though their words as yet meant nothing to him, seemed at the least a threat. He shivered. It was hot. He was afraid. Old and glistening like a toad in the middle of the square stood the cathedral, its big doors shut to, but with a little postern open. Edward stood looking at this postern and hearing the blood race in his ears. Then, gathering up the skirts of his coat, he ran outright across the square towards it.

Such darkness prevailed inside the cathedral that for a while Edward was groping blindly in front of him along the nave,

44

meanly lit by the old round-headed windows of the clerestory and the occasional wan pools of light from the candles and lamps in the chapels. He was content, nevertheless, to be thus alone at a time when sheer despondency would have made the well-meant interference of others intolerable. The dank, sooty, greasy hollows of the place seemed to him like the recesses of his own mind, with the same snug familiarity, flattering his loneliness. There was nobody here, the confessionals were empty, the sacristy was silent, the chapels were without even the customary old woman engaged in remonstrating dialogue with the saints. The gloom worked powerfully upon him, urging him freely to indulge his misery. He sat down on the steps before the rails of a chapel in the transept and burst into tears.

Sobbing and snuffling, he sat there for some time, happy to go on doing so until he should feel ready to stop. He remembered how, as a child still in long clothes, he had been taken, largely for exhibition, to tea with some friends of his mother's. She had left him in one corner of the room to play, and he had suddenly decided that he should like to wet himself. So he had stood there, watching the women and young men gathered around the table, and quietly wetting himself until his mother screamed for the nurse to take him away. That was what it felt like now in the encouraging darkness. He went on, crying and crying, until an arm was put round his shoulder and somebody told him to stop.

'I'm sorry, I'm sorry,' he blubbed.

'No you're not, otherwise why are you crying? There, don't, or I shall too, only I never have occasion to, as I have almost forgotten how. There, there, this is too wretched on any account. Don't, I beg you.'

'I'm sorry.'

'No, truly, it's I who am sorry. I should have left you be. But then maybe you'd have been locked in here and had cause to cry in earnest.'

'How do you know I wasn't crying in earnest?' said Edward angrily.

'That wasn't what I meant.'

'No, I'm sorry.'

'Please stop saying you're sorry. English people always say that and it means nothing. What you are really sorry about is

45

what you're crying for. The fact that I fell over you on my way out of the chapel has nothing to do with it.'

'What were you doing in the chapel?'

'Praying for my family – but mostly for myself, I suppose.'

'How did you know I was English?'

'Your Italian is too neat and practised. I found you out in one sentence. Anyway, were you praying before you started to cry?'

'No. I wanted to, but it seemed stupid.'

'That is what I feel sometimes. I watch others at mass, women particularly, and I think "I wish I could bury myself in prayer like that" – but perhaps they're only meditating on bonnets or lovers or whatever it is, and the Madonna and the saints are neither here nor there.'

'I only came in here because I didn't want anybody else to see me,' said Edward.

'Ah yes, I see, you were ashamed.'

'Probably I was.' He had not thought of it thus, but under the circumstances it seemed appropriate.

'It was the same with me once, years ago in Bologna. I was younger than you, I think, and living at my grandmother's house near the church of San Petronio. One week – it was in winter – my grandmother took to her bed and sent the servants out for draughts and pills, and the house was full of doctors and priests and I had only my youngest brother Carlo for company. One very cold morning a letter arrived for me from my brother Pietro. I thought it something that Pietro, who never had cause to write a letter to me in his life, should do so now, and guessing that it had something of importance I went away and hid with it in one of the empty rooms in the attic.'

'What did it say?' asked Edward.

'It started, oddly as I then thought, with poetry, some lines Leopardi had written to a friend of ours, one of the Pepoli, the passage which begins, as I recall, '*Lui delle vesti e delle chiome il culto*', and speaks of a fashionable person who never smiles and who, though young enough, has never experienced his own youth. The application was obvious. Pietro had made the verses into a portrait of himself. He was in Rome when we thought he was at Florence, he had been there all through the autumn and winter, and his letters to my grandmother were thus full of lies. He wanted a particular favour of me, he knew I should not refuse it, that Carlo was too young, that he had no friends in Bologna he could trust not to tell the rest of my family. And do you know what he wanted me to do?'

Edward of course did not. That sort of question always irritated him.

'In the house were his books, Latin and Greek mostly, for he was something of a scholar. These he now told me to sell for whatever I could get. They were, he said, the only valuable things he possessed.

'Well, such a thing seemed nonsense at first. If he wanted money he might have raised it on the security of our family's name or his expectations of inheritance. It was always very cold and bare at my grandmother's, I remember, and I sat on a hard chair with my toes freezing, reading on in bewilderment. Pietro wrote as though the books were treasure to be pawned, saying I must send the money at once by the fellow who brought the letter and was going back at once with whatever I could get. I'd understand, he said, why the money was needed. In all this there was a touch of the man of the world, and I perceived how little we knew each other that he should think me able to guess his reasons for raising money on old books. Then at the close of the letter he was so good as to explain himself.'

'And what was it?'

'He wanted the money to pay his Roman whores. He had nothing, he had sold most of his clothes and borrowed God knows how much he couldn't repay, yet each night he ranged to and fro like a pasha. He said he couldn't sleep unless he went to a woman first. And for this I was to sell his books.'

'And you did?'

'Yes. My grandmother thought she was dying and read through the daily offices with her confessor, so I told Carlo I was going to visit a friend and slipped out when he was having his geometry lesson with the tutor. Pietro's wretched messenger came with me, glad to earn something for carrying a load of books. It was bitter cold, hard, bright, tingling afternoon air. My nose and ears smarted with it. I was trembling also in case we met anyone I knew. But I went about inexorably from shop to shop, until I found one who gave a good price, a man who went over each one very slowly, riffling the leaves and muttering to himself, seeming almost to ignore my presence as he did so. Here and there were notes and jottings, and the sight of my brother's tall, spidery hand across the pages filled me with despair. I didn't want to sell the books after all. The man put them aside and paid me out the price on which we had agreed.

'When I left the shop I was miserably unhappy. I gave the Roman fellow something to eat with and told him to come back to my grandmother's house in the afternoon, when I'd give him a letter to take with the money to Pietro. Then I went into a church and sat down. There wasn't much money after all. What there was seemed the embodiment of my brother's desperation. We had never greatly cared for one another, and that bonds of interest and gratitude should be created between us in this way was monstrous to me. I looked at the money and started to cry, as you have done.'

To Edward the story, however well told, appeared to have no other point than that of calming him by preventing him from speaking. He was grateful for so honest a kindness.

'Oh, we shan't talk of it again. If it's of any concern to you, I should never be able to cry like that any more. That's why I'm jealous of you. I can't even say my prayers.'

Edward got up off the steps, took out his handkerchief and blew his nose positively. The two of them walked back into the nave towards the open door. They felt, as they neared it, the heavy layer of heat wafted in from the square. In the sharpness of the light outside Edward discovered that he had been talking to a round-shouldered, bright-eyed man with close-cropped hair and a face in which the strength of line seemed only to have got so far and then given up. Looking at him with a kind of envy which seemed to emphasize what he had said before, the man sighed, then laughed in embarrassment, shook him by the hand and was gone. He turned his head in crossing the square, as though expecting Edward to follow. Edward, watching him, was determined that evening to go and see Cristina.

 6

THE WOMEN PERCHED on the edges of the sofa like roosting birds. If I clap my hands, thought Edward, they will all fly up with a rattle of wings to the mirrors and the lamps. As though he had already done so, one or two of them looked at him in curiosity, but nobody moved. For the first time in Villafranca he was not wholly afraid, but bowed and walked past them into the broad, hot saloon where the footmen in their liveries of dingy green shuffled to and fro handing out biscuits and sweet wine. The red biscuits, hard and dusty as shards of terra cotta, and the treacly wine, which one of the Marchesa's servants had once frankly discouraged him from taking, he ate and drank now as though both actions were part of some familiar sacrament. In the same spirit he greeted the Marchesa and her mother-in-law, who sat, tutelary spirits enthroned, at the end of the room, notably unamused by anything.

Vaguely he peered through the brilliance of the wax-lights, his alertness for a moment dulled by loud, immoderate voices and the distant, unscientific thumping of a piano. As he made the tour, nodding and bowing in his nervous fashion to those he knew and to several he did not, he saw that it contained practically everybody he had so far met in Villafranca. His own tallness, and a general state of abstraction in the face of a single purpose, made it easy for him to look about and survey them, to watch their gestures, the very movements of their lips in speaking, to catch their unguarded expressions and the eloquent spontaneity of their lightest actions. He saw the old dowager Rangoni waving her flabby, mottled hands, while the Marchesa, in whom something had long ago quelled an attentive regard, pursed her lips and turned away. He watched Aldegonda punctuate a story with little hard taps of the end of her fan on a friend's folded arm. He saw Massimo yawning in answer to a question. In one corner, with her customary appearance of someone made forlorn in the hopeless quest for amusement, sat his aunt, listening miserably to Countess Molza's description of the *parti* she had found for her unmarried sister.

Only two other people in the throng seemed able to share his carefully determined remoteness. One was Signora Lupo, who sat quietly in an angle of one of the tall balcony windows open to the night air, watchful and alone. He took care, as far as he might, to avoid her glance. The other was his uncle, Count Castelvetro, solitary, almost spectral, in the interval of shadow between two candle-sconces. Yet though nothing else in him appeared to move, his eyes did so continually, scanning the company as if for one thing only, which had still to show itself. The three of them, thus, thought Edward, were the fixed points governing everything else here.

'She's gone, you know,' said Mariclò, who now confronted him, inexorably demure, hands folded before her.

'Liar,' retorted Edward.

'I meant only that you wouldn't find her here. She won't come in if she doesn't want to.'

'How do you know?'

'That's her way. She has nobody to tell her what to do.' Mariclò paused. 'Signora Lupo says nothing. And I think that is sad. We all need someone else to tell us what to do.'

'I suppose that is being philosophical. I can't make it out at all.'

Her earnestness was what most perplexed him when she said: 'She might listen to you, Edward. Not to any of us, but to you,' and then bit her lip in an unaccountable annoyance. They had nothing more to say to one another. Turning impatiently from her, he went to where he knew he should find Cristina.

She was alone, as he had expected, on the balcony at the back of the house. Her craving for solitude and anonymity always seemed the most artificial thing about her, and sometimes Edward longed simply to tell her that it didn't matter. What in others might have seemed eccentric was in her a mere freak of childishness, as if she were afraid of being taken for somebody else. Perhaps that was why, tossed to and fro between loathing and adoration, she had no friends.

She reminded him sometimes of a town he had once visited in Saxony, in the company of his mother and a dragoon officer she had taken as a lover. The town stood in the middle of a broad plain, and you could see it from several miles off. It was without suburbs of any kind, sitting encased within the immense complexity of its fortifications. The dragoon, who was fond of Edward in a nonchalant way, had told him the story of it. Of how the Elector had summoned a very famous French architect to create an impregnable system, and of how, when finished, its glacises, ravelins and salients had been considered the most perfect ever devised. Then there had been a war with Brandenburg and everyone had thought the Brandenburgers mad for daring to besiege the splendid, solitary, fortified city. But there had been no siege, nor, indeed, any shot fired. 'What happened?' Edward asked. 'Nothing,' answered the dragoon, 'for the city gates were opened by a trick and the enemy rode in unharmed when the people were asleep – so you see, all these banks and stones are quite useless.' Edward, looking at Cristina, wondered when she would ever be so betrayed into forefeiting her dreadful, encircling loneliness.

Not now. She had seen him coming, of course. He stifled the impulse to speak first. She had turned away as soon as he came close, and now leant, in what seemed a customary fashion, on the balustrade, peering over into the lane below. He could see something, a vein or a muscle in her neck, twitching as she breathed, and her lips parting and closing as though in a whisper to herself. Without looking up at him, she said:–

'So you are angry with me because I didn't tell you. Why? What business have you to be angry?'

'You were glad enough to tell me things before. In any case, it's not that which has made me angry with you.'

'What then?'

'Just that I love you,' he said, with a candour which made her stare. It was the first time he had ever seen her so astonished. That pleased him. It was a point gained.

'Edward, you mustn't think . . .' she began.

'Don't presume to tell me what I mustn't think!' he cried. 'Stop telling others what to feel. Show some feeling of your own.'

Her countenance darkened. They heard the piano thumping in the other room and the clattering hubbub of the guests. He was thrilled by her silence.

'I suppose,' he went on, 'that you want me to feel sorry for you. Everyone else is, you know, even Aldegonda. I, however, take the contrary part.'

'What is that?' said Cristina very quietly.

'That Tagliabosco is what you deserve. A dilettante, cold, passionless. I haven't the least intention of pitying you. Others in Italy have marriages arranged for them. Your own mother, for what I know.'

'Don't speak of my mother!' exclaimed Cristina in a sudden flush of rage. He wanted more of it now.

'Well, well, I won't, if you stop begging for pity.'

'I didn't ask for it from you, of all people.'

'Yes, you have. Not in words, but in what you are.'

'Ah, if I were what I am, you wouldn't know me, Edward.'

'It matters to me that I don't know you now. Listen to me, Cristina. I've told you everything there is about me that can possibly interest you. That my father is a brewer, that my mother is the sister of an earl, that I like tea and marzipan and marsala, that my favourite music is Donizetti's, that I read *The Vicar of Wakefield* whenever I can get nothing else, and that I'm embarrassed because I blush and burst into tears easily, and because I'm taller than common so my trousers don't always fit me as they should. These things don't matter a rap to you for what they are. My father's beer is made at a place called Burton-on-Trent in an English county called Staffordshire, but, good heavens, what Burton is or Staffordshire means even less to you than it does to me. And I've never set foot in England since I was seven. All that really seems to matter is that you know this.'

Her stare lay unflinchingly on him. She seemed as cold now as before.

'You know also that I find Villafranca languid and provincial, that I'm lonely and without friends.' He thought of Basevi and said, 'Well, more or less so. And you are the same, don't deny it. No doubt that was why, the other evening, you said you wanted

52

to trust me.' He waited for her to answer. She said nothing.
'Well, didn't you?'

'Yes.'

'Yes, oh yes,' Edward repeated bitterly, 'you were so deucedly
eager.' Again he paused, feeling the moment's weird buoyancy
under him. 'Yet you said nothing to me, ever, ever, about Guido
Tagliabosco. See if I believe in your trust, Cristina.'

The other evening all over again, he thought. The two of them
there, like abstracted souls in the enclosing gloom, with, behind
them, the noisy, merciless embodiments of ordinary life. Surely
they must both want the same thing. In the tall house on the
other side of the lane, with its single tall window, he could
see somebody moving about in the lighted room through the
chink of half-closed shutters. Suddenly Cristina began to
speak, as though with the prepared spontaneity of a figure in a
play.

'Edward, I can never love you in return, you understand. And
it may be that you only love me because there is no one else. You
want to possess me.'

'Am I truly any worse than you?' said Edward.

'Maybe not.' It was the first ground she had given. To grasp the
offered advantage, however, would be mere effeminacy.

'You needn't be afraid,' she went on, 'that I shall love Guido
Tagliabosco. We saw each other this morning. We had met as
children, ten years since. They have drawn up the articles
between us already. We shall marry in July, before everyone
leaves for the *villeggiatura*.'

'And if you refused to marry him?'

She looked blank. 'I don't know. My guardian would be forced
to pay him the dowry that is promised, if he insisted, but I think
he would not.'

'So you marry in order to accommodate your guardian.'

'No, Edward. To please myself.'

'That is absurd.'

'Have you never heard of those who marry without love?'

'Oh, I don't suppose my mother and father were ever especially fond of one another. And my aunt Castelvetro may love my
uncle the Count for what I know, but he doesn't care a brass
button for her. This isn't material. You could choose, so why
don't you? They won't shut you away in a nunnery.'

'I have no choice,' she said. 'It is for Guido to decide. You mustn't hope I shall refuse so as to oblige you.'

'You will never oblige me in anything,' said Edward, 'so I never hope for it. I don't know why I love you. You don't deserve it, from me or anybody. Your coldness disgusts me, it's stupid, empty, vain. I thought so when I met you here at the Marchesa's concert. That night at the Triregno when Massimo was driving the carriage home, you laughed, and I thought that perhaps you were beginning . . . well, to recognize the possibility of being happy in Villafranca. But laughter embarrasses you, I know, so you stopped laughing when Aldegonda and Mariclò looked at you.'

He felt her composure defying him. He turned his head away and looked across the lane, trying to avert dismay. In the shuttered room the figure was still moving. There seemed to be someone else there as well, but the light was too dim to make them out clearly. With a conscious effort he said at last:–

'It's no good, Cristina. Between us, I mean. I can't touch you, can I?'

'If you think so.'

Someone in the room opposite was moving the light to and fro. Then the other person passed in front of it. He put his hand down and felt himself hard under it.

'Yet I can try. Somebody must try,' he cried, seizing Cristina in the same instant and kissing her with great suddenness and decision. Tearing herself free, she caught him by the coat collar and smacked him smartly about the face.

'There, feel that, wretched, half-grown English boy! I won't change, I won't, I won't, for you or all the world.'

Cristina, as though furious with herself for such a betrayal of emotion, walked slowly off into the house. Edward did not follow her, but stood where he was, gently pressing his face with his hands. On the other side of the lane the shutter was drawn back and a man, or part of him, came and stationed himself in the little space thus disclosed. Motionless and amazed, Edward stared at him. Then the window was shut again and the light was taken away. Edward shrugged, scratched his head and returned to the saloon.

His face was still hot from Cristina's touch. The smell of her was on his collar. He was trembling and exhilarated from the thought of what he had just done. The hard, numbing dullness of Villafranca had been dissipated in a single act, something never before attempted. In the past he had been the mute watcher, the discreet minister, the silent applauder. Now, for some reason, he had learned obscurely to connect with this place itself, the order of things was changed by his own violent design. The sudden strength and boldness of it all alarmed him. What was he to do without shame or embarrassment to aid him? He supposed he had better brazen it out, yet, red-handed as he was, he could not nerve himself sufficiently to swagger among the guests as he had done at first. In a sudden access of his former shadow-like bashfulness he slipped into the throng, hoping that nobody would notice him, especially not Mariclò.

The company had thinned out a little since his arrival, and now stood or sat in scattered islands across the big room. Someone was singing 'La lontananza' and Countess Castelvetro was laughing. The noise of her laughter fell on Edward like cold water. He looked swiftly around him, catching Signora Lupo's glance as he did so. With her inimitable assumption of weariness she beckoned him towards her, and he saw that Cristina and Guido were there as well. In the smiles of both as he approached lay the hint of resolved complicity. The Signora said nothing but inclined her head in greeting, as if whatever business she had with Edward had been long understood.

'You must let me present you to Count Tagliabosco, Edward,' said Cristina in a strangely exalted tone. Guido got up and shook Edward by the hand. That morning's encounter in the cathedral was evidently not to be alluded to. It pleased him that Guido, by whatsoever means, had realized this, because it allowed him for the first time to deceive Cristina.

'You've been long in Villafranca, then?' said Guido, engaging him at once.

'Since the end of March. I'll go to Rome when my father is well again.'

'And forget Villafranca, I suppose. How can you endure it?'

'Oh, in much the same way that you all do.'

There was a sad little laugh at this, in which Guido joined.

'But I was born here,' said he. 'Without such a dimension I have no real existence.'

55

'I imagine that is why you are always going away,' Edward rejoined pertly enough. Guido's face brightened.

'But how can it mean anything to you?'

'It's possible to enjoy Villafranca if one has an object.'

'Ah, you have an object. I wish I had an object, or at least one that was more than half formed. What is yours?'

'I don't know yet,' answered Edward, glancing sidelong at Cristina, 'but I presume I must have one.'

Guido laughed. 'You're a fortunate fellow.'

'Then you have nothing to hope for?' said Cristina, as though she had at last discovered an ally.

'We don't hope for much in Villafranca. I might hope for the safety of my estates or honours from the Duke, if I cared for such things. But to form an expectation of anything beyond this, anything so sublimely vague as not to be bought and sold or got by the indulgence of an appetite – that's hardly conceivable. I've never known that.' For the briefest instant he and Cristina looked at each other, and Edward thought to detect a shadow of sympathy between them, until as suddenly they looked away. Guido reached out and touched Edward's arm affectionately. 'You're lucky, so you are. I envy you.'

Slight and sallow-complexioned, his thin arms and rounded shoulders, coupled with the hang of his unfinished face, gave him even more the semblance of an old ape, though he had scarcely two or three years more than Edward. The sense of something unachieved was everywhere in his contained being, its self-possession falling across whatever lay beneath with the smooth articulation of a trap-door. You wondered, looking at him, imbued as he was with moderation and good taste, whether he had ever been showy, spendthrift, coarse, blasphemous or petty. The conclusion, sadly and invariably, was that he hadn't.

'Don't envy Edward,' said Cristina, 'he's mad enough to care for Villafranca.'

'I imagine you'll never do that,' said Guido sardonically.

'One almost forgets one is here, though one can never forget why.'

'I'm merely beginning not to find it dull,' said Edward, holding on stoutly. 'The trouble with you, Cristina, is that you think this is how it ought to be, and so of course it becomes what you want.'

'You speak as if you know the city,' said Guido.

'Show it us, this precious city of yours,' cried Cristina, throwing her arms wide, 'I doubt it'll move me the more.'

Edward softly said: 'I shall engage to move you. Do you agree, Count?'

'Yes, show us your curiosities,' said Guido. 'Monuments and cabinets and galleries don't move me, but mine is all the ignorance of a native, so I may hope for something amusing.'

'There! You've been brought to hope at last.'

'By your merit, I think.' Guido looked at him oddly. Edward turned towards Cristina, who said:–

'For tomorrow, then, and whenever else we please. I have no objection to walking, as you know.'

Signora Lupo appeared more sybilline than ever, as if she had long ago guessed how this might all come about and what its outcome would be. Beyond her in the doorway, Edward glimpsed the thickset, brooding figure of Count Castelvetro. At least, he supposed that was who it was.

 7

So, FOR DAYS on end, he showed them the city. He might have gone on until they all dropped down dead from exhaustion, if Guido had not had to ride out to Baggiovara to look at an estate and Cristina were not whisked off by Aldegonda and her friends, in awe of her Milanese smartness, to pronounce on this season's bonnets. Edward was glad it had happened thus. He felt the brimmings of an intolerable satisfaction among the three of them and was ready to step back from it instinctively.

Yet he knew that the cause of it owed nothing to any sudden access of love between Guido and Cristina, and that, unless some preternatural transformation took place, they would never show more than a distinguished mutual regard. Following him about among the churches and cloisters, to the Collegio di San Carlo and the house where Muratori died, into the ducal library with its rows of books like dirty teeth, and through the dismal, brocaded horror of the palace galleries, where smoky Correggios and Van Dycks seemed ready to accomplish a modest decomposition, they were concerned not to speak to one another unless it was on a topic which he had introduced. Now and then, when one of them asked a question, the other would address the answer to Edward. In everything they deferred to him, though it was obvious that their deference was more in the nature of a command. He must lead them up and down Villafranca purely in order that they should not need to acknowledge each other's presence beyond what common civility required.

The exercise gave him a sardonic pleasure. He might as well have offered them both a ride in a balloon as expected them to be genuinely interested in the dusty marvels of Villafranca. He had never had any great hopes of Italians in that line, and had long ago reconciled himself to their scorn of the past. Yesterday in Italy, when it has ceased being merely unfashionable, becomes an incubus: to have engaged them too deeply on the Este family, the architecture of the Capuchin convent or the question of whether the Via Emilia strictly followed the line of the ancient Roman road, would have driven towards a vapid silence. Cristina and Guido were in this respect no worse than most, and a certain measure of taste and intelligence had given them a greater regard for such things. But, as Edward understood it, they proposed these daily expeditions for the shelter his company afforded, rather than for the sake of historical curiosity.

Though he could guess that they found a decided quaintness in his obsessive antiquarianism, they endured it as a means whereby the three of them might be always together. He liked theatrically to push back the door-curtains in a church and to throw out an expansive arm like a figure in an engraved prospect. He liked, too, leading them along narrow lanes in search of those phago-cyte buildings which can be taken in the act, as it were, of absorbing work more ancient, with arches and pillars perpetually not quite disappearing into the surrounding masonry. He liked, above everything, his own heroic perversity in connoisseur-ship. Raphael and Perugino could be admired without his direction, but who, lacking Edward's enthusiasm to guide them, would learn to love Lanfranco or his adored Gentileschi? He knew, nevertheless, that the apparent tameness of Guido and Cristina meant nothing more than a reluctance to let him go.

Cristina's diffidence was easy to understand. He had readily fathomed the apprehension with which she faced the actualities of marriage. That freedom and directness she so energetically cultivated with him sheltered the fears of a Cressida thrust among the Grecian tents. Nothing sustained her beyond Edward's presence, but, though she could not know it, the weight of his attentions was beginning to shift. Chivalrous envy of Guido's advantages was giving place to a more detached concern with the way in which Cristina herself confronted the unfamiliar closeness of her betrothed, and, more arresting still, with the vague unease beneath Guido's reserve.

His was not the restlessness of the man for whom some other woman promises a readier entertainment. Edward, so lately twitching to be at Cristina and embarrassed more often than not by the naggings of his own lust, was astonished at his rival's uncertainty. Any orthodox arrangement of the kind would have demanded the company of some benevolent aunt or younger sister, who might take care occasionally to be out of the way so that the odd kiss could be snatched. Signora Lupo, however, had been content to turn over the responsibility to him, but whenever he looked like proposing a discreet withdrawal the pair moved desperately in his wake as if retiring from the verges of some terrible disclosure.

Yet something there was which intrigued Guido in Cristina. His sophistication, so dense as to give him a kind of wax-coated deadness, melted somewhat when she spoke with taste and eloquence of colours, patterns or materials in discussing her Milanese dresses and bonnets. Knowing nothing of these things, while being constantly addressed with a 'don't you think so?' or an 'isn't that so?' Edward could notice Guido's suddenly-kindled animation. Small details, the shape of a cup, the suggestions of banded design in stonework, a flower, a surface of painted wood, pleased him more than those grander notions after which Edward's fancy ranged, so that, when Cristina perceived their beauties, she seemed to earn something from him which he would never have awarded to the brilliance of her eyes or the sweetness of her voice.

Whatever the cause, he engaged with women in a way Edward had never met before. Fearful though he might be of the immediate business in hand, there was already a common ground of sympathy between him and Cristina which went beyond even a simple matter of choosing silks. In this sense they seemed to have achieved a mutual completeness incapable of the least modification. It was only that they must not be told of it.

When, following the interlude of bonnets and Baggiovara, the whole thing looked like starting again, Edward saw that something would have to be done. Opportunity came in the church of San Domenico, tucked into the skirts of the palace and built of

the same melon-flesh brick. He had wanted to show Guido and
Cristina the curious series of pictures with which its nave is hung,
each an ungainly likeness of some member of the ducal family
celebrated for her saintly virtues.

For a time they wandered up and down, reading the inscrip-
tions picked out on large, plain tablets beside the paintings.
There was a queen of Hungary and an English princess who had
married a German emperor and a duchess who had founded an
order in Ferrara. After a while Cristina sat down on a bench near
the doorway. Guido stood with his back to her, his hand fingering
his lips, staring vaguely into one of the chapels. Edward looked at
Cristina, framed in the oblong of sunlight striking the wall from
behind the green door-curtain. She was quite still, her hands
clasped in her lap, her head cast back so that the shadow behind it
threw the smooth curve of her neck into relief. Pale almost to
transparency as she appeared, there was a brightness in her
glance and in the soft falls of her hair which gave her a warmth
that in all those scores of moments he had stared at her Edward
had never noticed before. Thus tranquil and motionless, in her
plain walking dress, she seemed fixed here in the church like an
effigy, yet at the same time a creature mocking serenity and
repose.

Edward's gaze fell on Guido, standing there in his nonchalant
harmonies of elegance and experience. What, in God's name,
was either of them doing here, with him or with each other? They
were the strangers, the interlopers, not he. Villafranca was
suddenly his own city, he possessed it, disposed of its comings
and goings, grasped its syntax. The glozing memory of Florence
was now just a sweet taste in the mouth. Villafranca, so seedy, so
venal, so hopeless, had become the territory of imagination and
desire. He knew this was what he had always wanted. Clenching
his fists in ecstasy at the knowledge, he slipped out of the church
into the street.

It was the dusty close to a hot day, yet the town, only now
unshuttering itself and opening its doors, already seemed very
full of people. Besides the little groups always gathered around
the sellers of melon and lemonade, there was a crowd scattered
all the way along the Via Emilia. Under the arcades the shopmen
stood at their doors, hands in apron pockets. In the cafés there
was a half-hearted playing with spoonfuls of granita and

ice-cream and an irritable rattling of cups. Men leaned on their billiard cues like alerted halberdiers. Women tapped their fans on the tabletops. In everyone's face there was the same expression of sullen, fretful expectancy.

'Please, what's happening?' Edward asked a man standing in the doorway of a sausage shop.

'Haven't you read the decree?'

'What decree?'

'The new one, of course.'

New decrees went up almost each week, like mourning notices, cross little bills with labyrinths of rubric and the ducal shield frowning at the top. Mostly they were about public instruction, taxes on property or sentences of imprisonment, and Edward, who had not yet been presented to the Duke, had come to suppose that he must spend an inordinate amount of time thinking solely of matters like these. The sausage-maker eyed Edward coldly.

'The Duke's doubling the garrison. Public order and suchlike. It went up this morning and the regiment arrives any moment from Mantua. He must have asked for it after what happened in Ferrara.'

Edward had heard something of this from Basevi. The sausage-maker cleared his mouth and very deliberately spat. It was frightening, somehow, to see him do this, with the knives on the counter behind him and the heavy grey salami and hams dangling from their hooks above.

'The potato-eaters,' he muttered, 'and '31 all over again. Filthy potato-eaters!'

In the arcades the crowd had thickened. The warm air was full of a tremulous impatience. Hardly anyone now spoke. Edward was bold to push forward and stand shoulder to shoulder with a young priest and a lady accompanied by her maid, both dressed in mourning. The four of them craned their necks to peer up the street. In a little while they could hear, faintly, a noise like a distant movement of the earth, followed by the vaguest murmur spreading towards them.

'They are coming,' said the priest softly, and the woman, without turning, gave a sardonic smile of acknowledgment.

Edward had stood in crowds and watched processions before. He remembered how grand it had been at Stuttgart to watch the

62

daily changes of the palace guard, with everyone so merry and *en fête*, and how jolly were the parades at Paris, with the fat king and queen and all the royal dukes and duchesses bowling out of the Tuileries among the outriders and hussars. But something like what now happened was altogether strange to him, unimaginable if he had not been there. It was a crowd in which you saw and heard nothing. People stood perfectly still, their faces suddenly blind and immobile. No one broke from the mass of onlookers or tried to press forward beyond the lines of guards which had formed along the pavements. Not the feeblest cheer was to be heard. There was that dreadful, congealing silence which Edward had learned to know and fear in Villafranca. The raging of its violent emptiness sickened him.

Slowly, and contained, as it were, within the people's cold scrutiny, the dragoons, with their wagons and gun-limbers, filed past. Though they had ridden that day from Mantua, a morning's journey at least, there was a freshness about them like a warning. The soldiers were mostly young Croats, with trailing yataghan whiskers, well-waxed boots and gleaming accoutrements. The grinding noise made by the wheels of the gun-carriages, the curious dull, flapping sound of sabre-hilts tapping rhythmically against the edges of saddles, the jingle of bits and the apparent infinity of the cavalcade were like challenges to the crowd's quiet. The menacing clench of reins in the fist and the bunching of muscle in horse and rider defied passivity. Yet it was only when the last of the canteen wagons had turned the corner of the Corso Canalgrande that anyone stirred, and even then there seemed to be a momentary pause, as if the dust of the soldiers' passing had somehow first to settle.

Wondering and subdued, Edward went home. The experience, with all its aspects of the minatory and the bizarre, was a reproof to his vanity of making Villafranca his own. He had been the only true onlooker there, one whose destiny was not comprised in the arrival of Croat dragoons. Miserably he thought now of having to return to his father and mother. In six weeks everybody would set off for the country and he would have to go down to Rome or Naples to follow, as was the custom, his parents' tedious imitations of pleasure.

The palace, when he returned to it, was full of that nice fustiness which a day's heat brings out of old chairs and frayed damask. Edward sat down on one of the spindly little sofas in the hall and felt himself sliding into gloom. He stayed inanimate in the shadow until the door by the staircase creaked open and Annibale came towards him bearing two letters.

'This one's from Naples, *milordo*. And the other was brought a moment ago from Marchesa Rangoni's.'

'Are they waiting an answer?'

'No, *milordo*, the boy was positive there was to be none and went off directly.'

Taking this for yet another of the Marchesa's peremptory summonses, Edward put it by without looking at it, and hurried instead to open the larger letter, which bore the flourishing superscription 'The Lady Augusta Rivers, Posillipo' beneath a coronet and wafer. His mother was not given to agreeable surprises, but this once she had excelled herself:

'My dear Ned,

Your father & I were so pleased with yr. last acct. of things at Villafranca – though I own I cannot *imagine* how you *enjoy* it! – that we have decided that it is best for you to remain there until the summer is quite over (I have written to yr. aunt about this) The Drs here – 2 are Swiss 1 is a German & *entre nous* (though *not* liked by yr. papa) *very* agreeable in his manners – have recommended that we do not move to Rome, or even to Frascati as we had planned, as the air is *putrid* &c & the climate here has a beneficial influence after the mild congestion of the lungs he has lately had.

So you will not mind, dearest Ned, staying at Vfranca till we are able to send for you in September, when we go to Lucca.

We were *surprised*, I must say, by yr. curiosity as to the circumstances of yr. aunt Harriet's marriage, but I see no reason why it shld not be satisfied. It fell out v. conveniently as far as we cld judge, since she met the Count when she was with us at Vienna (we left you with those dull sticks of Drumshanes at Schwalbach, I fear) & he was accompanying the prince of Villafranca, the Duke that now is, on a visit to the Emperor.

One has always, you know, to be careful with the people here over *money*. Nobility & persons of *ton* in Italy often promise more than they can perform (though I fancy it is more so here at Naples, where the *noblesse* is so v. numerous, than in Florence) but yr. grandfather was able to make enquiries & found that

Count Castelvetro was *substantial* & wld offer handsome settlements &c. Yr. aunt for her part was truly *éprise*, though I think the same cld not be said for *sua eccellenza*, who, I always felt, went into the affair a trifle coldly, more perhaps for the sake of respectability than with any real fondness for yr. poor aunt, & looking for a *parti*, whch he found.

As to whether she is *happy*, the speculation on yr. part is somewhat impertinent, though interesting. I never heard anything against the Count except a little *liberalism* in his politics, but since he is said to have saved the present Duke's life in the last outrages, he has not been noted much for that.

Of course yr. aunt's position is *strange*, though several noblemen at Milan & Turin have English wives, & she went into the match with her eyes *open*. Yet I don't deny she must miss English society & since he *never* travels now, sees little of the world.

Yr. uncle Cannock has written asking whether you would wish to go to them in London for the winter & to Marchington at Christmas. Uttoxeter is *engaged* to a daughter of Ld Bromyard's, so will be off a-visiting at Tedstone, no doubt, but yr. younger cousins are pleasant enough & fond of horses & music, whch shld please you, so you may write & accept & go there in November around yr. birthday.

We go on *splendidly* here & I am quite the *jeune fille* again. Yr. papa is as well as may be conceived.

Yr. affec. Mamma.

P.S. Apropos Ct Cvetro I think I ought to tell you that when we were at Florence I heard him *scandalized* for having been previously contracted to a lady at Vfranca with whom he broke the engagement to marry yr. aunt. Such stories are often owing to jealousy, but there may have been some truth in it, thus making yr. aunt a sad creature. A.R.'

Edward folded the sheet with something nearer satisfaction than any previous letter from his mother had ever occasioned him. Opening the second letter he found that it came from Cristina. He read it slowly, smiled to himself, stuffed both letters into his coat pocket and muttered:–

'Good.'

 8

IN LATER YEARS he would look back on that afternoon in the
tailor's house at Carpi with a curiosity undimmed by the
process of time, for there was to be no absolute understanding
why it should have been so important to him. The lightest twitch
of memory recalled its savour, and the talisman, with powers
thus invoked, became a measure of existence.

There was a hint of it even in the simple freedom tasted on
setting off along the high road from the city. He had ridden this
road a hundred times without valuing it, but the purely clandestine way in which, slipping out of the palace in the weakest of
the morning light without a word to anyone, he joined Basevi and
they trotted away like satisfied thieves, gave everything a
glamour he had never honestly known before.

With that equine sympathy which gauges what you feel before
you yourself have arrived at it, their horses, restive and skittish at
the customs post, flew off into the country; when the pair drew
rein and looked back, Villafranca was already a greyish-brown
indistinctness which could touch them no longer. They could
smell the fields, the larks were screaming, there was bugloss and
mallow in the ditches and their faces were whitened with the dust
of the roadway.

'This is why her parents don't trust me,' said Basevi.

'I thought they wanted you to marry her, with your prospects
and all that. My uncle will never turn you out.'

'Yes, but I told you, a Jew on horseback, that's what they don't like. Gentiles may ride, but Jews walk until they are rich enough for carriages. Perhaps that was why they asked about in the ghetto at Villafranca, to get a character for my family, like hiring a servant. They didn't believe a proper Jew could care anything for martingales and four-year-olds. It is the children of Israel whoring after strange gods, me and horses. But then Anna got to hear of it, and they gave in.' Basevi laughed.' She is very forthright, you know. At our weddings we have a custom which demands that, as they leave the synagogue, the husband and wife try to stamp on each other's foot, and whichever is first will rule the household thereafter.'

'Shall I like her?'

'She will like you. She'll say your hair needs brushing. Don't be discouraged, it's only her way.'

Edward shrugged.' Oh, it's always people's way, isn't it? I've been used to that for years.'

Anna never mentioned his hair, but in everything else she was as positive and direct as Basevi had given her out. Her questions sprang not, as so often among Italians, from a desire to banish idleness or boredom, but from a sincere absorption with his answers to them. Something in him seemed genuinely and without malice to amuse her, and her immediate assumption of familiarity was grounded in the truth of his own affection for Basevi.

It was this certainty of hers which marked the afternoon, as much as the zeal with which the company fell to eating, or the urgency with which the tailor's wife pressed him towards the various dishes, or the waves of discussion and reminiscence surrounding each mouthful. The diners themselves, what was more, were beyond anything in their enthusiasm, their unpremeditated eloquence, the amplitude of their movements as they reached and proffered across the table, and in the ultimate absence of reserve dictated by their preoccupation with the moment. He could hear, for the first time consciously and unmistakably, the noise of Italians at meals, cheerful in contention, delighting irrepressibly in the companionship of the table, loud without coarseness and vulgar merely in not giving precedence to refinement.

They deferred continually to him, praising his fluency of speech, filling his glass, inviting him to try what he had tasted already, in a thousand little flourishes of courtesy. It felt like the colossally vague embrace bestowed by a parent who cannot quite remember, for the time being, the name of one child among so many, but is content to display a general affection.

It might be that they did not care for him, or perhaps that they found his moments of bashfulness and reserve an unmerited slight on their lack of gentility, as they might imagine he supposed it. His greeting on arrival had perhaps been judged too cold or he had not manifested enough eagerness over the polenta. He felt the English clumsiness of his elbows and shoulders, that overriding sense of not knowing what to do with the limbs at one's disposal, of which the Italians are so serenely unconscious.

However burdened with his own unease, he could scarcely fail to acknowledge theirs. It was not difficult for him to realize that he must have been the first Gentile ever to have sat at this table, thus doubly an alien to them all. They were too polite to articulate such a feeling, yet he knew it was forever there, because he had it as well. In the act of sitting down together, he and they had, as it were, done for each other. It was impossible not to think of his parents' horror were they to discover that he had allowed himself to be entertained in the household of a Jewish tailor: his father, in the ultimate condemnation, would have called it 'being democratic', and Edward wondered what these Jews must feel on being told that they served such purposes of outrage. His had not been a calculated ruthlessness – he was there because Basevi had invited him and to indulge his curiosity – but in the very occasion lay something wonderfully irrevocable, an affront to every inculcation of dignity and respect.

It was the more ironical, then, that the company should have strained to do him honour. There was a remarkably stupid cousin from Leghorn, whose refusal to acknowledge Edward's fluency in Italian took the form of converting all her verbs into the infinitive and sedulously omitting the article before every noun, on the grounds that only thus might a foreigner understand her delphic utterances. There was Basevi's rolypoly brother Abramo, a fiddler in the theatre band, who made lecherous asides about his future sister-in-law to Edward while the dishes were handing round and quizzed him about the Rangoni girls, especially Aldegonda whom he had seen in her box and was smitten by. There was the hatter's wife from across the way, agog with questions about Paris, and a solemn, white-faced boy called Gioacchino, of whom the stupid cousin kept whispering 'Only twelve years old' each time he sought to engage Edward in conversation. There were two laconic gentlemen in tall hats, whose task seemed to be that of agreeing with everything the tailor said, and there was Anna's mother, Signora Limentani, who had taken it into her head that Edward's slightness of build was owing to the fact that his uncle and aunt were starving him, and plied him accordingly with the best of the chicken and the *sformato*, while his efforts to wave them away were merely viewed as the hypocrisy of English good breeding.

It was Limentani the tailor himself who ruled all. At the drawing of each new cork he sipped and swilled and pronounced, and, when an especially toothsome salad of rocket and endive was brought in, he furnished a discourse on spring vegetables which drew loud murmurs of admiration from the tall-hatted ones on either side of him. Had he only continued in this vein, his overbearing pomposity would simply have been irksome. As it was, he early singled out the English boy as a rival, to be ridden down as swiftly and thoroughly as possible. Thus the honour and delight which every stranger feels in his welcome among Italians, and which Edward, made much of as Basevi's friend, was ready to enjoy, soon became muddied with his host's mounting irritation at the way in which the dues of interest and concern were paid to a whippersnapper in a blue coat.

This very coat, like Desdemona's handkerchief, was a banner for jealousy. Limentani was a maker of braid for the uniforms of the ducal court, and Edward, with all the gifts of an engaged listener, had started on a polite question or two as to the mysteries of the work involved, but the tailor, determined not to be civil, slyly shifted the conversation towards English clothes.

'They say your broadcloth is the best, but I've never believed it,' he said, throwing these last words out to the company with a scornful grin. 'Stuff like this of yours will barely last you a season, but then if you follow the fashion like the rest of our young cubs you won't need it to.'

Basevi's face wore a look of ineffectual sympathy. 'It isn't an English coat,' Edward said calmly, 'it was made by Dufour in Via Rondinelli in Florence, who is generally thought of as the best.

He is a Swiss, I believe.' He looked Limentani straight in the eye as he spoke, kindling the tailor's fury by showing how much of the game he had already understood.

'This is the English mode, is it, of which we hear so much? For the English gentleman, with his horses and his dogs, eh?' Limentani was warming to his theme and, from differing motives, there was an evident quickening of interest around the table. Even the stupid cousin's husband stopped staring at his bottle and gazed gloomily upon Edward. Signora Limentani handed the *polpettoni* with a decidedly preoccupied air, while Abramo gave the friendliest of warning kicks under the table. Gioacchino's glance was chillingly philosophic. Nobody offered to speak; it was as if they had laid wagers on the contest. Edward, wondering how to deal with his own anger, began nevertheless to enjoy himself as he felt their mutinous affection surround him. Heedless of it, the tailor in his hubris pursued:–

'I never trusted the English. What have they ever done for us in Italy that we could not do for ourselves?'

The tall-hatted ones instinctively cast an eye towards the doorway. It was a sign that politics were on the table.

'Lord Palmerston is our friend, I think,' volunteered Abramo. Limentani scowled at him.

'Oh, you think, do you? I think Lord Palmerston is a bag of wind, and all the other lords with him, who come to us with their methods and their systems and go home and write books about the poor Italians who are not fit to govern themselves.'

'You seem to know a lot about it,' said Edward, 'a deal more than I do.'

The left-hand tall hat shifted in his chair and whispered:–

'Limentani has correspondents in Turin and Genoa. He is very intelligent.'

'Very intelligent, I should say,' echoed the right-hand, nodding almost till his hat fell off. The tailor sat back to enjoy the effect of this loyal demonstration upon Edward, but the result was clearly unsatisfying. His wife's face grew more and more sybilline. With a seraphic grin, the Leghorn cousin suddenly demanded:–

'You English lord?'

A polite denial was cut short, however, as Limentani, with increased asperity, renewed the attack.

'Was it not the English in Corfu who betrayed the Bandiera brothers to the Neapolitans?'

This was not the first time Edward had heard such an accusation, yet even if it were true he felt honour-bound to refute it.

'Was it? Their own imprudence was more to blame, though I suppose one may libel the English for anything these days. Whatever is done in the world is always England's fault, I've learnt that much. You never stop to consider France's share.' He felt himself getting warmer, as he knew Limentani wanted him to. The tailor's face gleamed.

'France is a different matter, and one which you cannot understand.'

'France is always a different matter,' muttered Gioacchino oracularly, staring at the tablecloth.

'Only twelve years old,' whispered the Leghorn cousin promptly.

'I haven't finished!' cried the tailor. 'The English must stop meddling and that is enough!'

'But the French have meddled ever since Buonaparte and nobody has told them to stop,' objected Abramo, 'and in '31 it was because of French promises that our Duke encouraged Menotti to revolt.' Again he kicked Edward under the table.

'Permit me to correct you, who are so noble in defence of our sovereign highness,' said the tailor venomously, 'but Menotti's failure in '31 owed nothing to France. And I think you'll find that England has been the greater meddler of the two. Our politics are like our cooking,' he declared, so majestically that the tall hats went bolt upright in veneration, 'simple to us, but incomprehensible to strangers, its ingredients plain, honest, unpretending, culled and prepared by humble, unassuming folk, for those who know how to taste them. As in cooking there is fish or meat, so . . .'

But the stupid cousin was too quick for him. 'English to eat fish?' she enquired portentously. Limentani, in a sudden release of rage, hammered the table, jingling the glasses and spoons. 'Listen to me!' he shouted. 'As in cooking, I said, there is either meat or fish . . .'

'Enough! Away with your fish and your meat!'

It was his daughter who answered him. She had sprung to her feet, incomparably rebellious, with an ardour which no parent,

Jew or Gentile, could have checked. In the brilliance of her unabashed gaze, in the lustrous blackness of her hair, in the sheer emphatic handsomeness of her, pressing the table as though to stop herself from flying at her father, Edward saw the very image of a long-restrained liberty.

'What entitles you to speak so?' she cried, her beautiful, sonorous voice rising to thunder. 'What do you know of Italy? Because you waved a flag at Reggio twenty years ago, you think it's given to you to speak for all of us . . . and to insult our guest into the bargain?' Anna's bosom heaved as she spoke. Her mother, clattering the plates together, glanced at her in furtive adoration. Basevi clasped her by the hand. Drawing back his chair, her father seemed to study her as something quite unpremeditated, to which his hitherto untroubled view of the world could not give a name. At that moment, Edward felt, she might have drawn a sword and bid them follow her till the last Austrian was driven beyond the mountains. Perhaps that was what old Limentani would not understand.

Between the pair of them lay an emptiness nothing could fill. She had spoken. He had listened to her defiance. So, getting up and placing his chair at the table with pedantic precision, he muttered the words 'Foreign innovations?' with all the scorn at his command, and stalked, not altogether without dignity, from the room.

It was a scene condemned forever to imperfect realization in Edward's memory. What followed was so patently at odds with it that the earlier vulgarities and embarrassments seemed put there to enhance the unexampled pleasure of the afternoon. Still smouldering, Anna sat down to receive her mother's quiet but insistent reproof. Leaning across to Edward, whom Abramo was patting on the back as if the victory were his, Basevi said:—

'I couldn't help you, do you see? It was impossible. He wasn't angry with you. In fact I don't think he even knew who you were. It is just that your presence is made the object of everything he feels. It's enough for me to have brought a Christian into the house for his anger to be kindled.'

'But I asked you whether my coming would offend him . . .' began Edward in genuine embarrassment.

'Bah!' exclaimed Signora Limentani, hovering with the *dolci*, 'our Daniele is a philosopher and thinks too hard about these

72

things. Eat, eat, *milordo*, you're as thin as a nail. Take a candied fig or two – they're good, though I say it who shouldn't.'

The figs settled it, as did the sweet wine and the coffee and a *nocino* on whose preparation the Leghorn cousin chose to harangue Edward when he ill-advisedly revealed that in England (for what he knew) walnuts were only pickled or else eaten from the shell. There was a pushing back of chairs and a stretching out of legs in token of vanished constraints. Anna, rising purposefully from the table, went to join her mother in the kitchen, pursued by the still voluble cousin. Among the bread crusts, the nutshells, the small improvisatory splashes of wine and sauce on the furrowed tablecloth, the men talked of journeys and money, of whether it might be better to live at Bologna than at Milan, of the coming opera season and if it were true that De' Bassini had been engaged and the scandal last year of the dancer who had arrived from Venice with her protector in tow and the terms he had tried to force upon the impresario, of the Duke's new laws against the contraband and the Pope's concessions. And, as they let Edward in and out of their talk, he felt coming upon him one of those singular distillations of happiness which derive from the plain fact of being foreign. It was as if he had found himself again, barely recognized but essentially the same beneath the trappings of an alien syntax and a rhetoric of gesture not his own, giving life to resources of eloquence and warmth he had never before been able to lay bare.

On some necessary pretext he got up and walked into the next room. He wanted solitude in which to absorb this new reality. Limentani's hectoring was like a baptism; Edward no longer felt any rancour, through a conviction that nothing of the sort would ever happen to him again. By such a means he had stumbled upon a territory with which Cristina, Guido, the Rangoni and the ballrooms and drawing rooms of Villafranca had nothing to do, and been given the freedom of it.

About to enter the room beyond, he paused at the threshold when he saw Limentani himself sitting in a shadowed corner, talking in low, earnest tones to Anna, their hands affectionately clasped. It was a scene he could not interrupt. He went out, musing, onto the balcony. The street below was empty, save for the cats asleep on its warm stones. The air was thick with that arcane silence which at this hour, in these towns of the *bassa*, is enjoined as though with finger on lip. Inside the house the comforting flow of chat from the men at the table rippled on across the shadow of the dining room. An arm came round his shoulder, and there was Basevi beside him with his coat off.

'Still angry with me, are you?'

'I never was for a moment,' said Edward. 'You did it for the best – as though you knew how it would all happen.'

Basevi's smile held a disarming guilt. 'I own it. Perhaps that was why I brought you here. Sometimes we must compromise ourselves to take a step forward.'

'Don't vex yourself, Daniele, I've done something of the same sort today,' Edward rejoined with a certain pride.

Glancing back, Basevi said: 'She has made her peace with him. She likes you, by the way.'

'I'm glad. It would be foolish of me to pretend that didn't matter. But I think she'll stamp on your foot first.'

'Why?'

'So that you can have your own way afterwards.'

'That's one of your paradoxes, is it? Well, I insist on your telling her so yourself before we go home, which must be soon. I'll send someone to see about the horses, and you must go and gossip with my scallywag brother. If you're good, he'll maybe stop raving about Aldegonda Rangoni and speak of music a little. Have you observed how people who play instruments for a living never like to talk about music?'

He strolled into the house, whistling softly. Drawing back a little, Edward watched as Anna emerged from the shadowed room where she had left her father. He watched her dust Basevi's waistcoat with the back of her hand and straighten his cravat. He saw the gesture become an embrace, he saw the way in which the pair, amused at their own caution, looked about, and then, with a sort of desperate enthusiasm, fell to kissing, and he realized all of a sudden that it was the first time he had ever seen it done. A spurt of envy went through him: not thus had he fallen upon the cold, unwilling Cristina. He saw Anna whisper something to Basevi which made him laugh, and the two flung themselves upon each other with renewed stealth and urgency. Suddenly Anna, pulling herself away, cried angrily 'Gioacchino, how dare you!' and the pale, hollow-eyed boy walked noiselessly past them, as if they were a vanity he had learnt to eschew.

Gioacchino came out onto the balcony and stretched a length of string, with a piece of wood attached to one end, over the iron railing and into the street. With enormous concentration he started to pull the piece of wood up to him and then let it down again, repeating this until Edward, leaning in the angle where the railing joined the wall of the house, said:–

'What are you doing, Gioacchino?'

But Gioacchino, being only twelve years old, saw no reason to answer.

9

I F IT FELT odd to have left Villafranca, it was even stranger to
return. Entering the city, he looked quizzically at everything
around him, thinking 'I lived here once' as the walls and doors
and pavements suddenly quickened with unfamiliarity. He began
to stare at people as he passed, wondering whether they would
recognize him. A mere afternoon seemed an age of distance. Yet
for all the ease and happiness which had come upon him at Carpi,
he felt safer here: it was as though, in going there, he had visited a
foreign country, where, for a season, they had garlanded and
feasted him, on whose flesh an hour afterwards they might have
banqueted.

He wasn't tired, only rather wooden from an hour in the
saddle. When he had given his horse to the groom he strolled
through the house into the dank, weedy little garden, with its
couple of spectral sycamores shadowing the windows of the
library, a few sad lemon trees in pots against the wall, and a cross
of straight gravel walks converging upon a fountain whose
drippings reminded him of somebody with a runny nose. Coming
out onto the mezzanine at the top of the mossy steps leading
down into the walks, he looked up at the sky, tinged with livid
patches of light under the mantling of cloud. The warm air
around him was thick enough to punch and there was a keen
smell in it like iron. Excited at the chance of thunder he went
slowly down the steps.

There was somebody else in the garden. Edward saw a man

sitting on the stone bench under the trees at the end of the walk, and recognized Guido. He looked as if he had been waiting there for hours, but it was perhaps only the habitual patient weariness of his expression, which made him always seem much older than he was. Giving Edward a thin smile he said:–

'They let me stay. It wasn't worth leaving only to return.'

'Was it so important?'

'Since it concerns you, I think so. Where did you go?'

The question startled Edward. What right did Guido have to an answer? There was something proprietary in it that he at once resented. Nevertheless he replied:–

'To Carpi.'

Guido's gaze suggested that it might as well have been Timbuktu.

'Alone?'

'No.'

'With whom, then?'

'A friend.'

'What friend?'

The note of irritation was something Edward had never noticed in Guido before. Such questioning irresistibly recalled Cristina, and it might have seemed as though he had caught the habit from her, if only there hadn't been something less arbitrary, more raw, in the interrogation. For her it was a rhetorical exercise: for Guido it was a simple wish to know. Nervously Edward moved away along the alley towards the fountain, wheezing and dribbling in the middle of the garden, and Guido came after him.

'Who was it?' he said softly.

Edward turned round. 'Oh, I don't know, Prince Metternich, Monsieur de Lamartine, the Emperor of the Brazils, for God's sake. I shan't tell you until you tell me why it should matter.'

Guido reddened and was silent. Edward suddenly felt the extent of his own power, though he was not sure yet what its nature was or how he would use it. He saw only that Guido must not be hurt.

'Cristina sent you, I suppose. If she wants to reproach me she should do so for herself.'

'No, Edward, she knows nothing of this. I came alone because I wanted to know.'

'Well, what precisely?'

He surveyed Guido composedly, understanding the sort of answer he would give. In an almost inaudible voice Guido said:–

'I . . . we . . . I was afraid that you wouldn't come back. I sent a servant twice to enquire for you. In the end I came myself and waited.'

It was a thing both obscure and absurd. There was even something sinister in the notion of having been sent after and waited for during the whole time of his journey to Carpi, his entertainment at the tailor's house and his return thereafter. The realization confounded him totally, yet in the end it was no different from any other devious proceeding in this corkscrew place. He said nothing, only shrugged and made a noise of impatience. Guido came closer.

'Why did you leave us alone yesterday? Why?' he said. 'Why didn't you stay?'

Edward was not going to tell him that. In a world of lies, reticences and obliquities he had every right not to speak. But something made him want to, if only because Guido's questions were once more so different from those Cristina would have asked. With her the question, with him the reply.

'That mattered to you both?' Of course he knew it had. Her letter was in his pocket to prove it. Guido, drawing his hand across his face in a vague, half-accomplished gesture of embarrassment, said:–

'Forgive me, but don't you see how it must have been? We couldn't speak to each other, she and I. It was the first time we had ever absolutely been alone together. I did not know what to say to her, nor she how to answer. It was horrible.'

'Ah, fiddlestick, Guido, I won't believe it,' cried Edward, 'the least common civility would have done. You could have shown her something in the church. Or there were the reinforcements arriving from Mantua, you might have gone out and had a look at those. Or bought an ice or a glass of lemonade. Or made her a present of a pair of gloves.' He stopped, exasperated at Guido's murky confusion. The idea of the two of them being left to deal with one another was piquant in the extreme. Yesterday he had liked it; now it was sublime.

'You would have done all those things, I suppose,' said Guido.

'You sound as if you envied me.'

78

'I do.'

'Deuce take it, why?'

'Because you have the power to act, and I don't. You speak airily of gloves and lemonade, as if it were only a matter of that. To you maybe it is. But do you imagine I could possibly see it in such a way? I or Cristina?'

'Ah, Cristina,' rejoined Edward, 'we shall put upon one side. See here, Guido, why don't you both give it over directly? You have only to say a word to her and she would agree, you know that.'

'Saying words cannot help,' Guido said sombrely. 'We might never utter a sound to each other again, but we shall be together for the rest of our lives.' There was something preternaturally hollow and infinite about the way in which he pronounced these words, as if their echo was to go on spinning in a limitless emptiness. As the realization of Guido's meaning became clear, Edward grew embarrassed by his own obtuseness.

'Then your families . . .' he began.

'Yes, you understand, it is our families.' This was not precisely what Edward had understood, but it did not matter. 'There is no question of our refusing.'

'Do you wish there were?'

'That's unjust. My wishes do not enter into it.' Guido stared hard at the fountain. 'Hope is permitted to you but not to us.'

'Hoping and wishing are not the same.'

'I have learnt not to do either. Do you understand?'

People were always asking Edward that. It was starting to lose its meaning, to become submerged among all the other imprecisions from which Villafranca appeared to take its essence. One day, in a burst of sincerity, someone would annihilate the vagueness for ever. Edward resumed impatiently:–

'So you sat there, the pair of you, in the church, with nothing to say? I suppose you could not have stayed there for long.'

'She asked me to take her back to the Piani d'Ungheria.' The name was captivating again in its colossal evidence of solitude.

'It sounds as though you never did that before.'

'You were always there, Edward. We were alone now. There were no carriages and Via Emilia was full of people after the procession. Cristina was . . . well, almost in tears and did not want anyone to see her, so we had to go through the back streets by the market. When we reached the Madonna del Popolo she was crying. By the time we were at the palace I had made up a foolish tale that she had been overcome by the heat and needed to lie down. Mariclò did not believe that, I could see. I felt stupid and worthless to anyone.'

That at least Edward could understand. 'Mariclò never takes anything on trust. Maybe that's why she always seems so interesting.'

The thick, metal-scented air muffled the reverberation of their voices. The leaves and branches around them were motionless, and above the line of the garden wall the roofs of the neighbouring houses glistened with an inauthentic sharpness of definition.

'I am not,' Edward said 'going to tell you why I left you as I did. And you may not ask me. Yet, at least. But you might at any rate tell me what Cristina said. Was she angry?'

Guido shook his head.

'Not even mildly angry? Or rather cross?'

Again Guido demurred. 'Her feelings were my own exactly. I had never seen her so before. That was the worst of all, the sheer unfamiliarity of it, the way in which she seemed to become what I was.' He waited for Edward to say something, but he was silent, standing with his hands in his pockets, looking at Guido.

'And I, I was afraid.'

'Not of Cristina, surely?' The thing seemed natural enough to Edward.

'No, of myself, because you were not there, because I was alone.' He looked away, suffused with embarrassment, his body wanting, as it were, to disappear rather than manifest the feelings which now overcame it.

'I was afraid you wouldn't come back.'

'You know that's impossible.'

Spreading his arms wide in one of those ample gestures of futility in which he was perfect, Guido said: 'Yes, Edward, but you can choose where you go.'

'Then I have chosen to remain here, if you really think I can make up my own mind about such things. But I'm starting to believe that it is not me, after all, who decides. These things are settled by others and I meekly comply.'

'Ah, you're too strong for that.'

'Would you say so to Cristina?'

'There's no need. She knows, all too well.'

He fell silent, as if choked by his own apprehensions. Next door the convent bell started up, and the ring-doves grated in the trees. Beyond the walls and the houses, far off across the plain, came a faint murmuring noise, like the approach of horses. At length Guido, carefully averting his gaze from Edward, said:–

'You must simply never leave us like that again. You must never go away without telling us.'

To Edward such things would have been incredible if he had not in some degree felt that Guido was more concerned for himself than for Cristina. As gently as he could, he answered:–

'I undertake nothing of the kind. Despite what I said just now, I must be allowed to come and go as I please. I'm only a boy, as Cristina never ceases to tell me. And a stranger. Villafranca isn't Florence or Rome, with lots of Eustace and Murray and Calignani and consuls and chaplains for the English. So you might smother me and be none the worse. While I remain here I must have the liberty to do as I like. That's all.'

'But you are necessary to us, Edward,' insisted Guido.

Edward had been on the point of remarking, not without a certain exasperated cynicism, that they had both much better need each other than him when his aunt came out of the house, accompanied by the Marchesa Rangoni and Signora Lupo. The Signora hung back a little under the trees, as though reluctant to move out of the shadow while there was yet some light. The Marchesa, with her usual air of saturnine complacency, bore majestically down upon Edward, barely pausing to acknowledge Guido's presence, while the Countess looked up at the sky and sniffed.

'Rain,' said she. 'How tiresome that is when we were all to have gone to the ramparts this evening.'

'I am glad we have found you, Edward,' said the Marchesa. 'The week after next is the Congedo, and Mariclò has particularly asked whether you will be there.'

'Of course he will be at the Congedo,' cried the Countess, as if some affront had been implied. 'He will come with me.'

'I haven't any idea what the Congedo is,' said Edward, turning to Guido for enlightenment, 'but I'm sure it will be jolly.'

'The Congedo is the leave-taking at the Palace before everyone goes into the country. They say that it's a relic of times past, when oaths of fealty were renewed to the Duke. It has died out everywhere in Italy but here.'

'Oh, it is quite charming, Ned. Chivalrous and stately, like something from Scott,' said the Countess. 'I always enjoy it.'

The Marchesa gave her a look that was almost pitying. 'My mother-in-law and I,' she said, 'do not go any longer, but we send the children.'

Then she added quietly: 'But it may be that this year Massimo will not go either. You, Count, do you still go?'

'I . . . well, I have not decided.'

'No,' said the Marchesa, as if knowing perfectly well that this was what Guido would say. 'Mariclò hopes, then, that you will come, Edward.'

'I shall bring him, you need not fear,' said the Countess.

Turning to Guido with a wry smile, Edward said softly: 'She will bring me, do you hear? Which of us is free?'

'You, of course, always,' rejoined Guido, laughing. The Marchesa made him an inclusive gesture.

'You'll come with us? We've the carriage waiting.'

He said yes, though Edward was wanting him to say no. The Marchesa had never in her life been denied, and Guido was respectful of that tradition. As they all went up the steps, Signora Lupo turned to look at Edward. He wished she would speak to him, instead of seeking to draw him out by means of her silent remoteness. Perhaps Mariclò was right in disliking her.

When they had gone, he told his aunt that he would go and read in the library until dinner time. Rather to his surprise, the Countess did not, as on previous occasions, try persuading him to stay. 'I shall be out here, if anybody asks,' she said, 'and you may tell them that I shan't go to the Taccoli's ball tonight after all. One gets too fagged at this end of the season.'

Once in the library Edward sat down with a volume of Parini's poems at the table by the big window that overlooked the garden, opening at the ode on smallpox vaccination:

> *O Genovese, ove ne vai? qual raggio*
> *Brilla di speme su le audaci antenne?*
> *Non temi, oimè! le penne*
> *Non anco esperte de gli ignoti venti?*

Such a pattern of daring Guido should have followed. Edward sat quite still for a while, his hand on the opened page, thinking of the mass of things a single day had allowed him to perceive. Now he felt tired, as though his arms and legs would drop off, and more than ever distant from his morning ride with Basevi and the meal at the tailor's house, whence he had trailed homewards to find himself sought about the town by those to whom he had supposed his absence could hardly have mattered.

The idea that Cristina should need him was tremendous, the more because he was beginning to experience that singular pleasure which arises when we realize we are no longer in love. Guido, whose sensibilities he had until now scarcely considered, was someone he did not yet understand.

Between them they had brought him to know where his strength lay. It was a force he had never imagined himself to possess and did not know what to do with. Yet it was something that in the simple act of leaving her alone with Guido, he had made Cristina cry. He was glad, too, that his running away to Carpi for a whole day had made them frantic without him. It was a stranger capitulation than any he had either wanted or imagined, but there appeared to be no limit to its offered possibilities. Edward yawned, wishing it were dinner time, and turned again to his book. Glancing through the window as he did so, he saw the Countess walking in the garden, waiting for the thunder, if it were ever to come.

I O

WHOLLY PREOCCUPIED WITH doing what was politically correct for her family while at the same time keeping an iron in the fire with the Duke, the Marchesa Rangoni had withheld Massimo and Aldegonda from polluting themselves at the detested rites of the Congedo, but delivered Mariclò at the Palazzo Castelvetro as a surety. With her brown complexion and immense eyes Mariclò was not thought a beauty, and her mother, in contriving to render her even dowdier than usual in a court dress that had patently been handed down, seemed as though she were using her younger daughter's plainness to abuse the very principle of legitimism.

Understanding in this the Marchesa's habit of demanding others to believe that the entire nobility of Villafranca was governed by the crook of her finger, Edward was happy to have heard from Basevi, only minutes before her arrival at the palace, that Guido had gone early into the country, having closed up his house and seen the servants on their way before he left.

'That is as may be,' said the Marchesa, clearly annoyed that Guido had not done as she expected. 'No one saw Cristina this morning, so perhaps she has slipped away besides, though I never knew anyone behave less as if they were engaged than her. I wish Signora Lupo had been more concerned, but she is calm, quite calm.'

'Whoever saw her otherwise?' rejoined Edward, very pleased

with himself. 'As for Signorina Cristina, she told me that she did not think it patriotic to attend.'

Mariclò spluttered into her large, crumpled sleeve. The Marchesa, not seeming to hear her, winced somewhat, but regained enough composure to look Edward in the face and say: 'How eccentric. It is not at all what one might have expected.'

'For myself I should scarcely have imagined anything else, but then I can't presume to judge on the degrees of patriotism, can I?'

At which the Marchesa, having clearly had enough, felt it was time to take leave.

'Did Cristina really say that, Edward, or did you just make it up?' said Mariclò as soon as her mother was gone.

'Of course I did. She hasn't any patriotism, except, you know, in a vague sort of way. Do you mind my teasing your mother?'

'She deserves it now and then. But poor Cristina!'

'How?'

'She cannot be patriotic when she has no *patria*. She is not a Milanese, though she has been brought up like one, and she affects to despise Villafranca. I think she might learn to love something, don't you, before it's too late?'

Edward stared at her, astounded. 'Do you mean that, truly?'

'Yes,' said she, as if it were the simplest of conclusions.

'And what do you love?'

'Oh, any number of things. The view from our house in the morning, across the Piani d'Ungheria to the theatre on the other side. Glasses of lemonade. The taste of cinnamon is nice. Arguing with Massimo. Dresses of plain muslin like the ones we wear in the country, and the straw hats we wear with them. For that matter I love watching you play the piano with Cristina. But she . . .' Mariclò shrugged, an operation almost monumental in the absurd superstructure of gala costume, 'she can love nothing. Hatred or contempt is easier. It's sad, I think.'

'You enjoy feeling sorry for her, don't you?'

'Yes. But not for any reason you can imagine, clever English Edward.'

'Why, then?'

'Because she seems destined to be friendless and alone, unpitied by any of us. And unloved.'

'Not unloved. There's Guido, at least.'

'Bah! Guido Tagliabosco, so tongue-tied, so refined, so eager to understand everyone else's point of view, and with no more passion in him than a calico handkerchief.'

'That's not true, Mariclò.'

'How can you tell?'

'I simply know that it isn't, that's all.'

'Massimo says that he is not truly Italian in his sentiments.'

'A fat lot your brother knows of it. According to him, no one is truly Italian in his sentiments unless they will point a pistol into the Duke's carriage. I'm glad he is not coming to the Congedo.'

Mariclò laughed. 'So am I. I think he is a silly boy, and I only said what I did just now because I wanted you to say something more in Guido's defence. Now I can be sure you're hiding something from me.'

'The practice is not unknown in Villafranca,' said Edward drily.

'Well, at any rate, Cristina is hardly likely to marry Guido now. They were to have wedded before leaving for the country. Instead of that, she and the Lupo are coming to us, and since our property adjoins San Gaudenzio, where you are going, and Falconara is on the other side of the river from it – that is where Guido lives – we shall all see each other, and everything will be as it was before. Which is to say that nothing will happen.'

'Unless one of them should fall in love with someone else,' said Edward. Mariclò looked at him with great shrewdness.

'Which you know is impossible.'

'Yes. Of course it is.'

The carriage was brought round, and the Countess came out into the courtyard with her maid and a footman, who handed her up and tucked in her dress before shutting the door. Whereas Mariclò in her finery seemed merely overburdened, the Countess appeared flamboyantly, almost crudely, girlish. It was the manner of a woman who had never been seriously looked at. Edward, learning sympathy towards his aunt, said at once 'How well you look today, Aunt Harriet,' and earned a grateful smile.

The ducal palace at Villafranca is a large grey building of little architectural distinction, placed ineluctably along one side of a square, opposite the oratory of San Marcello, whose delicately moulded stucco angels reproach the gruff, bulky atlantes upholding the portico of the gateway. Beneath this same gateway the

Castelvetro carriage passed into the colonnaded courtyard, where the Countess, Mariclò and Edward got down, shook a little of the street dust off their clothes, and went upstairs among the spotty old frescoes, in a milling crowd of others. However seedy their cattle and frowzy their coachmen, the good families of Villafranca had spared nothing in adorning themselves, and had done it, Edward considered, really very well. Where their clothes were not expensive they were at any rate in the last cry of fashion, and about everyone there was a characteristic air of natural proportion and artless elegance, as if they had lived purely in order to arrive at the harmonies proposed by the occasion.

There were several landings on the great staircase, and the Countess kept turning round as they reached them to see who was there. Plainly, as Mariclò observed, those who stayed away were of less account than those who came. Edward wondered if somebody was keeping a list.

It was not Count Castelvetro, whose grim station at the head of the stairs was like that of the executioner in *Marino Faliero*. Even the ribbon and gold embroidery of a court chamberlain could not mask his threatening spontaneities, apparent in the shifting of his feet and the restless flexing of the fists sticking out of his scarlet sleeves. To Edward and Mariclò he nodded slightly, with a kind of mocking deference. To the Countess he said, clearly yet so softly that almost she alone could hear:–

'My dear.'

Edward watched her shiver slightly, as though something akin to pleasure were evoked by the sound of her husband's voice. He saw the look of infinite contempt which passed across the Count's face. Then an attendant with a white wand moved forward to shepherd the three of them away.

The usher stepped ahead of everyone down the corridor in a fashion which suggested that he might soon be going to lay an egg. At the end of it he led them into a long saloon, lined, like other such rooms, with mirrors in bristly gilt frames and little tables with tops of pink marble. There was a dais and a canopy surmounted by a huge coronet, like a stork's nest on top of a house. On the platform stood a number of empty chairs, and behind these hung heavy swags of rose-coloured damask. No one, however, advanced beyond the oviparous usher with his white stick, who stood halfway down the room, full as it was with flunkeys and soldiers of the ducal bodyguard. Edward, who had been in and out of palaces with his parents, knew what to expect on this sort of occasion, and was not at all surprised at having to stand about in a throne-room for three-quarters of an hour while the Duke and Duchess were settling the question of whether or not to appear.

He looked around him at the crowd, genuinely amazed that there should be quite so many people in Villafranca to be thought worthy of receiving in this manner. Several of them he had indeed never set eyes on before, but Mariclò assured him that they were from the true-blue families seldom seen at her mother's evenings, except when the Rangoni, feeling a need to assert their primacy, gathered the tribes about them regardless of politics.

'What happens now?'

'Something tiresome but soon over with. How sensible of Cristina to stay away. I wonder where she can have got to. Why do you laugh?'

'Because I can hear an orchestra tuning through those doors over there. Moments like these always make me want to guffaw.'

Mariclò began laughing likewise, then said: 'We oughtn't to, you know, because of your aunt. She looks as if she were going to faint.' It was true. The Countess stood some way away from them, alone among the islands of nobility, her face seared with emotion. Edward was starting towards her when Mariclò laid a hand on his arm.

At that moment the damask curtains to the left of the throne were parted by two of the flunkeys to disclose the sovereign and his family, attended by persons of their household. There was something religious, almost idolatrous, about the way in which, at a barely perceptible sign from the usher with his staff, the entire crowd behind him billowed to earth in a profound reverence towards the group upon the platform. In a voice high-pitched yet completely inaudible, the Duke pronounced some words apparently designed to express gratitude, one of the chamberlains took up a position beside him with a roster, and at length, in a movement of remarkable swiftness, the soldiers of the bodyguard placed themselves as markers along the line of carpet which led to the throne. The doors at the further end of the room were cast open and the orchestra was heard discreetly playing a pot-pourri from *Anna Bolena*. The usher, standing to one side but looking more constrained than ever, motioned the little troupes of Molza, Taccoli, Bonacini and Falloppia one by one towards the party spread across the dais like people taking the air on a terrace.

Edward had read of the obeisance of the Persian satraps at Persepolis or the kowtowing Chinese at Peking, but nothing quite so abject was required from the aristocracy of Villafranca by their liege. Each of them went down in a perfunctory little bow or curtsey, from which they were lifted by an extended finger from the Duke and Duchess. There was a pause for conversation, another bow and bob, after which the presented family cantered off into the next room, where Edward could dimly see a row of buffet tables laid out and servants ambling about with bottles and glasses.

It was all, on the face of things, a far more friendly and sociable affair than he had expected. No wonder everyone was so willing to come. Yet, as always in Villafranca, there was the sense of something missing or held back, a tremendous unmade gesture which was wanted to finish the occasion. You saw it in the way people looked and carried themselves. It reminded Edward of the crowd on the afternoon the soldiers arrived from Mantua. There was the same expression of hungry, feral expectancy, as though things were always going to happen, and an equal intimation of much more taking place within the preserves of fancy than would ever show itself in any visible fact. Here, certainly, the phenomenon was more subdued: the anodynes of ceremony and good manners had killed half its force before it began. Yet its presence, hidden behind gravity or good humour, could not be denied.

Nor, as Edward realized, had this anything to do with loyalty. You felt the sensation as much in the countenances of those whose devotion was unquestioned as in the faces of the few whom an unquenchable self-interest had driven to court despite their implication in every seditious enterprise that might be going. It was simply a wish – vague, formless, undirected maybe, but looming and positive nevertheless.

Their turn at length arrived, and the three of them, led by the Countess, moved along the carpet towards the platform. Edward found himself looking at the frivolous gathers of lace decking his aunt's shoulders, and was reminded instantly of the look she had given the Count as he appeared at the top of the stairs. Recalling that eager glance, he understood now why she was dressed like this.

'Her excellency the Countess Castelvetro. The *nobildonna* Maria Clotilde Rangoni. Mr Edward Rivers,' said the chamberlain, sepulchrally reading their names from his list. The two women ballooned to the floor, and Edward gave what he thought was a nice, dignified bow, extending one foot slightly, as he had seen people do to the Emperor at the Hofburg in Vienna. The Duchess gave the Countess the tip of her finger, and the Duke held out a chubby paw to Edward. Nobody offered anything to Mariclò, who might not have been there at all for the pointed disregard shown to her.

It was clearly something to have an Englishman at the Congedo, and the Duke, who chose to address Edward in French, seemed determined to make what he could of this. As they spoke, Edward looked at him with careful interest. This was the man Basevi and Massimo Rangoni and, very occasionally, Guido had talked to him about, the man who, when barely of age and on the throne, had signed the execution warrant for Basevi's brother, had exiled Massimo's uncle, had sent the Marchesa's sister to a convent for embroidering a patriotic flag, set police watches on the Tagliabosco family and searched Count Castelvetro's library for seditious volumes. This was the man whose name was at the head of all the little new laws, rescripts and proclamations that covered the walls of the city, who searched, censored, prohibited, pursued, confiscated, sequestered, banished and condemned. It was disappointing, not to say annoying, that he should now seem so thoroughly agreeable. His face was like a not unamiable cheese, with just so much liveliness and imagination in it as a cheese might be thought to possess. The Duchess, on the other hand, was thin and stringy and disappointed over something, and her mouth, as she spoke, seemed altogether to be worked by the sinews in her neck. Behind them stood a pallid collection of princes and princesses. One of them was a boy of Edward's own age, with exactly his colour of hair. The moist, fishy look in his eyes was remote and unseeing.

The Countess and Mariclò made another curtsey and they all

hurried away into the next room. The band was playing 'Cielo, a miei lunghi spasimi' and everyone was helping themselves to the cakes and sweetmeats piled on the banquet tables. Even here, despite the chatter and music, there was the same perceptible air of incompleteness as had hung over the crowd in the presence chamber.

'Thank goodness!' cried Mariclò. 'All done for another year, and I did not even have to talk to the horrid, scraggy old Duchess. She doesn't ask me now why Mamma won't come. Our servants tell other people's servants, who tell the police, and the police tell Baron Stappler, who passes it on to her – for what use that may be.'

Her voice was loud and defiant, wanting to be heard. Insulted as much by her mother as by the Duchess, she needed a moment in which to proclaim her dignity. I like you for that, thought Edward.

Together they began to sample and compare the cakes, jellies and ices around them. Mariclò took a couple of macaroons and deftly put them into Edward's coat pocket.

'Why on earth do you do that?' he asked, 'I don't care for macaroons.'

'Everyone does it, it's the custom. Only nobody must see. Watch, and you'll catch them at it.'

It was quite true. In an astonishingly light-fingered fashion, the marquises, counts, barons, their wives and children pilfered and prigged among the plates and stands. You saw things disappear into extraordinary places, under sleeves, into the tucks and gussets of dresses, into the tiniest of waistcoat pockets. One man stood talking to his wife while blandly cramming a glove with sponge fingers. An old lady had made her shawl into a cunning little bundle filled with crystallized fruits. Edward, who could laugh freely now, was seized with irresistible delight at the absurd mischief, yet found time to notice that his uncle stood aloof from it all, at the door, looking directly, and with unconcealed interest, at him and Mariclò. Notwithstanding his blushes, Edward looked back at the Count, a figure from a world before he was born, when Waterloo was newly fought and Rossini's music was in fashion and they were chasing the Turks out of the Morea and sighing over Foscolo and Mme de Staël, in his braided collar and knee-breeches and hair cut *à la Titus*. At thirty-eight the Count looked like someone who, having mislaid his youth, had busied himself too much with searching for it ever after.

'Is it true about my uncle saving the Duke's life?' Edward bluntly enquired of Mariclò.

Pausing for a moment, as if with slight reluctance, she answered:

'Yes,' then, moving closer for confidence's sake, she said:–

'It was in return for a favour. I don't know what that was, but he warned the Duke of a plot against him.'

'He betrayed names, then?'

'No – that is why they absolved him. The Duke and Duchess were going to the theatre, and were to have been shot at from a window in the narrow bit of the Via della Croce just before the square. But he warned them to take another way, and they were saved. Then the Duke offered him a favour.'

She stopped, looking around with much circumspection, then, edging him a little towards the band, where she could the less easily be heard by others, she said:–

'But it was never granted, because they expected him to name the conspirators and he would not. He was made a chamberlain so that the Duke might always keep an eye on him. And the two, so the talk goes, have never forgiven each other.'

'Is that all you know?' asked Edward, convinced that it was not.

'That is all mamma considered fit to tell me. Massimo knows more, but won't say anything, as he does not want mamma and grandmamma to find out, because they are frightened he will be shot, he is so wild for Pio Nono and the King of Piedmont.'

For a while Edward kept on staring at his uncle.

I I

SAN GAUDENZIO LIES barely a league and a half from Villa-franca along the Bologna road, and you can see the city quite clearly across the plain on the other side of the river. There is a village in the Emilian manner, which is to say a straggle of dusty houses round a square with an *osteria*, a church that looks as if it were wholly unacquainted with anything so mean and has withdrawn a little way into the fields to prove the fact, and beyond the church the sweep-gates and the avenue to the manor house and farm of San Gaudenzio.

The neatness and elegance of the house took Edward wholly by surprise, though he later realized that he must have passed by it on dozens of occasions during his afternoon rides. It was nothing more or less than a little castle, with crenellated walls and a turret at one corner, all of which had been improved some sixty or seventy years since by a French architect from the court at Parma, who had straightened the windows and laid out a parterre for walking after dinner. There was a pair of steps from the parterre into a park after the English fashion, with Portugal laurel and ilex and two handsome beech trees, and at the end of the park an avenue of limes led out into the open country. You could survey all this at ease from the open platform at the top of the turret, to which Edward ran up almost as soon as he arrived. He sat in one of the angles of the parapet and stared delightedly out across the parched yellow land, with its silent farms and melancholy grey vines, towards the city, insidious and phantasmal behind the screen of heat. He had no special longing to return. What he had to do was better accomplished here, indeed, than in the atmosphere of vigilance and ceremony in which he had first set it on foot.

He heard someone coming up the steps below, and the nut-cracker face of Basevi presented itself like somebody appearing through a trapdoor in a play.

'This is where you'd be, isn't it?' he said. 'Well, your uncle arrives in an hour, so you had better come down and be civil to him at dinner, as your aunt has a headache after the journey.'

'I never know what to say to him,' rejoined Edward. 'We have hardly exchanged more than two words in all the months I've been here. I'm afraid of him. At least I think I might be if I knew him better.'

'Have a cigar.'

'Thanks.'

Basevi interspersed the stages of taking his match-case from his pocket, striking a match, lighting his cigar and passing the case to Edward, with going and peering intently down the stair-well of the tower and craning over the parapet. Then he sat down close to Edward and said, in a quiet, ruminative way:–

'You see, we knew, of course, why he married your aunt. It was not merely because she was the sister of a *milordo* and entitled to call herself Lady Harriet. And not for anything like love. I remember my first sight of her. It was when I was preferred to the Count as his steward and presented myself at the palace. She was standing in the hall with her maids, busy opening some boxes of dresses that had just arrived, and the Count presented me to her. We'd heard of Englishwomen before, even if none of us had met any; they aren't much known in this region. So I'd expected someone marble and aloof, an effigy of pride and self-possession, anything rather than your aunt. I looked at her, a thin, anaemic, girlish creature with weak eyes and big hands, the Countess Castelvetro, my new master's wife, and I felt pity for her at once.

'I expect you know how we use contempt in Italy. It is one of our most powerful instruments. We look at a person's shoes, or their carriage, or the horse they ride, or the jewels they wear, and such things will either justify or condemn. And, if they condemn, then it isn't to hatred or vituperation – we're too tender-hearted

94

for that – only to scorn. A man is judged not by his scruples, but by his boots.'

'That's how they judge my aunt, the women who come and drink tea with her in the afternoons. I've heard them whispering as they go downstairs.'

'Well, that was how I saw her, despised among her equals, a plain, vapid Englishwoman, no longer young, and destined to a childless solitude in a world where friendship is replaced by good manners. He wanted an heir, certainly; who that has land does not?'

'And was there . . . ?'

'No, not the merest sign. A child or two might have restored her credit. She is still of an age for such things. And to want them too.'

'So it was the dowry after all?' said Edward, remembering, not without a sense of the visiting irony of circumstance, what his mother had had to say of the matter.

'The poor thing might as well have been sent to Greenland as to Villafranca. And who the heir is has not yet been settled, though it is expected a cousin at Reggio will be named. Whoever it is, he will have the palace, all the farms, some property at Sassuolo, and this, which is everything from here to the bridge.'

'And who is it that lives opposite, on the other side of the river?'

'That is Falconara, the Tagliabosco estate. And over there, behind the church, is Scarabello, which was a fortress once, in the days when the Rangoni were more wicked and less feckless than they are now. Have another cigar.'

'No thanks. They're so good they make me feel sick. Where did you get them?'

'Guido Tagliabosco gave them to me. He bought them in Bologna: the tobacco's always better in the Papal States. "*Dove c'e frate, belle fumate,*" you know. I did him a favour.'

'You're a deep one, aren't you?' said Edward.

'So are you. That's why I give you my cigars. Wasted on boys of nineteen.'

Edward got up, laughing and stretching himself. The afternoon's denser heat was loosening under a light breeze that stirred the tufts of foliage on the poplars and ruffled the dead flat square of the fields.

'I'd better go down and give myself a polish before dinner.'

'So had I,' said Basevi. 'I shall need to be ready with the farm accounts for the half year to present your uncle with. He receives tomorrow, by the way: having done that, he feels he's discharged his obligations to the *villeggiatura* and can carry on like a hermit.'

'Who's coming, then?'

'At least a dozen families. All the Rangoni, the Lupo and your Cristina as well, the old Marchesa, the young Marchesa, Signorina Aldegonda, Signorina Mariclò and the precious Marchese Massimo, whom I loathe.'

'Why?'

'Because he makes me feel that I'm a Jew. Every word, every look asks me why I'm not whining and fawning, as he expects Jews to do.'

'He is a patriot,' said Edward, 'you ought to respect that.'

'Bah! that kind of patriotism is useless, we don't want it. Boys like Massimo are patriotic because they are given nothing to do. That sort is the most dangerous.'

'To whom?'

'Oh, everyone, me, your uncle, even you, I presume. And the Duke, for that matter. Speaking of whom, they say he has ordered the *Due Foscari*, to start the season in September, on the day after we all return to town.'

'Ah, "Speranza dolce ancora", I can't forget it. Three times I'll have seen it. In Vienna, I recall, the audience laughed because the trio sounded like one of Lanner's waltzes.'

'What do the Austrians know of our music?'

'They seem to know a great deal about everything else that goes on here.'

The Count arrived but did not come in to dinner. Edward, hungry and impatient, told the majordomo they should serve, and went and sat at the dining table in the lonely pomp to which he had grown accustomed. From the long windows he looked out at the evening folding across the park. The earliest stars appeared, and the bats began their strange, tumbling flight. In the city he was used to the continual rattling and calling from the streets around the palace, but here the stillness gave every movement the clear definition of an attendant noise. The pouring of wine or water into a glass or the rasping of a fork across a plate were vivid sounds, falling eloquently into the silence. An occasional cough from the manservant who waited on him reverberated through the room like a little explosion. Edward felt uneasy, and before the last dish was brought he got up, pushed his chair back and walked out onto the terrace.

Darkness had come with its habitual abruptness after the long Italian twilight. The sound of them clearing the table in the room behind him and the quiet in its wake made it seem as if the house had twitched in an infinite sleep. As for the chirring of the crickets, that was a mere drawing of breath.

He settled himself on the warm steps among the lemon trees, and thought hard about tomorrow. If, as Basevi had intimated, all the Rangoni were coming, then it would be harder for him to have words with Cristina alone. What was more, he had an idea that she knew, with all her infuriating perceptiveness, what he was now attempting to do, and that her aim would be, as far as possible, to avoid him without giving any open offence. Guido must not arrive before they had had some time alone together, for who knew whether she might not seek refuge in some trivial conversation or other, so as to prevent an opening on anything more dangerous? The implicit ironies were not lost on Edward. Barely a week ago she had been looking to him to shield her from needing to speak to Guido. Now it was Guido who could stand usefully between the two of them. Yet they would be, he was certain, as stupidly constrained with one another as ever they had been before.

There must be some way of putting an end to this. Simply to tell Cristina what she should now do would not be enough. Edward's influence weighed with her, but it smacked to him too much of humbug to read her a lecture on the virtues of marrying Guido at once, and to expect that she should take instruction from him as though he were a priest. He felt the need of some gesture, some moment, whose blatant finality would accomplish his purpose. A word or a look would answer. It was something Mariclò would have understood. He wished she were here now.

Hoisting himself to his feet, he went down into the garden, and walked slowly into the enfolding gloom of the avenue of lime trees leading towards the open fields. He was one of those whose imagination peoples the dark, but the torpid serenity of a summer night in the country had eased him of all save the mildest vestiges of fear. Now and then some stirring in the shrubberies on either side of the avenue made him pause nervously. There was no moon, and his eyes grew steadily accustomed to the walls of shadow holding the thin, tall spread of blue between them.

At the end of the trees, beyond the low bay hedge that marked the purlieu of the park, the country lay in the waste of anonymous blackness upon which the city's distant glow flickered like an imaginary creation, creeping across the horizon even as your gaze blinked at it. Out there in the fields by the river, Edward distinguished the low-pitched, comfortable bulk of Falconara, where a tiny gleam of light at one side of the house was perhaps Guido's study. A little to the south, but on this side of the river, stood a long barn, a clean carcass of tall arcades, with a sharp, ridged roof. He thought, for a moment, of picking his way across to it, but the unfamiliarity of shades and surfaces in the ground between held him back. He stood for some time where he was, looking at the barn and the house and the town, and leaning on the little field gate.

He had stopped loving Cristina as swiftly as ever he began, though it was only now that he felt able to acknowledge the fact to himself. It was not merely the shock to his vanity of Guido's arrival which had achieved this, but, far more important, what he himself had done to destroy his earlier feeling. That clumsy, fudged kiss he had given her was not the result of passion or affection, but of a desire to offend. She had made him feel like a boy, much as Massimo made Basevi feel like a Jew or the Count made his wife feel like a fool, and the images he had entertained of her were properly a boy's. There had been afternoons in Villafranca when the heat made even sleep impossible and he had lain stiffening himself and tousling the bedclothes with the idea of her, not as she was, but as she answered his sensuality. Desire, under these conditions, spent itself easily, and a sort of compassionate interest in her fate had begun to take its place almost as soon as he understood the agonizing limitations placed upon her and Guido by their shared reticence.

Mariclò was right and Cristina was to be pitied. Edward had seized his moment of retaliation. Now he must be magnanimous without humiliating her. He turned towards the house. The silence of the fields and the dead shape of the barn were starting to make him afraid. He moved quickly along the path. As he gained the gravel walks of the garden, he noticed something on the ground which surprised him. The still-glowing end of a cigar.

12

IMPATIENT TO BEGIN the day, he awoke very early and padded across the cool floor from his bed to the window. He turned the bolt of the shutter stealthily, so that nobody sleeping elsewhere in the house should hear it creak or clatter, leaned his elbows on the broad sill, and looked out across the park. There was a heavy dew on the grass, and the plain beyond the river towards Villafranca was curdled with a thin layer of mist, out of which the vines, with their spreading arms, rose like attitudinizing dancers. Off the fields, grey in the dawn light, came the calling of a curlew. In the garden was that damp green smell he loved so, which the denser heat was soon to kill.

He thought soon enough of what he had to say to Cristina, and of the difficulty of saying it to her. The idea at any rate had remained congealed in his meditations of the night before, on which he had so uneasily slept. It was all very well trying to be magnanimous, trying to avoid a false piety in telling her that she should make up her mind to marry Guido at once or else give over and go back to Milan, her conscience salved by the solicitous Lupo, who could contrive to suppress the deeds of settlement to everyone's advantage, but such condescending altruism as he could now produce, free as he was from love for her, was useless against her unfathomable obstinacy.

What then was to be gained, supposing she did not mean to accept Guido, who, to his credit, had returned to Villafranca for the purpose of receiving her, by staying here and trifling with the conjecture and expectation of her relatives? The Rangoni, as Edward knew from watching them, both adored and resented her, sneering at her cold taciturnity yet desperate not to lose the solitary evidence of a world denied them through shabbiness and suspicion. Perhaps it was this sense that Cristina in some way belonged to them that had so far prevented her conduct towards Guido from being criticized, though Edward could scarcely believe that.

For himself Guido was no less intractably mysterious. It was easy to imagine, knowing him a little, that his adherence to the engagement was the fruit of a hopeless resignation. Massimo Rangoni had called him a coward; the irony was that Guido's cowardice was of a nature that such as Massimo could never understand. It was easy to think of Guido with his eyes bandaged before a line of rifles in a prison yard, or festering in defiant exile, or fluttering some tricolour rag on the end of a sabre. These were simple matters of yes and no. But to think of him declaring himself, abandoned to sincerity, in the cause of love, jealousy, anger, pride, ambition, despair, that was impossible. Yet the extraordinary delicacy and regard he invariably showed towards Cristina suggested more than a mere gloomy submission to the demands of a settled estate. He seemed to want the artifice of it all as much as she did.

As Edward, looking out into the pale morning, now considered this, he realized for the first time how callous he had been that day when, in San Domenico, he had left them together. In confronting each other they must also have acknowledged their own falsehoods. He thought of Cristina's passionate concern for frankness in others dissolving under the weight of her own confusion. He imagined Guido faced with the need to be sincere. He saw them both, inside that darkness, wanting to run but made immovable by a restraining propriety. At first he had not believed Guido as he described the agonies of their mutual embarrassment. At that instant all that had truly interested him was the fact, incredible as even that appeared, of Cristina bursting into tears. What now made it seem merely an incidental thing, born of the intolerable moment, was the supervening idea of them both staggering through the back streets with Cristina supported upon Guido's arm, each in a state of violent fear and amazement.

I did that, he thought, may God forgive me, and was proud of

101

it. Ashamed, he drew back from the window, as if somebody down there in the garden had noticed him. From where he stood he could just see, beyond the trees at the park's edge, and across the river, the shape of Falconara, still blurred in the mist. Guido must, he supposed, have forgiven him. Though he had every right to condemn, it had perhaps not occurred to him to do so, and Edward, realizing this, grew even more abashed. Thus almost with desperation he saw his impending interview with Cristina as a means of making amends to Guido.

He heard the servant come in with a basin of water and towels. He did not answer the good-morning, but stood where he was, long after the man had gone and the door was shut, brooding on the day, which after all, would be very hot and interminable. Then, stripping off his nightshirt, he soaped and sponged and slopped water angrily over himself. He dressed carefully in loose clothes that would keep him cool and paused to stare for re-assurance into the glass, wetting down a recalcitrant curl in his reddish brown hair, tucking up the edges of his tie and hitching his trousers into place. He would never be an Italian because his nose was too long, but he fancied he didn't mind that.

Towards midday the guests began to arrive. Edward had not expected quite so many, or that it was to be an occasion which so manifestly ignored political partialities, uniting opposites like the Reel of Tullochgorum. It might have been supposed that families like the Grillenzoni and the Bonacini would all be there, but to see Count Rosselli, so impeccably legitimist, and the pious Marchesa Menafoglio with a brace of priests at her heels, and no less than three of the Austrian garrison officers, suggested an uncommon flourish of hospitality in his uncle. If his aunt thought it strange, she said nothing, but wandered about directing the servants as if to entertain half the country on some freak of her husband's were the most natural thing in the world.

Tables were spread under the trees and along the western side of the house, and the stone benches in the garden were covered with faded yellow cushions. Two or three of the better sort of women from the farm had been pressed into service with the footmen who, wearing their country liveries for the first time, smelt strongly of lavender and pomade, and the majordomo stood at the hall door grinning and fidgeting between each batch

102

of guests. In the room nearest the garden the Count and Countess waited to greet them, while Edward, a little to one side, reflected that this was the first time he had ever seen his uncle and aunt do anything together. Even now, indeed, it did not seem as if they were man and wife, so patent was their detachment in confronting every arrival. There was something unsettling in the Countess's serenity of demeanour: it was the Count who was the more excited.

Hard on the heels of a servant with a note from Guido putting off because he had to go suddenly to Scandiano came all the Rangoni party in a drove, like the Tartars arriving on the frontiers of China. As always when together they were in high glee, shrieking with private laughter even as they tumbled through the doorway toward their hosts. The two older women looked Edward up and down with evident approval, as though they had never seen him before in their lives, and Aldegonda, staring in her bald, supercilious fashion for fully half a minute, said, with the air of announcing a novel conclusion, 'That is a new waistcoat you've got on'. It wasn't, but the point was scarcely one on which Edward considered it worth undeceiving a girl like Aldegonda.

His waistcoat at once attracted the notice of Massimo, who asked him point blank, in best Rangoni fashion, where he got it and how much he paid for it.

'I paid nothing,' answered Edward. 'My mother got it for me in Florence as a farewell present.'

'Well, how much did she pay for it?' asked Massimo obstinately.

'I don't know. I don't suppose I thought of asking her.'

'Ah, I wish you had. One might look up and down and not find such a waistcoat from Bologna to Venice. You had better ask her, you know, next time you write, and then I can send to Florence for one. I have cousins there.'

'He has cousins everywhere,' said Cristina, who came in with Signora Lupo, hard on their heels. 'Hullo, Edward.'

'Hullo, Cristina.'

It would not, he saw, be easy to say anything to her, less because of the distracting presence of the others than because of the look of resolved insouciance she now wore. No sooner did he begin to wonder whether someone, either the young Marchesa or

Signora Lupo, might positively have demanded an explanation of her delay with Guido than he started to suspect that it must have been so, and a chance to get at the truth presented itself with the arrival, after the others had gone, of Mariclò.

For a moment, as she appeared in the room and came towards his aunt and uncle, themselves struck by the change in her, Edward could not speak. He had become aware, in a handful of waking hours, that this was a place where, for whatever reasons, people altered, in manner, condition and semblance, but he could hardly accept her as the same Mariclò he had seen on the previous morning, frizzed and monstrous in her court *tenue*. Now a kind of freedom played about her, like light glancing off water, which defined and commended everything so as to make Edward feel that he wanted to describe her to herself, the way in which she no longer seemed to hang lopsidedly off her right shoulder, the way in which she did not any more look ashamed of having to own to her hands and feet, the way in which her chin and her forehead, which had always before looked like parts of someone else's face, were made to belong inalienably to her simply by the falling down of her thick black hair, which now and then she raised a hand to throw back as she chatted and laughed with the Countess. And for once he did not find it especially irksome when his aunt, clearly delighted, said:–

'My dear, you must be very thirsty, coming over from Scarabello in such dust and heat. Edward will take you into the garden and find you something to drink.'

'Why didn't you come with the others?' asked Edward as they went down the steps.

'Because mamma and Aldegonda were very severe on my refusing to put up my hair. They said I wasn't a girl any more, which of course is true, but I said, which is quite as true, and which they know, that we do things differently in the country. In the end we were so cross with one another that I wouldn't come in the carriage, though Massimo ordered me to and I said no, so we boxed one another's ears in front of the servants. Now, you see, if I had been Aldegonda and had my ears boxed, I should have gone back into the house and put my hair to rights in front of the glass. As it was, I gave it a tug or two with a comb and came over by the fields.'

'You walked? Alone?'

104

'Yes, but very slowly, so that it shouldn't seem so to your aunt when I arrived. Am I glowing a little?'

God, thought Edward. 'You're . . . that's to say, no, not glowing. I mean, at any rate . . . well, no matter.'

'They have probably forgiven me by now.'

'I'm sure of it. They were laughing when they arrived.'

'I thought as much. That is always what happens in our family. Massimo or my grandmother will say something funny and we dissolve. In any case, it is not me they're cross with, but Cristina.'

'Ah, I thought as much.'

'You see, mamma was very angry with Guido for not having gone to the Congedo. It upsets her ideas for people when they don't behave as she thinks they ought. She would talk about nothing else until we arrived at Scarabello, and there of course we found Cristina and aunt Lupo, who had both left in the morning in that smart yellow carriage of theirs that Massimo covets so. Our coachman drives so badly, as you know, and Massimo's no better as he goes so fast, so both mamma and grandmamma were very cross indeed by the time we reached the house, and you may imagine how furious they were to see Cristina and the Lupo sitting under the pergola in their summer bonnets drinking lemonade. The *fattoressa* makes it for us every year, for our arrival, and Massimo gets a glass of old Rolando's foul wine.'

'Such profanity of them – and in summer bonnets,' said Edward, and they both laughed.

Mariclò went on:–

'No, truly, it took little enough for it to start. Mamma told Cristina that it was her duty to satisfy the family's expectations and marry Guido at once. Massimo even hinted that, if she didn't, we should have to find somebody else for her to marry.'

'Himself, for example.'

'I think he would marry anyone who gave him a yellow britzka.'

'The notion's absurd!' exclaimed Edward angrily. 'And I mean nothing apropos of yellow britzkas. Cristina cannot be compelled in this fashion.'

'She will do what's expected of her, if she has any regard for us,' rejoined Mariclò, then added slyly, 'but, of course, if I were Cristina, I should do exactly as she has done already. Yet I think it must be interesting to marry Guido.'

'You talk as if she has broken off the engagement.'

'Oh, anyone can see they are engaged because anything else would be intolerable. They require each other's company.'

'Come, Mariclò, that isn't true. I have been present on every occasion at which they have met in the last month, and even then they have said nothing of any consequence. Indeed, they have scarcely held a conversation that hasn't required my assistance to make it go.'

Staring at him hard, Mariclò said: 'Then you don't see what has happened?'

'I understand merely that they're afraid of talking to one another.'

'It is not a question of words, Edward,' she cried, with a little gesture of angry impatience, then paused suddenly as, turning into the lime avenue, they came upon Cristina herself, in conversation with Count Castelvetro. It was surprising enough to see the two of them together, but Mariclò gently checked Edward from going any nearer. He saw at once what she intended and, still keeping the pair within view, they moved a little way back along the walk by which they had come.

'Would you like us to go away?' said Mariclò.

'No, would you?'

'No.'

But the 'no' died on her lips as Edward, gripping her hand, whispered: 'Look!'

For in the entrance to the narrow path leading back through the park into the garden, and unseen as yet by the Count and Cristina, there appeared the thin, melancholy figure of the Countess. Even from such a distance it was obvious why she paused and then came on towards the pair with an air of blankness in her countenance, as if, however temporarily, she were yielding to them the rights of her discovery – or at any rate the discovery she supposed herself to have made. Edward could imagine the recompense she hoped for, and in that moment felt against his uncle a sincere rage for denying it to her. As for Cristina, she seemed overcome with confusion, and in turning away from the Countess she faced her witnesses, who very deftly untwined their fingers as they came forward. Yet, to Edward's amazement, it was the Countess who now said: –

'Your uncle was showing Signorina Bentivoglio the vista along the avenue, Ned. She had never seen it before, you know, and on days like this a little shade is delicious.'

'Ah well, it must be,' he otiosely returned.

'I believe – though I can't be sure – it was planted nearly a hundred years ago.' She stopped, and that smile which was not a smile, like pushing open the door of an empty room, came into her face as she turned to the Count, saying! 'Or was it later?'

It was as if she had offered to murder him. He held out his arm challengingly, and Edward heard once more that softly murmured 'my dear?', with the hint of a veiled, unaccountable question underneath, that had so chilled him at the Congedo.

Slowly they returned towards the villa in a little straggling, hesitant group, one or two of them falling behind from time to time so as not to have to speak to the rest. The Count was nervous and distracted. It was the first time Edward had seen him caught so plainly unawares, yet it was obvious that he was preoccupied by something more than his wife's sudden apparition.

Their absence had hardly been noticed by the throng of guests, who were by now settled into the dozy conviviality that follows a luncheon in hot weather, and lay scattered about on cushions and chairs under the trees. One or two had already gone to sleep, until their servants should decide it was time to go home and come unceremoniously to wake them. Edward was in no mood for this, however, and with the appearance of Signora Lupo to claim Cristina and the resumption by Count and Countess of their former garb of empty, smiling blandness, he could be alone with Mariclò once more.

'That was horrible,' he said at last.

'Yes, I'm ashamed. Are you not also?'

'Dreadfully. Are you hungry besides?'

'No, I ate something before I came away. Are you?'

'Not particularly. Let's go into the house and be out of everyone's way.'

In the garden room's dank shadow, where the shutters had been drawn, the two of them sat for a while in furtive silence. Edward rested his chin on his hands. It seemed there was nothing left to say to Cristina on the subject of the engagement. The fact of what he had just seen, regardless of its true nature, threw everything he had proposed to himself this morning into confusion. The likelihood that those two should have had anything to say which required them to be alone together on the edge of the park was something he had never even thought possible. Though nothing in the Count's manner suggested an immoderate interest in Cristina, it was as if their meeting, with its air of secrecy and assignation, had been deliberately calculated to scotch Edward's altruism before it was even able to show itself.

'Damn!' he cried suddenly, making Mariclò start. 'Damn, damn, damn!'

'I don't understand you.'

'Oh, as if it mattered what I had to say to anyone. Why isn't Guido here? My uncle's right and the wretched fellow has cried off on purpose.'

'No, he hasn't,' said Mariclò in downright Rangoni fashion. 'And, if he has, it is out of honest fear, not for shame. But he had better make up his mind soon.'

Edward gazed at her through the discreet veil of shadow which rendered them as conspiratorial here as the others had appeared in the park. 'What did you mean' he asked, 'when you said earlier that with Guido and Cristina it was not a question of words?' Turning her head away, she put up her hand as she did so to smooth back her hair.

'I was going to say . . . That is, it's not important, merely my foolish idea.' She was unwilling, evidently, that he should accept this as a finality.

'Ah, then . . . ?'

'Guido hasn't, you see,' she announced, 'any interest in women.'

'And yet he is preparing to marry Cristina.'

'Yes, preparing. He has been the whole summer preparing, and a pretty preparation he has made. To marry a miserable heiress, with a paltry handful of unmortgaged lands. One who is merely beautiful and happens, by some trifling accident, to speak French and play the piano to a marvel. Such a preparation, *Madonna*!'

'It is as much her fault,' said Edward stubbornly.

'But of course you would think so. In the end it rests with him.'

'Now they have spoken plainly to Cristina you feel sorry for her. I see.'

'So do you, Edward, don't deny it. They have already thrown boys in Aldegonda's way: it is thought she might marry young Count Grillenzoni Falloppia. Then they'll set themselves to find a husband for me, which won't please them half so much. But it is the custom.'

'Oh, rot the custom, sink it, drown it!' he cried. 'Why does nobody in Villafranca do as they please for a change? Marry your coachman, run off with the raggle-taggle-gypsies-oh, but this resignation, it's disgusting.'

'At any rate I promise you I'll marry to please myself,' Mariclò quietly answered, 'which is more than Cristina can do. Yet . . .' she sighed, 'Guido Tagliabosco.'

'Well?'

'Have you noticed that he never looks at women? By which I mean that he is not like you at all. When you first came to us, you stared at Aldegonda and me as if you would eat us. You may not have intended to, you may not even have known yourself to be doing it, but you did and we noticed. I recall asking Aldegonda if she thought you handsome. She said you were better looking than some, though she didn't consider you handsome.'

Edward let go by another question he had thought of asking, and she continued:–

'Guido, you see, never does that. Women are nothing to him.'

'You can't judge simply from his being timid and modest.'

'Yes, you can. At least I do. I am only eighteen, but I know. Girls understand such things. Not all men are vain with women, like my brother, who thinks he has a killing air. You are modest, or at least you pretend to be, but in the end you're no different from Massimo. But with Guido it is something else.'

'I suppose you've talked about that also with Aldegonda.'

'Indeed I have. We both guessed it. It is precisely because Cristina is what she is that Guido fears her. His grandmother wanted him to be a priest, you know. He would have done better to don the cassock and purple stockings and be a little *abbate* with an elegant interest in music and books. We have such in Villafranca: you should see our confessor, Don Prosdocimo. Though he does not wear lavender gloves like Guido's.'

'Don't scorn him, Mariclò.'

109

'Oh, truly, I don't. He doesn't know what to do, he'll never know, will he? And if somebody tried to tell him, that would be worse. How much easier if Cristina were a man, then none of this would happen and they could be friends.'

'Then she must know as well,' said Edward. 'Yet perhaps that is important to her. How can either of us tell? It is as if they both need to be told what to do in order that they shouldn't do anything more foolish.'

'It makes me feel grand and old to be talking about it like this,' said Mariclò.

'I feel only very stupid and incapable, if what you say is true. I'm supposed to do something here, though I haven't the least notion of what it is. I wish I'd never come to Villafranca.'

This seemed to amaze Mariclò. 'Can you be serious, Edward?'

'Well, do you wonder at it? I might at any rate have been allowed to rot in dullness and neglect rather than being taken up and made necessary to you all in ways I can't possibly understand. It has come to the point at which neither Guido nor Cristina can set foot outside the door without consulting me as to the expediency of doing so. What is it I'm supposed to do, tell me?'

'I don't know, Edward. It may be only that you have to go on as you are, as we want you to be – as they want you to be – until the need for you has gone. Does that sound cruel?'

He looked at her through the depth of shadow which surrounded them, but could see no clear expression in her face. She stood up and threw open one of the shutters, as though perfectly understanding his wish. The light from the terrace momentarily transfigured, for Edward, her action of brushing back her fall of black hair and smiling at him as she did so. There was a beauty in so light a gesture that he had scarcely begun to connect with her.

'This is something else I have learned,' she said solemnly, 'that certain people become necessary merely for what they are, not for the things they do. I'll go now, or else my mother will send Aldegonda to fetch me, and that would be tiresome. But please come and find me again, won't you, before we go home.'

When Mariclò had gone, Edward sat for some time in an entranced passivity of thought. It was not impossible to believe what she had told him. The fact, indeed, that the perception was hers lent it a larger substance of truth, for he knew that, however much he bantered her on the point, in the end she was incapable of lying to him, despite her reasons for wishing to lessen Cristina's influence.

Little of that influence, in any case, was left now, and its residual traces were of no importance. By reviving dulled sensations and laying bare springs of feeling Edward had not known to exist in himself, Cristina disclosed to him all the blankness and shadow of her own nature. He could see how she needed to feel, how she envied in others the ordinary spurs to anger, joy and desire they possessed, as if, having swept up what belonged to her and set off with it, she had suddenly remembered something left behind and always wanted to be going back to fetch it. Or, as he now thought, sending others to fetch it for her.

After all, he said to himself, she doesn't know about the man she is to marry. And, if she did, what on earth would she understand by it, more than she guessed already? That women unnerved Guido, that if he could he would have run from her, from Villafranca itself, from all the ties which kept him there, save that something made him cling to her as she to him, the pair circling each other, dodging, waiting, in awed compulsion, while Edward, musing, watched them.

To watch, it seemed, was his present commission. He pondered the curious episode witnessed in the park and felt even more fearful for his aunt. She had assumed the worst and must now feed on it, since it offered such an easy palliative to her sense of injury: no longer was it merely a matter of flourishing her neglect in the drawing rooms of the city and hoping for scraps of nonchalant compassion from those she invited to her Tuesdays. The smallness of Villafranca meant that she and Cristina would inevitably be flung in each other's way, and that everything Cristina did or said would be treated as an offence. It was a connexion Edward had long assumed her to suspect, and his affection for Cristina made him want to protect her as much as he ever wished to shield his aunt.

Sitting there in the stillness, he became aware of little noises under the hot, thick texture of silence that enveloped the garden. Somebody crossed the terrace and went down the steps. A man and a woman passed the window in talk whose words Edward could not distinguish. Then he heard someone shut a door and go upstairs on the side of the house nearest the tower. Feeling

111

restless, he got up and went outside into the parched afternoon, where his uncle's guests lay slumped in the shade like cows. One of Marchesa Menafoglio's tame priests shuffled to and fro reading in his breviary, and the vigilant Austrians paced the walks in a manner irresistibly suggesting a patrol, saying nothing to one another but peering now and then into the gloom among the trees. Their presence unsettled Edward. He wondered where Basevi was, and instinctively turned back towards the house, going round to enter by the courtyard gate on the other side.

He picked his way among the carriages and the knots of dozing coachmen and grooms and hurriedly crossed the yard into the house. Uneasily he wandered about the cavernous rooms, half hoping he would come upon Basevi. There was nobody there. The house was still. Then came the noise of someone sliding the bolt of a door. Supposing this might be Basevi at last, Edward moved rapidly towards the sound. As he passed from room to room he caught sight of a book open on one of the tables and paused to glance at it. A volume of Tacitus, it lay open at a page of the *Agricola*, where a passage had been underlined in red ink: 'Under Domitian more than half our misery consisted in watching and being watched, while our very sighs were marked against us, and the whitened faces of us all were revealed in deadly contrast to that one scowling blush behind which Domitian hid from his shame.' Pondering the discovery, Edward was so thoroughly startled by the sound of someone coming into the room behind him that he dropped the book.

It was Cristina, who now said to him, with her customary abruptness:–

'Edward, there is a favour I have to ask of you.'

13

BUT THERE, JUST as she was about to tell him what it was, the others hurtled into the room with cries of triumph at finding her and sweeping her off with them. Armed by long experience against such disappointments he allowed the recollection to slip from his grasp and settled gratefully enough into the life of featureless indolence ordained by the parched, wrinkled August country. At evening, when there was the scrap of a breeze, he used to go and sit up on top of the turret, whence he could look out over the landscape and mark the houses and churches dotted across the plain. The two nearest were always Scarabello and Falconara, the one thrown forward almost into the roadway, a dirty, ramshackle place, the other neat and furtive on the far side of the river. Thus it pleased him, as the shadow spread like moss over the fields and trees, to think of the three of them, himself, Cristina and Guido, as each a wanderer, each an exile banished twice over. And when a thicker darkness fell, and he could see lights in the windows of both houses, these were to him like distant signals of warning or alarm. For if he turned and faced in the direction of the city, he realized that in the vague blackness which divided them from it lay some kind of a frontier, to which he himself was closest.

Soon the hunting season would begin, and all that week the woods and coverts were full of men exercising dogs. One morning very early he was rooted out by Basevi, looking more businesslike than ever in odd gaiters and a hat with a hole in the crown, and saying:–

'Come on, won't you, your uncle's Lord knows where, and there are the pointers to get out, and Guido's downstairs, so let's be off,' and in a trice, as it seemed, the three of them were out in the meadow beyond the park, their boots glistening wet and the dogs making dark trails through the dewy grass.

Guido was a foreigner here as everywhere else. The gleam upon the country round them before the heat deadened it made him look newer than before. He said little, letting Basevi talk while he stared hard at Edward.

'Wanted to know where I was, I suppose,' said Basevi, resuming a question Edward had asked him some three or four days ago. 'At his honour's, of course,' gesticulating at Guido, 'who did well to stay away. Your uncle was a fool. No, I'm sorry, but he was a fool if he thought such a proceeding would convince anyone.'

'But it's his custom every year to invite neighbours on the first afternoon of the *villeggiatura*, you said so yourself.'

'Neighbours, yes, but *these* neighbours, spies, parasites, priests, Austrians, what a set! He will have gained nothing but contempt by it.'

'Well, at any rate they appear to have enjoyed themselves. My aunt told me that there was practically nothing left to eat or drink in the house by the time the last of them was gone.'

'We know why he did it at least,' said Basevi, determined on remaining disgruntled. 'For exactly the same reason that he goes to court and wears his chamberlain's uniform and takes his hat off to Stappler and the ministers of state. Wants to be thought respectable.'

'Why? He has no need of it.'

Basevi gave a snort, as though to say 'much you know!', and cut at the grass with his stick. Edward glanced furtively at Guido to see whether he was still looking at him and found that he was. Irritated by this, irked too by Basevi's gust of bad temper, he walked on after the dogs until he came to the margin of the river, where the banks fell away in a series of dune-like humps below which lay the broad gravelly bed incised by a few shrunken channels of water. In silence the three picked their way downwards and started to walk across in long, calculated strides, with a leap here and there where the rivulets were too deep and muddy. To the left of them one of the dogs started up a heron, which flew away into the fields with an angry clapping of its bill and a great shaking-out of wings. Down here, sheltered momentarily from coolness, they felt the heat starting to gather.

'This is where it runs deepest,' Basevi called back. 'I'll go upstream a little and find a spot where we can jump safely.'

The others stood and watched as he paced along among the sand and stones. Guido fingered his chin gingerly. Edward was almost certain of what he was thinking, and said kindly: 'Don't worry, he is bound to find somewhere safe,' but was rewarded merely by Guido's solemn, heavy-eyed gaze. Then Basevi took off his broken hat and waved it at them.

'I'll cross first and then I can help you over.'

He landed easily enough on the farther side. Edward did the same, and they both turned to watch Guido. It was obvious that he was dressed too elegantly to fall in the water. He hovered on the sandbank, twitching the skirts of his coat nervously and making half-hearted attempts to pose himself for jumping. Clearly, like so much else, he had never done this sort of thing before and knew that he looked ridiculous.

'Come on, your honour, give it a try, won't you?' cried Basevi, addressing Guido with a characteristic mixture of politeness and impatience. 'If you slip, it'll only come up to your waist, and the water's like warm broth at this time of year.'

But it would not do, and Guido still stood dithering, until Edward, reaching out towards him, cried:–

'It's all right, you know, you've only to jump and I'll catch you.'

Upon which Guido smiled at him and with a clumsy, flailing movement, fell, as it were, over the river to clasp Edward's outstretched hands on the other side.

They were now in the bounds of his estate, and as they came up to the top of the bank they saw the gates and grounds of Falconara ahead. With the larks startling the air and the sun gleaming on the leaves of the poplars by the roadside and the yellow of the flags in the ditch beside which they walked, there was a kind of preparatory beauty, like a warning to Edward, in the landscape of which the house was the inevitable object. Whereas Scarabello was rendered only hideous by its age, and

115

San Gaudenzio, for all its appointments, was never more than handsome, Falconara, on the gentlest of hills, occupying what the French call 'a smiling position', looked, when viewed close to, incomparably spruce and appropriate, as if the plantations which surrounded it had somehow withdrawn of their own accord so as to accommodate it more easily. There was no courtyard, but the house was flanked by small crenellated towers like toy fortifications, with, at their feet, a sort of defensive outwork of lemon trees in pots. The green shutters and little balconies along the upper windows and the iron grates on those below gave a southern look to the place, on which Edward remarked as they passed the sweep-gates.

'Ah, you would notice that of course,' rejoined Guido. 'My mother, who rebuilt the house, was a Neapolitan.'

'I should have remembered,' said Basevi, as if this explained something else.

'Oh, you ought to know. You know everything about my family.'

'All that's necessary.'

'You'll stop and have something to drink?' asked Guido. Edward said yes, more out of sheer curiosity than from a wish to oblige. With Basevi it was a less easy matter. He pretended at first that he was not thirsty, and then pleaded that something must be done about the dogs.

'But you'll come in and take something,' Guido pleaded.

Basevi bowed somewhat distantly. 'As your honour pleases.'

'We'll take the dogs away and join you,' said Edward.

They watched Guido enter the house, and gave the dogs to an old coachman who was engaged in mending the axle of a gig. As they were walking back, Basevi knelt down to button a gaiter, and Edward said:–

'What was that rigmarole just now? I have never seen you stand on your dignity in that fashion.'

Still kneeling, Basevi grinned up at him.

'You are a young ass, Edward, if you think I did it because I was ashamed to enter Falconara by the hall door. Why, last week Guido and I were drinking brandy together while your uncle did the civil to the Duke's spies.'

'Well, why did you do it?'

'For Guido, of course. To save his embarrassment, poor

fellow. He wants to talk to you alone, but does not know how to manage matters without seeming ill-bred. Believe me when I tell you that last week, when I slipped away from San Gaudenzio on the pretext of taking a horse to be shod in the village, and came over here for the day, he would talk of nothing else but you. He asked me all sorts of questions.'

'And what did you tell him?'

'What does one tell people?' Basevi finished with his gaiter and straightened himself. 'Now here is a piece of advice for you. Are you too proud to take it?'

'Not if you aren't too proud to take a drink from Guido.'

'Never tell anyone everything you know. Always keep something back for yourself. Especially here in Villafranca. It's your custom and it's a good one.' He paused. 'I swear to you, Edward, that I told Guido only what I thought he wished to hear.'

'Oh, I believe you,' said Edward, 'not that it matters – except to him.'

There was little enough time, once they entered the house, for Edward to admire the handsomeness of its proportions, since Basevi had no sooner led him across the hall towards one of the stone-framed doorways which gave into the rooms beyond than Guido burst out at them as though from hiding, his face suffused with alarm. Seizing each of them by the arm and leading them back a little, away from the door, he whispered:–

'I had no idea they were here. They never said a word to me of their coming today. And so early. What shall I do?'

'But who is it?'

'Signorina Bentivoglio and Signora Lupo. Massimo Rangoni has driven over to San Gaudenzio in their travelling carriage and left them here. He will come back in two hours – two hours! – to take them home.'

At least, thought Edward, she has not shrunk from the encounter. It was time to act firmly.

'You will do as you ought to do, Guido,' he said, and Guido looked at him in desperation, as if destiny depended upon his command. 'You will give us all something to drink and sit down with us and we shall pass the time together until Massimo has had enough of my uncle's cigars and that confounded yellow britzka. And perhaps it will be more than two hours, three, four maybe, a whole day, with meals along the way. We shan't desert you, I promise.'

'Very well.' Guido seemed crestfallen, expecting, perhaps, to have been told that Edward and Basevi would send the women away, like bailiffs seeing a pair of trespassers off his grounds. Edward wanted to give him a comforting buffet on the shoulder, but felt that, if he had, Guido might have dissolved beneath it. As it was, Guido looked up at him, a lingering misery in his gaze.

'Come on,' Edward said ruthlessly, 'let's not be too ill-bred,' and they went into the drawing room.

It was a long, bright, uncluttered space, marked at the corners with tall green vases of the kind that always looked to Edward as if djinns and afrits were ready to leap out at a mere twitching of the lid. The chairs and sofas, all of a piece, had a severe republican elegance, the background to some gesture of classic abnegation or stern integrity. On one of the sofas, indeed, sat Signora Lupo, and Cristina with her back turned, so that the pair, in the lightness of summer dresses, were like the rowers of a boat. At the other end of the room, Edward noticed with pleasure, was a piano.

Guido's embarrassment was making him almost tearful. He seemed to have shrunk in size, and the immense liquid darkness of his eyes was the only substantial thing about him. In a sort of hoarse whisper he contrived to present Basevi to the two women, and to confuse their names as he did so. Basevi looked on compassionately as Guido attempted to ask everybody whether they would take something to drink. Overjoyed at finding that they would, he positively ran out of the room in search of a servant. A look of acute concern resolved itself in Cristina's face. Edward was delighted to see it there.

'We must apologize to Count Tagliabosco,' she said at once. 'It's entirely Massimo's fault that we are here. He wanted, you see, to drive our carriage, so we agreed on condition that we were passengers. But he drives so very fast that it was enough for us to come this far, and we thought that the Count would not mind us being refugees.'

'Oh, I'm sure he is pleased to see you,' said Basevi with a touch of archness. He must have caught Signora Lupo's gaze, for she smiled. Cristina, however, chose to take him seriously.

'Are you?' she said. 'I think not. We should have gone on to

118

San Gaudenzio and taken the consequence of a few broken bones. It was wrong of us to come, I see that.' Then, as if to explain what she had just said, she added: 'So early in the day, and uninvited.'

There was a large silence among them as they awaited Guido's return. The continuance of anything like conversation seemed to depend to an almost preposterous degree upon his re-entering the room, in which the stillness was so intense that they could hear the sound of birds rustling in the shrubbery beyond the open windows. When he at length appeared, followed by two spruce young men bearing wine and biscuits, everyone perceptibly twitched with animation. They saw that he had apparently regained composure, for he smiled as the glasses were handed about and seemed quite determinedly at ease. Cristina's face was tinged yet again with that gentle anxiety Edward had admired earlier. Though she could not understand the causes of Guido's nervousness, she could gauge the extent of its hold over him, enough to create a real sympathy. She sat watching him, ignoring the glass on the table beside her, tapping her foot on the floor in doubtful impatience. At last, unable to bear any more, she got up and flung across the room towards where he stood, a little removed from the others.

Basevi had begun to talk to Signora Lupo in a way which made it possible for Edward to lean back discreetly over his chair and watch Guido and Cristina. Though he could not hear what she was saying, he could sense the fervour and sincerity with which she spoke, and the corresponding gravity of Guido's response. He had never before seen them so mutually preoccupied, and the sudden apprehension of this unsettled him, like something that had run on too fast for him to catch. Annoyed to miss what was being said, he moved his chair closer, the sound of which made them at once turn round. Edward felt chastened by his own intemperate curiosity. Rising forthwith, he glanced in the direction of the piano and said:–

'Do you have any music, Guido?'

'Yes, there is plenty in the drawers of that cabinet over there. You are going to play? It's in tune, you know. Old Roncaglia, the master who taught us as children, comes out and knocks it together for me. It's Camploy's best. Please play something.'

With a backward look in their direction in case they should

119

begin again, Edward started to riffle through the music. Among the sheaves of studies and sonatas he came across a number of opera songs and exclaimed:–

'We'll sing, so we shall! Here's "Mira, o Norma" – that's for two women, that will hardly do – and "Suoni la tromba", we might do that, I suppose – and the duet from *Linda di Chamounix*. No, this is even better.'

'What have you got there?' asked Basevi.

'It is the trio from the *Attila* of Verdi that they gave last season at Milan, a magnificent piece by all accounts. Oh, let us try it, please! We may do it slowly, you see, and Cristina and Guido and I may all sing, and, Basevi, you may play the accompaniment.'

'I may attempt it at least.'

'It is nothing but a few chords and arpeggios. Guido, you will take Foresto, the tenor, and Cristina is to sing Odabella.'

'And you, I suppose, are to be the baritone,' said Basevi sceptically.

'Why not? Because I am nineteen years of age doesn't mean that I may not sing in the bass clef.'

'What are we to sing, pray?' asked Cristina, who had been too preoccupied with Guido to listen.

'Oh, nothing in the least difficult: it is "Te sol, te sol quest' anima" in *Attila*. Extremely slow and not taxing to the voice.'

The notion must have seemed outrageous to them both. The idea of singing in one another's presence was terrible enough, but to have so critical an audience was even worse. Cristina was adamant that she would not, that Verdi was too difficult, too rough-grained for a weak voice like hers, and Guido, emboldened by her, held out resolutely, protesting that he was not a tenor at all and would only make a fool of himself. Basevi compliantly sat down and began to try the instrument.

'Give us a sonata, Daniele,' said Guido.

'God forbid! I am the sort of performer whose execution offers a discreet comment upon the music. I don't claim to play what is written, and thus I mustn't be listened to, for fear it should be taken for the composer's inspiration.'

They all laughed at this clever put-off, then Edward, turning once again to the pair, said, in a way which made it less of a request than a command:–

'Please do as I ask. For my sake.'

He had never felt so thoroughly meretricious before. It gave him a shameful pleasure. He had decided that they should sing, and in order that his desire be fulfilled he had made a calculated demand which was absolutely certain to be complied with. So he was almost angry when Cristina, with a truculent air, said: 'For your sake, Edward, of course.'

They went to the piano and stood looking over Basevi's shoulders at the music. Signora Lupo watched them. Edward wondered what interested her in all this, and made up his mind to ask her outright one day. Basevi began, as he had forewarned, very discreetly, so that Cristina made a false start and they had to set off once more. As she sang, Edward realized that he had never heard her in such fine, clear voice before, nor Guido, plaintive, throaty, something of the south rather than of this region. The two seemed to lead each other on, so that when at last it came to his turn, as Ezio, to chide them with their delay, he felt like an intrusive, unwelcome presence, as though what they sang held more truth than the mere words of lovers in an opera air. It was a momentary fancy, no more. For, as they started the repeat, he saw Guido glance away from the music towards him and smile, complicitly as it were, and almost as soon saw a dark, cross look come into Cristina's face as she noticed it. He knew then for the first time, without either wishing or contriving it, that he had made her jealous.

He was more certain of it when they finished the piece, in that atmosphere of mutual congratulation which suggests a sense of distinguished achievement, for she barely paused to thank the others before turning to him and saying: 'Will you take me into the garden, Edward?' and leading him without further ceremony from the room.

The garden at Falconara was no different from others in the country seats about Villafranca, save that it was better kept. Dotted among the Portugal laurels and ilexes were several mournful male deities in lichen-blotched stone. Edward wondered whether nymphs and goddesses had been considered too corrupting a presence among the virtuous Tagliabosco. In the middle of the park stood an icehouse under a mound, within a clump of poplars whose long, serpentine roots had broken up the surface of the ground. Their walk towards this place was silent, but for the rustling of Cristina's dress sweeping the stones and

121

mould of the path. Without summoning his assistance, she climbed to the top of the mound and sat down, in a movement of breathtaking grace and assurance. He had never seen a woman do such a thing before, and could easily admire that with which he was no longer in love.

'And now,' said he, 'you're going to tell me, are you not, the particular favour you were about to ask.'

She laughed. 'Yes, I am. But I saw no reason to announce it to the world. More especially since it concerns your uncle.'

'I thought so. It came so very soon after we saw you together in the garden.'

'Ah, yes,' said Cristina, frowning, 'and what was made of that, I wonder?'

'My aunt, I think, has made something of it.'

'Your aunt, well, what shall we say to her? Not that it truly matters. In such cases people think what they please, and it's no use undeceiving them. Mariclò has said nothing to me about it.'

'Do you think she would have been so foolish?'

'No, none of the Rangoni is so stupid. And you, Edward?'

'It was strange, I admit. But not in that way.'

'Good,' said she firmly. 'You understand. Your uncle would not . . .'

'I know. But what then?'

'It was the first time he had ever truly begun to speak to me. He found me among some friends of my grandmother's, and contrived, I don't know how, to get me away so that we could talk unobserved. I thought at first that he would frighten me, he is so . . . so ardent.'

The expression amused Edward. Ardour of any kind was not something he ever associated with his uncle.

'He asked me . . .' She paused again. 'He asked me about my marriage. He said that Guido was an honourable young man, whom he much respected. It was quite as if he had been my father giving me his blessing.'

'Everyone, I believe, approves of the match,' said Edward softly, as though reminding her of what she had forgotten, and thinking of the Rangoni's earlier impatience.

'Then he asked me about my aunt Lupo, and whether she had always been as good to me as appeared. And then, as if I should understand the connexion of the one with the other, he said that in three weeks or so I was to expect a letter from him. It was to be a summons to a meeting between us.'

'But, Cristina, you said . . .'

'There was not the slightest hint of indelicacy in the idea. The innocence with which he spoke convinced me of that. He assumed that I understood and would act upon his instructions.'

'You agreed to go alone to see him?' Edward was horrified.

'No, not alone.' She turned to face him. 'You will come with me. That is the favour.'

'But how shall I know when or where? In any case, what affair is it of mine?'

She paused before answering, not, as he could see, because of having to think of what she was going to say, but because the entire nature of his question had startled her.

'Everything here concerns you, Edward. We have made you our confidant, we have trusted you as we trust nobody else.'

The notion repelled him. He saw himself suddenly as some faceless creature in a French tragedy, condemned to call people *seigneur* and *madame* and to the manufacture of deferential alexandrines – '*Ah, quel heureux destin en ces lieux vous renvoie?*'

'I never wanted to know your secrets!' he cried, 'And, as for saying that you have trusted me, that is nonsense. Perhaps I believed it at first, but not now. Why, you don't even trust yourselves.'

'Edward, I did not mean . . .' Cristina conciliatingly began.

'Oh, you meant precisely what you said. You meant that I had become a repository of such confidences as you chose to place in me. You meant that because I am not an Italian, that because I shall go away shortly and never see any of you again, you deem it safe to tell me certain things. Well, I shall tell you something now, Cristina. There are only two people in Villafranca who have never made me feel that they want anything from me, and have given their friendship freely. One is Daniele Basevi, and the other . . .' He stopped, unable to resist the pleasure of delaying in order to see whether she had guessed and what her response would be to the name. But he was himself taken aback when she exclaimed:–

'It is Guido, isn't it?'

123

'Good God, no, of course not. It is your youngest cousin, Maria Clotilde Rangoni.'

Her glance mingled relief with incomprehension. Remembering what had just taken place, he realized that his earlier judgment was correct, and began to wonder if Cristina's jealousy of Guido had anything to do with her having suddenly fallen in love with him. Something miraculous, if that were so, had been achieved, though he doubted it profoundly.

Massimo was coming towards them along the path among the statues, flaunting his customary irrational elegance in immaculate boots and breeches and a smart stock of custard-coloured silk. Envy and detestation of his florid, presuming handsomeness had always made Edward nervous, and now he was even more so at the idea of being found alone with Cristina. She, it appeared, had no qualms about remaining where she was and surveying Massimo coolly from her eminence above the icehouse as he stared at her in reproof below.

'I have come to take you home, Cristina,' he announced, as if he were saving her reputation by doing so. 'If you like, Edward, we'll give you a ride to San Gaudenzio.'

'No thanks, I'll walk back with Basevi. In any case you have just been there, no?'

Surprise clouded Massimo's face for an instant. Then he said:–

'Ah, già, they told you. Yes, I had estate business to discuss with your uncle. Things of that sort. You're coming, Cristina?'

It seemed to Edward that she would have liked to say no, and knew she could easily have done so, but instead she got up, shook her skirts a little and held onto his offered hand to steady herself as they clambered down the slope of the mound. Massimo rather peevishly took her arm and they went back together towards the house.

It was Guido who met them on their return, with his smile of that solicitous kind which looks over the shoulder. Something had not pleased him in Cristina's peremptory removal of Edward, and he contrived to impose upon the ceremony of handing the ladies into their carriage and walking beside it down the drive with Edward and Basevi an oppressive air of thwarted expectancy, implying that the whole business of their leaving cut short a due of explanation – from whom was not clear.

They parted just outside the gates. Massimo was evidently too preoccupied with the absorbing duties of a daring charioteer to say more than a curt farewell. Edward's leave-taking was mingled with the reflection that he had given neither a yes nor a no to Cristina's request. Signora Lupo acknowledged him with a slight inclination of the head. She said nothing. She never did.

14

THERE WAS TIME enough, after all, to take stock of things in these August days at San Gaudenzio. Had he wished to study the answers to the celebrated questions of the Emperor Tiberius, he supposed he might have arrived at them, if only through the sheer leisure for contemplation which the place afforded. He was not lonely as he had once been in Villafranca, and he felt no craving for entertainment or society more than the country offered. In order not to finish all the books he had brought from the town, he borrowed others from Basevi and sat in the shade of the park trees reading and thinking by turns, reminded continually by what he read of the suspensions, withholdings and suppressions which surrounded him.

He could not understand why Guido and Cristina needed him so much. Once he thought he had known it, but the certainty had swiftly dissolved. In the end, far from being flattered by their attentions, he was disturbed by their assiduity. He wished they would leave him alone, yet the freedom and solitude to which he had looked forward on coming into the country was not to be found even here. Rather their need seemed to intensify through a sense of his closeness to them. He was there at San Gaudenzio undefended by the put-offs and forgivable hypocrisies which so easily obtained in the city. They knew he could not run away, though they must have guessed that he wanted to. What was more, he could not, without rudeness, refuse to visit them, even

126

if, at every visit, he felt as though yet another part of himself had been devoured.

That they should do as they were both expected to, that they should at last marry and leave him to go back to Naples, was too simple now to be imagined. Yet, as he understood it, Cristina would not refuse Guido. She had arrived, it was not clear how, at the acknowledged existence of a desire. What Guido felt Edward hardly wanted to consider, though he knew it was not love for Cristina.

As a humdrum refuge from all this, he never declined any of his aunt's invitations to go driving or visiting. The drives were dusty and always along the same roads, but a feeling that he was himself a prisoner of custom made him share her restlessness at least in this. In that idle, languid manner which was a common heritage with his mother, she would answer his questions about England as they bowled across the causeways between the fields and tell him about her childhood in Staffordshire and his grandfather, Lord Cannock, who was held to be the best rider in the county and from whom, as she believed, Edward must have taken his good horsemanship. As she spoke of Marchington and Rugely and Dove Bank, and the Vernons and the Ansons, and old nurse Wood who had dressed them all up as gypsies and taken them for a frolic to Uttoxeter races, and of how they had told Lady Garle's fortune as she sat in her carriage and she had crossed their palms with a shilling each and never recognized them, his imagination seized upon everything with a transforming power which gave it a kind of romantic inaccessibility, so that an envisaged Staffordshire became Borneo or Japan.

Dull and vapid though the visiting was, to people who, had the Countess died that day, would have forgotten her existence within the week, and whose florid protestations of pleasure at seeing her – but it was a century, no, truly, but how beautiful she looked in her morning dress, but how young! – always embarrassed Edward, it saved him from the responsibility of having to confront Cristina or Guido on any but the most distant and ceremonious footing.

Visitors came and went at San Gaudenzio besides, interlopers upon the territory of quietness enclosing it. The servants, noisy and familiar elsewhere, moved about the staircases and corridors of the villa as though interpreting its mute discourse, opening and

127

closing doors stealthily, creeping into a room with a basin or a dish borne like the instruments of a murder, slipping the catches of the shutters with an evident grudge against the intrusive vulgarity of the heat and warmth outside. Getting accustomed to the sounds of the house within its silences, Edward had grown used to a sense of people entering and leaving on private business with his uncle at the oddest of hours. He never spoke to his aunt about this, but he knew, from certain hints she let fall, that it concerned her.

Anything, indeed, to do with his uncle concerned her. Whatever she did or said seemed to act as a mask to this unending preoccupation, in which all else was mingled and submerged. Edward wanted to open the subject with her, but, supposing she would think it a mere impertinence, was content to realize that she could understand, in her vague, instinctive fashion, why he was respectful.

She seemed to cling to this dogged, thankless affection because there was nothing else. None of the things which are ordinarily held to engross women of her rank, music, books, fancy-work, bonnets, letter-writing or gossip, had the same grip upon her. She must always be hoping that some grace of action, which the Count could never have suspected her to own, would turn him, surprised and penitent, towards her.

Not even religion offered a palliative. At her marriage she had nominally been received into the Roman faith, but Edward soon discovered that, with some curious vestige of fear for her soul, however she might dimly conceive its essence, she had remained loyal to the rites of the Church of England. Yet she gained no special consolation from their exercise: what mattered was to keep on with them in case anything more dreadful should happen to her by leaving them off.

Edward willingly joined her at prayers. His religious constancy was, it is true, always the stronger when his parents were close at hand: his mother had gone over to Rome years before, and his father found churchgoing of any sort a deuced bore, so that his own adherence to Protestantism was often more an act of filial defiance than anything else. Yet here at San Gaudenzio something of the savour returned, as together he and the Countess retreated, like stealthy lovers, to an empty bedroom in the least occupied corner of the villa, and read solemnly through the order

128

of evening prayer and the shortest of the psalms for the day. In the responses he was the clergyman, choosing the lessons, reading the collects and giving the absolution besides.

At this ceremony, though the Count must surely have guessed at what was taking place, he never disturbed them, but always, as they followed the service through its various stages, Edward could detect in his aunt's low, urgent manner of answering and saying the prayers a sense that in some incomprehensible fashion the entire sacrament was being directed at her husband, almost as if she were longing for him miraculously to appear among them in the dry-smelling bedroom with its piles of mattresses and pillows.

One afternoon, when the garden trembled in the heat and the cicadas scratched, they were leaving the room and Edward, having hidden their prayerbooks on top of the wardrobe, was slipping the key into the oiled lock when they both froze at hearing a footstep in the corridor. It was his uncle who now stood facing them in the shadow as they turned, guiltily silent, towards him. He too said nothing for some moments, as though reaching for appropriate words.

'Edward, do me the favour,' he began at length, 'of opening that door again.'

Edward did as he was told, thinking 'now we're for it' and casting a backward glance at his aunt, rigid and helpless against the wall.

'I have to speak to Edward alone,' said the Count, 'so you may leave us, my dear.'

The Countess slunk away, without turning to look back, and, when uncle and nephew had entered the room, the former, ordering the door to be locked again, walked towards the window, where he stood for some time with his hands behind his back, looking out into the garden below.

'Edward, do you know that what you and your aunt are doing is against the laws of the state? You need not think I am unaware that you read Protestant prayers together on a Sunday, and that the Countess has been in the habit of doing so since we were married. The Duke allows only the Catholic rite in his dominions, and the fines on those following heretical observances are most severe. You, of course, are exempt, as a subject of the Queen of England, but the Countess, in becoming my wife, has become an Italian . . . I mean . . . that is to say, a Villafrancan. I hope you understand what I imply. There is a position to be maintained. As a court chamberlain I must be above suspicion.'

The irony was too much for Edward, who rejoined:–

'Yet you have done nothing to stop either her or me from pursuing this custom. Why not?'

His uncle now turned swiftly round towards him. The expression on his long, pallid face was one of near delight. It was as if, by challenging him, Edward had passed over some apparently necessary but wholly tiresome element in their interview which could now be safely put aside.

'This was not what I wished to speak to you about. Sit down please.'

They had another pause, as Edward obeyed and the Count turned once more to the window. Several times he drew breath as if to speak, and then checked himself. Finally, with a certain obvious effort, he began, to his nephew's complete astonishment, with the words:–

'We are all very fond of you here. You know that, don't you? Your affability has made you universally liked in Villafranca. It is not something to which we are accustomed in English manners. My servants call you a true gentleman because you are not gratuitously rude to them. I'm grateful for that. Do you like me, Edward?'

Edward was amazed into dumbness, but the Count pursued:–

'No, I expect you don't. I can't say I give you cause to. The matter is of no real importance to me, though it would please me to earn your esteem. I've a great many things just at present to concern myself with. Estates, the court calendar, private affairs of one kind or another. By the way, my steward Basevi trusts you. That's worthy of note, don't you think? When I took him on, you know, people said "Oh, he is only a young Jew, in a few years he will have fleeced you of everything", but I knew better, he is one of those to whose fingers money sticks, an honest man after his fashion. Everyone's honesty has a reason, no?'

He turned again to Edward, who could only mouth:–

'Oh, perhaps.'

'And what do you think is the reason for Basevi's honesty? Well, it doesn't matter, does it? Do you love Cristina Bentivoglio? No, of course you don't. I'm glad of that, it would have come to nothing, such things do. She has fallen in love with Guido Tagliabosco. You must have noticed. She feels sorry for him because he is being forced to marry her. He must ask her soon, but I think he is afraid. It's easy to see why. Such men usually are.'

The Count took a case of matches from his pocket and lit a cigar, which he puffed to keep alight, but otherwise simply held in the air, punctuating his discourse with it by the description of circles and figures of eight.

'You see, we must believe in something. It doesn't matter what, only to believe is important, to be constant to some sort of possibility, not merely to things as they are. We are nothing without it. I think you know that.'

He moved away from the window and came towards Edward, holding out his hands, one of them still clutching the cigar. There was an extraordinary pathos in the gesture, which Edward had never imagined it possible to apprehend in someone hitherto so remote from his sympathies.

'You and I, we have not spoken much, have we?'

The novel suggestion of intimacy in this made Edward cringe, and only grew worse when the Count said:–

'You mustn't be afraid of me, you know. I'm told it's a fault I have, that of making others afraid.' He laughed joylessly. 'They say even the Duke is frightened of me, though I cannot tell. One may not know everything, do you agree? Yet I should be glad to be assured that you were happy. I always thought it very important, when I was young, to be assured of happiness in others. I may have been wrong – indeed I very frequently was – but I believed that to be important.'

What it all meant, this muddled, obfuscate collection of sentences, he could not guess. It might be that the Count was mad. He looked up into the elongated face, with its hollow grey eyes like the worn marks on the back of a plated spoon. Suddenly the Count grasped his hand and said:–

'Believe me, Edward.' Then, taking the key which his nephew still nervelessly held, he unlocked the door and was gone.

Upon instinct, Edward made up his mind to go over to Scarabello and see Mariclò. He ran out of the house into the blaze of the day and charged through the sweep-gates, across the road onto the path which led between the ditches to the verge of the Rangoni estate.

In the fields he slowed his pace, enjoying their bright openness in contrast to the shadow he had left behind. Most of the corn had been harvested already, and here and there were flocks of buntings pecking among the stubble. On the edge of one of the watercourses a solitary stork was poking in the reedbeds for frogs. Edward stood and watched it for a moment, rather amazed at its temerity in venturing into a countryside where all wild animals and birds existed solely to be killed because they were either edible or a nuisance. He thought of himself as somewhat of that kind and wished the stork well.

Jumping easily over the boundary ditch, he clambered up into the field. Scarabello, a blotchy pink huddle of crenellated walls, lay beyond a park which neglect had transformed into a wood, through whose tracts Edward picked his way towards the grim stone terrace at the back of the house. He was not surprised to find nobody to welcome him. The Rangoni kept two old servants in the house and three or four men and women on the farm who might be called upon to harness the coach and hem the bedsheets when needed, but nothing was ever offered to the visitor in the way of polite entertainment by the household.

The hall at Scarabello smelt of horses – at other times of the year it smelt of cows and pigs – and the visitor seemed to carry wafts of these smells with him wherever else he went in the house. Edward noticed that since his last call on the family, four days earlier, someone had made a hole in the bottom of one of the pictures of ruins which hung on the wall opposite the fireplace. Massimo's hunting dog was gnawing a bone at the foot of the stairs, and there was a sound of clattering about in the kitchen and those spasmodic moanings and gaspings of the sort made by people who feel that the world must be told how hard they work. Going out onto the brick platform under the mulberry tree at the southern end of the house he found Mariclò.

She was alone, seated in musing indolence on the stone parapet of the wall above the overgrown garden. As Edward came towards her she put up her hand to her face to smooth back the swatches of hair which had fallen across her cheek.

'You look as if you expected me,' said he.

'I suppose I must have hoped you'd come. The others have

132

gone to Soliera with the Boschetti. I didn't want to go, so I stayed here and waited for you.'

'I'm glad you didn't go. You probably wouldn't have enjoyed it anyway.'

'Oh, I might have done. Shall I go into the house and ask them to bring you something to drink?'

'No, thanks. I only came across because I wanted to talk to you, and I'd rather not be hobnobbing with your mamma before dinner.'

'Are you still frightened of her? You shouldn't be. She likes you enormously. She thinks you would have "done" for Cristina, if it hadn't been . . .'

'I'm sick to death of you all liking me,' said Edward, and started at once to tell her what happened that afternoon. She listened with none but the most trifling interruptions, then paused for a long while before saying anything at all, looking away from him and smoothing back her hair.

'None of it surprises me. It is precisely what we'd expect of him. How well did you know your uncle before you came to Villafranca?'

'I never knew him. I don't truly know him now. Even less after what has happened today. Yet, Mariclò, I was not afraid of him.'

She smiled. 'Ought you to have been? They should have told you about Count Castelvetro's sorrow. People, you know, have sorrows. I hope I never do. The sort of thing, that's to say, which possesses me and makes me dull to everything else. I don't wonder at him asking whether you liked him. Nobody here does, much. He's far too eccentric, and that sort of thing doesn't answer in Villafranca.'

'Either edible or else a nuisance,' said Edward. Mariclò, looking up at him did not understand, but, realizing why she did not, laughed to herself. 'I was thinking about a stork,' he said. 'Tell me about the great sorrow.'

'It was in 1831, the year after I was born, so of course I don't remember it, and mamma and grandmamma always said I had no business to know about such things, but in the end I got one of my Rosselli cousins to tell me. The Count was little older than you or me – about twenty – and had fallen secretly in love with a woman whose name nobody knew, or if they did they wouldn't say, because she was someone among our families in Villafranca. You understand, they were going to declare it openly, but something prevented them, the Count not being of age, I think, and just when they were emboldened to do so the affair of Menotti took place and the fighting, and she, whoever she was, poor thing, died of a fever she got when her family took her for safety into the country.'

'And her name? You must know that.'

'My cousin said it was one of the Bonacini, but I asked Caterina Bonacini and she swore it wasn't, and Countess Coccapani, who is the greatest tattler, says it is a secret in the family but that we're all honour-bound not to speak of it. So it is one of those things which everybody knows but nobody mentions. Your uncle is said never to have recovered from it.'

'That, I suppose, is why he married my aunt,' said Edward bitterly, 'and I'll wager he never told her about his great sorrow. What a dismal place this is!'

'It isn't our fault, good heavens!' cried Mariclò, nettled. 'We learn to keep silent. Would you rather it weren't so? Such things happen elsewhere than in Italy.' She stopped, staring hard at the ground, then looked at him, demanding an answer. 'If you think that, why don't you leave us, Edward?'

He had been afraid lest she, of all people, should ask this question. The birds rustled among the leaves. Someone called across the fields. Now he said slowly:–

'You know that I shall leave you, after we return to the city in September. But that's neither here nor there. You know as well what my feelings are towards this place. It isn't my uncle and aunt, or what I used to feel towards Cristina, or this quixotic notion I have of contriving to get Guido to fall in love with her, or any . . .' He paused. 'That's to say, Villafranca, don't you see, is what you all are. Sometimes I really detest you . . . well, not you, Mariclò . . . but everyone else, so greedy, so enslaved by manners and forms and noise and useless chat and vapid nonsense about food and dresses and horses and theatres, and none of you opening a book or thinking a thought that isn't connected with something you can touch or see or eat or ride or wear. But sometimes I think I'd like to die in Villafranca. Sometimes I think I've died already.'

'It was what you wanted,' she said, with a gentle insistence on the point.

134

'Yes, it was what I wanted. Either edible or else a nuisance, therefore to be killed. There's the britzka on the road. I remember when I saw it first.'

'It takes at least ten minutes for them to come round by the church and up through the fields. Do you want to stay and see them?'

'I shan't mind,' said Edward, as he leaned forward to arrest her hand in the act of smoothing away her black hair.

15

UNDER THE SHADOW of an imminent parting, they got on with the business of being in love, united by a persistence which derived as much from the consciousness of those countless obstacles which might divide them from one another as from that resilience which was so strongly marked in the character of each. It was not as Edward had supposed it would be, a sophistication of what he had experienced in his days of hankering after Cristina. That, indeed, seemed to have taught him nothing save the authenticity of his feelings for Mariclò. Almost everything else appeared new, by virtue of her responsive affection. The calculating opportunism which lies at the root of every unanswered passion, the incidental tyrannies of appetite and expectation, the negligent exposure of self as part of a sustained war of attrition with the disdainful lover, gave place to an actuality of pleasure gained from dwelling within an existence shared exclusively by Mariclò.

There was little possibility that their attachment would be countenanced by the Marchesa or by Massimo, even at his most mercenary. While Edward might have been considered, in Mariclò's phrase, to 'do' for Cristina, the Rangoni, according to ancient custom, must marry among their own kind. Thus he and Mariclò had to devise the various means of communicating without detection. Notes and letters were out of the question unless carried by Basevi, and he, though readily admitted to a secret he had already half fathomed, must find it hard to contrive a pretext for visiting Scarabello purely to leave them where they could be taken up by Mariclò.

The indulgence of secrecy ought to have been amusing, yet it consistently wasn't. As each several solution for a meeting or an invitation was arrived at, the pair, excavating possibility like moles, felt the full load of weariness in the destined outcome. Subterfuge, while sharpening the edge of love, irked them with its embarrassing absurdity. In the long evenings, when the ladies sat fanning themselves on the weed-grown terrace, and Massimo, who grew more tetchy and impatient with each day, paced up and down before hurling into the house to scold the servants for delaying dinner, Edward's hand would stray with practised furtiveness towards Mariclò's, to feel the quick, intense pressure of her fingers upon his. As the family went in, the two of them would linger to be the last, so that with the backs of Signora Lupo and Cristina in front of them they could turn to mouthing kisses in the shadowed rooms through which they passed. The one thing they could do little of was merely to look at each other. Glances carrying any feeling whatever had to be stolen out of relentlessly swift seconds of opportunity. It was as though Villafranca, drawing Edward into that mesh of duplicity he had once so detested, was bending him to its customs, denying him all possibilities of openness so as to make him more gravely aware of the intrinsic strength in his attachment to Mariclò. He was not grateful for such ironies.

'You feel it too, don't you?' he said to her one day, when a precious quarter of an hour left them together in the park at San Gaudenzio.

'Sometimes, yes, but I am inured to it. I expected things would be like this when I began to hope you liked me. I even thought of ways in which we could go around it.' She laughed regretfully. 'So far successful, no?'

'We must be wary of everyone. Aldegonda saw me looking at you when we were out at Baggiovara the other day.'

'I wish I'd seen you. Why didn't I? What was I doing?'

'Taking a cup of coffee from the footman. You smiled at him in that way you have which makes everyone feel that what they have done for you is something remarkable, and he smirked with pleasure so that I wanted to break his nose, the puppy. You don't know you're doing it: if you did you'd

137

never do it again. So I stared at you and Aldegonda saw me.'

'You mustn't mind Aldegonda.'

'I don't, truly, in fact I have even begun to like her. She has no imagination worth speaking of – forgive me – but she knows what's expected of her and does the best she can.'

'She is a kind sister to me. If she suspects anything, she'll tell me so at once. In any case it is not her I fear but Massimo.'

'Why?'

Mariclò looked about her, as if the very trees and bushes were sheltering her brother's spies.

'For his sense of what is due to us, the Rangoni. Of the good families in Villafranca we are the oldest, and it has been a kind of religion with us to keep up a certain place in the world. We are bred to it.'

'Even you? I can't accept that.'

'There is nothing I can do about it, Edward. Our houses are falling down, our servants only stay with us because they are too old or because they have nowhere else to go, we quarrelled with the Duke years ago so we are perpetually pried into and informed upon, and every penny Massimo gets from the estates that isn't used to pay off a debt is spent on keeping us in new clothes. We squabble and complain at each other incessantly, and we're never truly happy but when we're rude and unfeeling. Yet I can't help being proud of what I am.'

'With Massimo that's an obsession.'

'It is what I'm afraid of. He is selfish like the rest of us, vain as well – his friends call him *Il Bello* and mean to be sarcastic by it – but his selfishness and vanity have a single object. Everything he does is for our honour.'

'And my love for you is so dishonourable?' exclaimed Edward. 'My uncle's an English earl, with thousands of acres in Staffordshire and Derbyshire and a town house in London and five parishes in his gift, and my father has been rich enough to spend fifteen years travelling for his health. I'm ashamed to urge these things: I should think it vulgar to have to do so with Massimo.'

Her face clouded, not, he knew, because of anger but because of the implications of what he had said, implications of which he too became suddenly aware.

'We cannot expect him to pardon us if he discovers it,' she

138

returned inexorably. 'I told you long ago that they may already have chosen a husband for me. If not, then I am to be a spinster all my life and stay at home as a companion to my mother. When my grandmother dies she'll be all alone, and they will marry Aldegonda in a year or two to Count Grillenzoni.'

The bleak realization of the truth in what she had just said fell slowly upon Edward. He hardly knew which was worse, the thought of losing her to some formal fool of the nobility, to have her trust betrayed and her intelligence stifled, or the notion of an eternal secrecy, with clandestine meetings once or twice a year and the occasional letter like a hand held out from the other side of an abyss. Staring at the ground, he muttered: 'What shall we do, Mariclò?' and then, taking her in his arms as though even now he felt her being snatched from him, he cried, acknowledging his own defencelessness, 'I couldn't help falling in love with you, please, please understand me,' as for a while they hung silently upon one another, engulfed by a mutual misery. Drawing disconsolately away from him, Mariclò said:–

'We can do nothing, Edward, except endure. It's a torment even to think about it. Promise me you won't brood upon what you cannot avoid.'

'I shan't, I swear it.'

She looked at him with an expression of hopeless indulgence, as if knowing him like herself.

'Ah, if I could only believe that,' she sighed, 'and for my own part besides. How weak I am! Massimo would say I was not worthy to be a Rangoni.'

'I'd rather have you weak than a Rangoni if it means that you love me,' said Edward, folding her in his embrace once again. The park and the fields beyond it lay perfectly still. The pair heard time falling away, and battened upon it even as it slipped from their grasp. Basevi, coming down the path among the trees, did not see them until it was too late for him to retreat. They turned, in instinctive momentary shock, facing him in half-smiling embarrassment while he assumed an air of discreet complicity.

'I'm sorry,' he said, 'it was hardly intended I should find you. I was on my way across to see Count Tagliabosco. Will you forgive me?'

'You are laughing, aren't you, Basevi? Admit it,' said Edward.

And Basevi did indeed laugh. 'But not at you. At things I remember doing myself, things I do still, God knows. But be careful, I beg you both, everywhere here is dangerous. When I can warn you I shall. Yet I am going to do something very rash, and ask you a favour which may compromise the pair of you for ever.'

'We'll give it already,' said Mariclò, 'since you have put yourself in danger for us.'

'A few letters here and there are nothing, *signorina*. This is different.'

'What, then?'

Basevi looked away and rubbed his hands together. It was one of those touches Edward loved in him, that though he might appear shadowy, devious, subtle beyond outwitting, a strain of unconquered bashfulness gave his true nature away.

'Well, you see, I am getting married the week after next, to Signorina Limentani of Carpi, whom you know, Edward. And the law of Villafranca requires that a Jewish wedding be witnessed by a Gentile, who must put his signature to a document. And so I have to ask . . . if you would . . . that's to say . . . if you would both come to our wedding.'

'Why should we not?' cried Mariclò. 'A Jewish wedding, that's capital! What would Massimo and Aldegonda say if they knew? Oh do let us go, Edward, please!'

'We cannot go alone,' said Edward, 'there must be a chaperone. And a fine old time we shall have of making our plans so that nobody finds us out.'

'Your family must not know, *signorina*,' said Basevi, 'that you have gone to the wedding of a steward to the daughter of a maker of court uniforms. It would not answer.'

Mariclò laughed cynically. 'There, that's what being a Rangoni means. But I'd come to your wedding if you were a pair of gypsies marrying over a brush, and be none the less a Rangoni for that.'

'Give you joy, Basevi,' said Edward, shaking him by the hand, 'but now it's for me to laugh, after all the scorn you've poured on that cousin of yours at Cento who is studying to become a rabbi. And yesterday, when we were out riding, you ate *coppa* at the inn at Bastiglia. Come now!'

Basevi grinned ruefully. 'Do you think the worse of me for following the custom, Edward? I could hardly marry in a church, and civil marriages are invalid in Villafranca.'

'No, Daniele, I think the better of you, for what my esteem is worth. I don't think I ever felt so important before. But what will they say to your Gentile witness being only nineteen and an English heretic into the bargain?'

Basevi did not answer, only shifted his spectacles and looked at Edward with quizzical sharpness until, realizing what it meant, he burst out:–

'Oh, aren't you the deep one!'.

On their way back towards the house the three began to lay the ground for the almost impossible project of conveying Mariclò to a Jewish wedding at Carpi and bringing her home again without anyone being the wiser as to her absence. Two weeks seemed scarcely long enough in which to make all safe, but the sense of urgent occasion worked strongly upon their fancies.

'Talk about it as little as possible between yourselves,' said Basevi as they reached the steps of the terrace. 'In that way you'll guard it more jealously. And now, *signorina*, the Countess has asked to see you with messages for your mother. She was most particular.'

'I'll go at once,' said Mariclò, 'because I know she is most particular when it's least important.'

Watching Edward watching her slip into the house, Basevi exclaimed:–

'*Ah già*, you're in love at last. I always hoped for that.'

'And wasn't I in love before?'

'A little infatuated for a time, yes, but there was no reason to call it love.'

'Oh, Cristina, Cristina! What is one to do about her? I've almost forgotten that I meant to make her marry Guido.'

'It was about Guido that I wanted to speak to you. Your aunt wasn't that insistent about seeing the *signorina*, but since the matter has to do with her brother . . .'

'Massimo? We have spent far too much thought on him today already,' rejoined Edward testily.

'You will have to listen and act as I bid you, for everybody's peace of mind, Edward. I've discovered, through a little observation and a trifle of chicanery, that Massimo Rangoni and other young hotheads, Ferdinando Taccoli, Leopoldo Sighinolfi, you know the sort of fellow, have been trying to persuade your uncle to act in concert with them in something – I don't yet know what –

141

that is to happen when we all return to town from the *villeggiatura*.'

Edward was silent, initially more amazed than he afterwards realized he should have been by the news.

'They have been coming here on certain days, more or less secretly, to induce the Count to join them. So far he appears to have refused.'

'But how do you know this, for God's sake?'

Basevi gave a resigned smile and spread his arms wide.

'Must I tell you? Must I honestly tell you?'

'Yes.'

'I must then. I carry letters for others besides you and the *signorina*, and I am not so respectful of their private character, you understand. What the thing to be attempted is I don't yet know. But we hear news now, from Rome, from Milan, from Venice, which makes us wonder why we have slept for so long. And the settlement with Tuscany over the territory at Fivizzano has angered a great many of our patriots. Can you be surprised that these foolish noble sprigs should think it a prime moment to act in?'

Remembering what Mariclò had told him, Edward simply muttered:–

'Damn Massimo Rangoni, damn him, damn him.'

'He has not yet brought your uncle about, but he may pull him too far, because the Count always admired his spirit. He once said he wished he were his own son. Fortunately for us there's someone else he admires as much.'

'Guido Tagliabosco, he told me so himself.'

'Yes, and he will listen to Guido in the end.'

'Then why does Guido not know of this?'

'I've acquainted him with every detail, but I cannot persuade him to act. One prudent word from him would steel your uncle against any thought of embroiling himself in such desperate nonsense, from which he has so much to lose.'

'What is it, Daniele? What are they going to do?' Edward was flushed with excitement, both at the thing itself and at the consciousness of how far his friend was once again trusting him.

'Madness!' whispered Basevi furiously. 'Every time I break a seal on one of those letters – I have the Count's ring, as his steward, to make a new wafer, and the rest I stick down with flour

142

paste under the wax – I wonder if they'll spell it out and confirm my worst fears, but as yet it is all mad talk, like plotters in a French play. But by God, Edward, they mean it, believe me. I am a patriot, yet I'd betray them tomorrow to Stappler and his police if it were the least honourable to do so.'

'Then you wish me . . .' Edward said apprehensively.

'To speak, yes, to Guido. He'll be led by you, always. He loves you, you know.'

'Too much, I believe.' Basevi was wholly taken aback as Edward went on: 'That's why I don't want to be a part of this. Your patriotism is not mine, Daniele. This is not my country.' To which Basevi simply said: 'Yet.'

There was a silence between them. Edward knew, even as he had uttered the words, that he could not refuse, yet a sickening fear of the roots of his own power over Guido had started to take hold of him. He seized Basevi's arm imploringly. He felt again very young and untried.

'Don't make me do this. You, of all people, must know how it appals me. I can't work Guido by what he feels towards me.'

Basevi answered in a tone of unrelenting calm. 'And by the same token you hope to get him to marry Cristina. Oh, Edward, you don't yet fathom your own strength. You're the only person to whom Guido will listen, and he is the one man who can bend the Count from a purpose Massimo and the others are hardening day by day. One word to him. Please.'

Though the entire matter disgusted Edward, any choice was out of the question. Basevi alone seemed activated by honourable sentiment, even if he did not scruple to manipulate Edward in the same cause. As for the rest, his uncle was already half crazy, Massimo was hag-ridden by preposterous claims of family duty, and, for Guido, who knew what drove him this way or that?

'I shall do it because you have asked me, because you're my friend. Mariclò is something more now, if only Guido could be made to know it. But I want you to understand that I do it disinterestedly, not as one of you, nor as caring for your politics or your revolutions . . .'

Basevi broke him off with a cold firmness. 'You are one of us. Villafranca has taken you to itself and you cannot turn your back upon it again. Now go in and be pleasant with your aunt. She deserves it.'

16

IT WAS SOME minutes before he could bring himself to mount. He went round the horse slowly, pretending to tighten her girth and lengthen the stirrups, and patting at her bridle as if he needed reminding that it was there. The groom, sensing that something was the matter, said solicitously:–

'I'll take her out myself if the *milordo* is not feeling well today.'

Edward smiled wanly at him. 'That's kind of you, Giacomo, but I can ride her just the same.'

'She likes you, *milordo*, you can see that. You don't pull on her mouth the way your uncle does sometimes.'

'My uncle's a hard rider, isn't he?'

'Works his horses, he does. Understands 'em, but works 'em just the same.'

Edward stroked the mare's neck, half hoping that she might, after her fashion, have divined what he felt. Then he swung himself disconsolately into the saddle, making himself comfortable as he asked:–

'Giacomo, is there a longer way over to Falconara than by this road?'

'Not unless the *milordo* wants to go round by Soliera, and that takes you right through the town. Looks as if it might come on to rain shortly, so I wouldn't try it myself. And better not to go across the fields if the gentlemen are out with their guns.'

They could hear the hunters' fowling-pieces going off in the distance. There was a chilly little gust of wind or two and the sky

144

was mottled with odd, yellowish clouds. It was a day of the kind in Italy when the summer shakes itself out to begin afresh, laying one coating of dust to start another. He knew it would be wrong to go haring about the countryside under a shower, but just now he would do anything to defer the fulfilment of his journey.

'There's a cloak in the harness room if you want it, your honour,' said Giacomo, running and fetching it without further ado. 'This'll keep you dry. It's the Count's own.'

Edward accepted it reluctantly, as though it were the shirt of Nessus, and bundled it over the mare's withers with a firm determination not to use it. Then he set off down the track and onto the road in the direction of Soliera.

The morning light was already starting to fade as the sky darkened and the storm came towards horse and rider across the plain. The landscape had a worn, sickly look, enhanced by the baldness of those patches where the harvesters had finished their task. Everything appeared as he had seen it at first, in those days of dismal solitude when he rode out among the shuttered villas and up and down the files of poplars, an unloved stranger. Yet in this instant he felt hungry for that time to come again if it only meant avoiding what he had to do now.

There was something meretricious in the very act. Edward knew, by Basevi's instinct of surprise, that he had not guessed at Guido's feelings – whatever character they were supposed to assume. Justly and reasonably he had appealed to Edward's sense of Guido's regard in order to save Count Castelvetro, and, by implication, others, from ridicule and disgrace. He could not have observed, in that very same regard, a depth of concealment which daily made itself plainer to Edward, who himself now shamefacedly approached the task of unmasking Guido's evasions only to smother them hastily when the business in hand was completed. As he pricked glumly onwards into a strengthening breeze, he realized that he had only one weapon to hand, but that its aid would be almost an indecency. If the need arose, however, he must invoke it.

Deadened to external sensation, he handed his papers to the customs officer at Soliera with a mechanical motion of his free arm, and set forward through the main street of the town at a shambling walk. Sepulchral quiet encumbered everything. The few people to be seen moved here and there in a monastic self-absorption, their footfalls hardly summoning an echo. From time to time they looked anxiously at the sky. None of them looked at Edward. A little way beyond the last houses and into the open country again, he felt the first cold splashes of the rain.

It was pointless now to turn back. He could see the rutted lane going down towards Falconara, and steered his horse, with a grim resolve, between the crumbling brick pillars of the gateway. Useless also to disregard the force of the storm, which now emptied itself upon the plain with implacable singlemindedness. Cursing, Edward dismounted, put on his uncle's great cloak, enough almost to keep the mare dry as well as himself, got up again and trotted her on in a consuming fury at everything, until the lane meeting the track up to the house itself allowed him to canter her the last few yards to the stables.

Fortune had at least ensured the presence of a man sheltering in the barn to run out and take his bridle. In a mere five minutes the weight of the rain was so great that Edward simply fell from saddle to ground, blinded momentarily by the water dripping off the brim of his hat.

'*Milordo*, is it you?'

'Yes. Take her in and give her a rub down, for the love of God. Where's your master?'

'In the house, *milordo*.'

'Is he alone?'

'Yes, your honour. He has not stirred all day.'

'If anyone else should come, tell them he is from home. You'll say nothing about me either. Here's something for your trouble.'

The man pocketed the coin and hustled the glistening mare into the stable, as Edward moved nervously towards the house.

It was so dark in the hall that somebody had lit the candles on either side of the two great glasses. Before one of them Edward took off his hat and cloak and peered at himself to see what sort of figure he must cut after his ride. The effect was grotesque: a damp ring around his head made it look as if someone had been apprehended in the act of garrotting him and run away with the cord, his stock had come adrift from the pin and floated in wild streamers across his waistcoat, and his face was mottled with little blotches of congealed mud. He wondered perversely whether, steamy and malodorous as he was, he might not be sufficiently repulsive to Guido to make their interview easier than expected. Acting upon the surmise, he hurried towards the *salotto* and flung open the doors, determined to finish with it all as soon as could be.

Clearly his entrance was more dramatic than he intended. Guido rose towards him from the shadows of the room with an expression of ghastly surprise, occasioned, perhaps, by having hoped that he would come.

'Your man disappeared as soon as I got into the house,' said Edward, 'and I thought . . .'

'Why did you come?' Guido spoke as if it were a premeditated outrage, the effective fulfilment of a dream whose material accomplishment was the object of a morbid dread. At that moment Edward was for him the thing itself.

'If you want I'll go away.'

'No, please, not now.' Guido sprang towards him, clasping his hands almost to break the knuckles.

An embarrassed silence fell upon them. Some preternatural daring or simple desperation made Guido cling to Edward's hands as if they had been ends of rope. Again his face in the gloom was full of pitiful accusation as he almost whispered:–

'What do you want?'

The question did not need an answer, but Edward knew that if he wished to save himself he must reply. Yet baldly to state his business on behalf of the Count and Basevi must seem unpardonably cruel. Shocked by his own prescient wisdom, he said:–

'Only not to offend you, Guido. My hands. Please.'

A shade crossly, Guido dropped them like toys he had been asked to give back, allowing Edward to walk away into the middle of the room and sit heavily down on the edge of the piano stool. Already feeling exhausted, he could at least bring himself to say:–

'I've come to ask for a favour, one which is yours to grant.'

This sounded impressively vague and lofty. He hoped, good God, that something would make Guido understand. Evidently, however, he did not, standing there beside the delicate vase upon its tripod, defenceless in his neatness and waiting for the answer he was not to be given. Oh the deuce, Edward thought, oh the deuce take it. It seemed to be he himself who made Guido say:–

147

'I'll do anything you ask, you know that.'

'Anything, yes, that's it, anything, whether it is worthy of you or not.'

'Do you despise me?'

'When you say things like that, yes, it is contemptible. Think of what you are! You can't cast yourself away upon such a submission, it's craven, shiftless, stupid.'

Stand up, fight me, don't yield now. But Guido, turning away, began slowly to pace up and down, pressing his hands together as he spoke.

'Then you despise me. But to myself I am not contemptible. I've loved you from the first, more than a brother, have sought your company and trusted to every feeling I ever entertained for you. And that is wrong? No, Edward, I think not. I'm not free like you, but within myself I may make allegiances where I choose. Thus I . . .'

'Stop talking to me about freedom,' cried Edward. 'Do you imagine I come among you like an invader, like one of those Lombards with ridiculous names, those *ardo*'s and *ulfo*'s and *baldo*'s you're all so pleased to count as your ancestors? I'm no more free than you are.'

'Oh, you'll escape us soon enough,' Guido said resentfully, 'with your English liberty. A subject of the Queen of England, protected by your consuls and your constitution.' He stopped where he was, looking steadily before him to where the rain, in its absolute Italian way, pelted the garden trees. 'I shall die if you go.'

'Gammon, Guido, you'll do nothing of the kind. Listen to me.'

Edward rose deliberately, went towards Guido and stood behind him, placing both hands upon his shoulders. He felt the body under his fingers tremble as if it would totter to the ground.

'You have no choice but to survive. These things are ordained. You are not of a kind to cut your throat because such as I leave Villafranca. You'll do as you're bidden and marry Cristina and . . .'

It was too much for Guido. Crying 'Stop, oh, stop, for the love of God!', he turned round and buried his head in the coat of the immovable Edward. 'I don't love her, I haven't even tried. I only love you. In all the world.'

It was what Edward had most dreaded to hear. The words

came like a sickening and grotesque parody of that capacity for sentiment he most prized in himself. Not merely did he fail to grasp even the possibility of truth in Guido's feelings, but the nature of the infatuation itself, abject and clinging, made him cold with disgust. Yet he knew, young as he was, that what he determined to bring about could only happen if he stood his ground. Stiff with embarrassed revulsion, he made no move to touch Guido, sobbing and babbling against him in the pool of shadow. Finally, when it became too much even for his artificial resolve, he drew back, saying:–

'Do you know that Cristina is jealous of me? There's nothing singular in that, though of course she would never admit it. I see it whenever we three are together. She adores you, Guido. I made her do so.'

'How! You . . .'

'Yes, I wrought her to it, it was a way for me to fall out of love with her. That day at San Domenico, when the Hungarians were arriving, that was when I knew. At least I was almost sure of it. Then, when you told me about her crying, I understood. I wanted it to happen, to save her. She must be saved, like Iphigenia, from a sacrifice to your terrible customs. I prayed that she should at least love you before she married you. And now it's so.'

'But why? Why should she love me?'

'Enough that she has even begun,' said Edward, with angry conviction in his voice. 'She had no feeling for anything when she first came here, a rich, proud, cold, scornful girl, accepting a destiny. Oh, I've no doubt she knew about passion in others. Half Milan would have offered itself to her for the sake of those unmortgaged properties at Lodi. Maybe for her beauty as well. For she is beautiful, admit that, Guido.'

Guido nodded in weak assent.

'She quite turned my head,' Edward went on, 'but not for her own sake. I realized that at last. Yet falling out of love does not end friendship. Something fixed between us drove her towards emotion. She felt sorry for you because she understood you to be in the same plight. I believe it was the first time she was ever truly compassionate towards anyone.'

'Her pity is useless to me!' cried Guido vigorously.

Good, thought Edward. 'Yet you ask for mine, and you expect it, what's more. How dare you reject hers? Nobody's pity, if

149

honestly given, is ever useless. She offers it freely, she sees that you don't want this marriage, and she has grown to love you precisely for that. She knows you aren't any young trifler of the nobility, scattering your nonsense before her in the hopes of securing a fortune. In short, Guido, she knows what I know.'

'And what do you know?'

'You are different, aren't you? Singular, if that's the word. When she marries you, there's one thing she'll find hardest of all to bear.' Edward paused, suddenly grasping the truth of the realization forming even as he spoke. 'And it is not your pre-occupation with me, or even that, considered as she is, she may not interest you. No, neither of those things. It is your solitari-ness, the fact that you are always alone when she most longs to love you, that's what will frighten her most.'

'I cannot change that. It has always been so.'

'Yes, and by the same token you have flung the poor creature into such a welter of affection as she has never before thought to experience. Easier if you were old or poor, or lived in that shabby, reach-me-down way bachelors have. I've seen it when we lived in Paris and my tutor, Monsieur Drocourt, used to take me to call on his friends, doctors, lawyers, journalists and suchlike. Stale breadcrumbs on the table and old cigar-ends and greasy, half-finished coffee cups on cracked saucers, which the servants are too shiftless to take away. But you don't live like this, your men all wash their faces and pomade their hair and have clean liveries, there's not a speck of dust in the house, every room smells like a rose-garden, the chairs and sofas are comfort-able – for a wonder in Italy – and wherever we may look there is something to admire.'

In the lamplight he saw that Guido's features had assumed an unaccountable hardness, a fixed expression of agonized outrage which challenged his own headstrong pursuit of advantage. Ruthless still, Edward exclaimed:–

'Oh, after all, why can't you love her? She is the only person living who understands you as you ask to be understood, who speaks your language of subterfuge and vanity and self-love . . .'

'You would say that of me?'

'Of you both. You say you love me, but it's not me you love, simply what you wish me to be, for you, at this moment. Neither you nor Cristina cares a rap for what I am. If I left tomorrow, your lives would both close over me without the tiniest scarring of memory, and you'd comfort yourselves as all really selfish people do, by loudly proclaiming your own unfitness for me and wrapping yourselves in the safety of your acknowledged weakness, declaring that I was stronger than you are. So that, of course, would make it easier not to care.'

Guido stared at him in amazement, his massive eyes glistening like oysters.

'Edward, how can you know all this?'

'I don't know. It's just something I understand. But it is true, isn't it?'

'After a fashion, yes,' answered Guido, 'I'm not honestly interested in anyone else, though I never dared confess it before. Some sort of change is taking place within me which demands all my self-absorption to stop it destroying me. It can do no harm to tell you that. I have the fame of being gentle and hospitable to everyone, yet I wonder whether I give a straw for those to whom I show such condescension and friendship. Your going, Edward, will hurt me harder than you can guess, but in the end it is as you say – I love you, yet I care nothing for you.'

Of course, Edward realized too late, Guido would strike back. It was the natural salve to barred affection, and he must be made to feel that, since in himself he was of no account, his rejection of love was, at the last, a mere tiresome interference in a long string of emotional calculations. To Guido, he now saw, he mattered only as part of a system, significant in proportion to the other man's view of himself as a solitary element of truth in a world where others had no genuine substance. Edward contemplated his incomparably neat head and body reflected as the single contained or definite shape in the wells of darkness within the looking-glasses surrounding him on the edges of the room. The rain had slackened now, and gleams of light, penetrating the shadow, began throwing familiar objects into relief. The yellow vases, the ebony chairs, the clock with the figures of Diana and the sleeping Endymion, the piano with a song opened on the music desk, these, the whole house indeed, were what Guido's sacred loneliness had devised. And, precisely because of this flamboyant, intransigent loneliness, Edward became possessed of a longing to defy the sovereignty of such a spirit. Yet the longing, he knew, was a capitulation, for Guido's was that

151

deliberate solitude which, louder than everything else, calls on you to take notice. 'Notice me!' said the song on the music desk, 'notice me!' said the flowers of the Turkey rug, 'notice me!' said the elegantly arranged heaps of books and papers upon the table.

'And Cristina?' he said at length.

'Cristina . . .' Guido smiled. 'Do you want me to marry her? I'll do so if you like. We shall not be happy – but it'll satisfy people's sense of arrangement.'

'Well, it is not what I like, is it? I don't know why she loves you, in the end. Maybe she knows you will never be unkind to her, as my uncle Castelvetro is to my aunt, and that you'll always treat her with respect.'

Pausing on the brink of speech, as though the idea, after all, was not as repulsive as it had seemed, Guido said:–

'You truly believe she loves me?'

'I think she had rather die than tell you so. Girls are like that. It's nonsense to say they cannot keep secrets. Men do not know where to begin with reticence.' Then, emboldened by what he imagined was some positively directed impulse towards acceptance, Edward added: 'You admire her, you've told me so a hundred times. So . . .'

'So?' Guido once more turned his bitter stare to Edward. 'Cristina has taste and elegance in all she does. Perhaps I envy that. She has the grace to hide her sophistication lest it embarrasses us too much. Yes, she is beautiful, enough to make the young men here afraid, but that does not mean that I can persuade myself to fall in love with her.'

He got up, with the air of one who announces by such an action that the interview is at an end. The folds of his solitude were once more drawn about him. 'I shall marry her to unite our estates. I shall marry her because contracts and customs ordain it. I shall marry her to . . . to disembarrass you of my feelings.'

Stung as he was meant to be, Edward cried:–

'Guido, that is unjust!'

'You complain of injustice! What justice have you done to me? Don't you see that you alone could have freed me from this obligation? A word from you and I should have abolished everything between the Bentivoglio and me. Oh, don't fret yourself, I'll marry Cristina, and we shall be as unhappy as may be. I'll father an heir, if you like. I wanted you to give me

152

courage, Edward, not to treat me as part of some glib solution tied up in a bundle of settlements.'

'But you must have known that I'd reject your craziness,' Edward flung back, beside himself with exasperation at Guido's sudden turning. 'And your plan was as glib as mine. How could I have saved you?'

Guido fastened on him a complete, withering coldness.

'Please go,' he said. And Edward, seeing there was nothing left to say, went out to his horse, mounted and rode back by the way he had come. Only when he was beyond Soliera again, with San Gaudenzio once more in view, did he acknowledge his failure to undertake the all-important errand of persuasion with which Basevi had commissioned him.

17

As soon as he got home, he called for a basin of water, went up to his room, washed himself very carefully all over and changed his clothes. It was the one positive thing he had to do. He felt he never wanted to leave the house again, and went downstairs and sat in his uncle's bookroom idling his way through the *Gerusalemme liberata* until it should be dinner time. He read over and over, with a poignant sense of its appositeness, the seventh canto's sublime opening, in which Erminia's headlong flight through the forest was like his own that afternoon across the country, and found himself yearning for the same sort of moral repose vouchsafed to her in the meeting with the shepherds. Yet, as if to remind him that he could not find it here, nearby lay the volume of Tacitus open upon the table with the red-marked passage from the *Agricola*, and once more his alert ear caught the noises of movement within the house. How would he now face Basevi, when even at this moment his uncle was being lured more closely into the meshes of some grotesque intrigue?

He heard the footsteps, as he had heard them before, upon the little stairs leading down to the garden. This time curiosity mastered discretion, and he crept out into the hall. At first it seemed as if there had been nobody there after all, but in an instant, hearing voices above, he shrank back under the nook of the stairway. It struck him all of a sudden that it could do no harm were he to show himself, as though by accident having strayed from the bookroom and happened upon them passing. He slipped back, therefore, towards the door and, shutting it loudly, moved with a resolute tread along the hall, where they awaited him, six of them, transparently masked with apprehension. Beside the Count and Massimo Rangoni, he saw the young Marchese Sighinolfi and his brother, whom they called Carluccio, the slouching Count Bonacini, whom he knew for a crony of Massimo's, and a Taccoli cousin of theirs whom rumour had long given out as disaffected because the Duke had dismissed him a year or so before from his post as gentleman-in-waiting, with no reason given.

Edward felt his stomach rise into his mouth with fear. He should have gone back into the study and kept still. Conspiracies of noblemen were things to be read about in romances and brought upon the stage: he remembered a play of Schiller's about a Genoese plot, and the scene of the blessing of the daggers in Meyerbeer's opera: here was the thing itself before him, not enacted for any notional quality of the picturesque, not to be dismissed as fanciful or preposterous, but immediate, palpable, vivid beyond any mistaking. There was no reason, nor had there ever been, to doubt the truth of what Basevi disclosed.

'Ah, Edward,' said his uncle, with the merest hint of reproach, 'I thought you had gone out riding.'

'The weather made me turn back, uncle, so I've been reading all afternoon.'

He wondered afterwards why he had told a lie. Something in the prevailing atmosphere, inevitably nurtured upon falsehood, seemed to summon it into being. He realized, too, that the Count must have known this at once. Yet when Massimo said, 'We have been meeting to arrange a shoot for next Thursday at Baggiovara,' Edward almost cried out, 'Don't insult me by your nonsense!'

'Massimo is going back to Scarabello, Edward,' the Count said. 'Perhaps you would like to go too. I can send one of the carriages to fetch you in time for dinner.'

He thought he had better do as his uncle suggested. Perhaps they would cut his throat if not. Massimo scowled, but offered no pretext for refusing. To go to Scarabello was the last thing Edward wished to do, the more because he knew that Mariclò

155

would not be there, having gone visiting that day with Aldegonda, but, after a leave-taking among the six men perfunctory
enough to suggest to his active imagination that they must
already have determined their next rendezvous before coming
downstairs, Massimo and he clambered into the smelly old
barouche of the disgruntled Taccoli, who, it seemed, would set
them down at the end of the Scarabello sweep before bundling
off home.

Better to have stayed reading Tasso, thought Edward, than to
be lurching along the road with a brace of idle scamps for whom
his presence acted as a gag upon any but the most trivial
conversation. Was it, in fact, for this that the provident Count
had despatched him, as a guarantor of necessary silence? None of
them, indeed, said anything as the carriage pulled out onto the
highway, still gleaming with puddles of rain, though now and
then Taccoli, looking fiercely at Massimo, made a sucking noise
which bespoke his crossness. At length he deigned to address
Edward.

'In your country,' he slowly said, 'is it true that women write
articles for the newspapers?'

'I believe it may be possible,' answered Edward. 'They write
books. I haven't been in England since I was a little boy, so I
cannot say.'

'In Italy women do not write books,' said Taccoli. 'It is not
considered proper. In my view they should not be taught to read.'

Edward inclined his head. 'Or to write?'

'Especially not to write,' said the other solemnly. 'In my view a
lot of harm is done by people being able to read who should not.'

'No doubt of it,' rejoined Edward, barely able to contain his
amusement. 'Do you read much yourself?'

Taccoli, who was not altogether unintelligent, looked at
Edward as if he would kill him. Massimo too appeared rather
embarrassed.

'In my circle we have no time for reading. We prefer actions to
words. Your uncle is different. He, I think, reads too much, and
that's bad for him.'

'Have you told him so?'

'Yes, but I don't think he understood what I meant.'

That was that, until the carriage stopped with a jerk beside the
sweep-gates of Scarabello, and Edward and Massimo got down.

156

He had nothing to say to Massimo, but then he seldom did. His feelings towards this brother of the girl he loved best in all the world invariably ended in a species of humiliating envy of him for his unceasing elegance. Endowed with that infuriating Italian grace and symmetry of figure, he could do nothing coarsely or clumsily, yet such gifts went wholly unaccompanied by any preternatural excellencies of heart or mind. Thus jealousy was always mitigated by the sense that here was only a beautiful morsel of earth. For a while they passed on together in silence. Then Massimo said:–

'You went over to see Guido Tagliabosco, I gather.'

'Yes.'

'How do you find him these days?'

'Much the same as he always is. How do you find him?'

'Scrupulous. It's a fault in his family. He carries it to excess. He is so refined one can never persuade him to anything. At least I never can. I suppose you might, though.'

Lord, thought Edward. 'I don't fancy I can have any influence there.'

Massimo snorted. 'It seems to me you have a great deal of influence with us all. My mother and sisters respect you far more than they do me. It's not right, but they do. You should be pleased.'

'I ought to,' said Edward, 'but I'm not. If you must know, I find it tiresome the way you all use me as an oracle. I'm only nineteen years old and I don't know anything useful.'

'Are you sure?' said Massimo, as though detecting a lie. 'At any rate you might tell my cousin Cristina that it is high time she engaged herself.'

'I shall do nothing of the kind,' said Edward resolutely. 'In fact I shall write to my mother next week and tell her I'm returning. And you can look after your own affairs.'

Beside himself, chiefly because he knew that Massimo was the one among them who would least understand his feelings, he could say nothing more. They got at length to the house, and he had half made up his mind to walk home straight away when Cristina herself appeared in the hall, and Massimo, with the unceremonious abruptness reserved for his family, left them alone together.

Numbed with the burden of factitious responsibility, Edward

157

gave her his arm. Her acuteness of perception caught at once what lay behind the gesture and she smiled compassionately.

'You are not pleased to see me, are you?'

'I'm always pleased to see you because you are Cristina Bentivoglio, and because of the way in which our friendship was made. But just now I can think of no one to whom I have less to say.'

He would never have dared to utter this to another woman; she alone could gauge his meaning. When she laughed and slipped her arm more comfortably through his, he felt the conviction suddenly sweep over him that she must not be lost, that those generous impulses set free in her must not be wasted, that even if Guido only admired her, that at least would be something. She was to be made happy.

'The garden's too muddy,' he said. 'Shall we be alone here? Are your aunts about?'

'They are all resting. Grandmother had a headache and took valerian, and the others read her to sleep. So we are quite alone unless Massimo chooses to disturb us.'

'Sit down then,' he said, and she did as he asked, on one of the stone benches that flanked the doorway. Edward stood still for a moment, rallying himself, before turning towards her and saying: 'Cristina, are you . . . that is, do you think that you might be in love with Guido? If it pains you, you need not answer. And whatever you tell me I promise to keep secret.'

There was something in the complete, trusting frankness of her gaze that he flinched from as she looked up at him. Suddenly averting her eyes, she stared beyond him, as if the effort of trust on her side also had been too great.

'Secrecy,' said she, 'is no longer important. At least not to me. I love him. I have loved him from the first. I know he can't love me in return, he is not framed by nature to do so, but that only makes me love him the more. Perhaps you don't grasp that. With me it is a dedication – the earliest I've ever known, and, it may be, the only one I am likely to know. Tell me, do you despise Villafranca?'

'People often ask that. No, as it happens, I do not. I used to, but it has grown over me like leaves.'

'Well, I try not to despise it, but I do.'

'I suppose that's because it is more provincial than Milan.'

158

'I despise the Milanese as much. There is no more dedication there than here. We do things in Milan only to prove to ourselves that we are not all dead. Once or twice sincerity appears among us and is fashionable for a season, then we kill it by neglect, or the Austrians shut it up in prison or silence it or banish it. I wasn't old enough to know that it was precisely that sincerity I admired until I came here – and found it in you.'

'Me?'

'In you, Edward. You are sincere. I don't think I like what you have done among us, but you meant well at any rate.'

She had succeeded, as somehow she always managed to, in making him feel unworthy of her commendation.

'And thus I found it within myself, in my . . . love for Guido.'

'But if it's hopeless, Cristina, how can you feed upon it?'

'You mean that I should turn to somebody else! Who is there to set beside him, with half his singularity and gentleness and discrimination? He is far removed from everyone here, there's nobody to appreciate him except you, and you are the only person he truly cares for.'

Even that was not certain now, thought Edward, wrily recalling his earlier interview, but he let it pass, moved beyond amazement by the unstinted fervour of Cristina's declarations.

'I'm jealous of you,' she said, 'as if you were my rival. You may have been acting for the best with us both, but there have been times when I wished . . . That day at San Domenico, for example, when you ran away. Why? It was cruel, to turn my own passions upon me without any defence.'

'I'm sorry, Cristina, God knows, I only thought . . .'

'Yes, yes, you imagined you'd have a sport with us, isn't that it? – like some vulgar matchmaker in a play.'

'No!'

'Yes, it is! What could I do? A woman cannot tell a man she loves him with the same absoluteness that a man uses to a woman. At least I cannot. There and then to say "I love you, your image is before me sleeping and waking, every choice of a pair of gloves or a book or a piece of music to play my grand-mother to sleep in the drawing room after supper, everything is done for you". And he, what was there for him, Edward, without your protection?'

'I can't always be deuced well protecting Guido!' cried Edward

159

savagely, conscious of having said something of the same kind already during the day. 'I cannot perpetually be coming between you both like a plenipotentiary between nations. Do you think I can save you from yourselves? I saw him today, and it was useless. Or rather I was. You're right, I've done nothing good in Villafranca. I should never have come here. Idleness in the end is evil.'

She had risen to her feet and was clasping his sleeve, desperate for answers he was powerless to give. 'You saw him? What did he say? Ah, did he . . . ?'

The prospect of what he had achieved filled Edward with less surprise than sadness. He had, after all, met it already, but mere pride had forbidden him to acknowledge it.

'So you love him, and it's my confounded fault, every mortal bit of it. My game with you both, as if I'd any right to that. I'm only a boy.'

'And that is the last time you will ever dare to make such an excuse, Edward, to me or anybody else.' She had drawn herself upright, directing upon him the force of a merited reproof. 'You were never a child: I judged you falsely from the beginning. If you had been, you would not have dared to do this.'

For a while he could say nothing, and stared at the worn brick on which his feet were planted as though tracing his confusion in its lines. Then, without lifting his head, he muttered:—

'You could not have done without me, I think. You both made use of me, as travellers make use of a courier to get rooms for them at inns and posthorses for their carriages and seats at the theatre and interpret things in languages they are too idle or grand or frightened to learn. You engaged me, each one of you, that was your part in all this, not mine. When we first met on the road – do you remember? – you were enchanted, goodness knows why, because I told you the tale of the bucket in the belfry of the Ghirlandina, that Tassoni wrote the poem about. And that's the way we have been with each other, Cristina, ever since, you and Guido the travellers, I the courier, the interpreter. I played with you, yes, and I was wrong, but which of us three is the least innocent? That's why I claim the right to say that I'm still only a boy. Whom experience hasn't – no, by Heaven – yet hardened.'

He paused, awaiting her rejoinder. Then, since there was

none, he dared to look up, and saw that she was shaking with tears. Something in her tallness and in her, for him always, inextinguishable beauty made her the more entirely desolate, and he reached out and took her to him and held her trembling in his arms. And it was thus that Mariclò and Aldegonda found them as they came into the house.

18

ALDEGONDA HAD BEHAVED magnificently. Edward could take it for granted that Mariclò would know what to do, could assume that she would see nothing amiss in Cristina leaning against him sobbing, but Aldegonda, he must own, surprised him. Of all the Rangoni she was the most orthodox, the least unsatisfied. She would wed her young sprig of a Count Grillenzoni Falloppia in due time, when Massimo could furnish a dowry, and content herself with teaching her children the paths of noble righteousness, with the preservation of those honours due to her rank, and everything the rest of them either partook of instinctively or else cared nothing for. Yet, though Edward knew she found Cristina ever more incomprehensible, some untarnished impulse of cousinhood made her run towards the weeping girl and carry her away to cold compresses, extra pillows and aromatic vinegar. To complete his astonishment, she had, what is more, refused absolutely to say anything to her mother or to Massimo.

There was indeed no more to be said, by Edward especially. He knew he had failed, and felt now that comfort which failure always brings, in the sense that he was not obliged to do anything further. Vain, in the end, even to hope that justice might be done to Cristina's suddenly disclosed passion, however much he might believe that his first capricious meddling was instrumental in revealing it to her. He would go away leaving nothing accomplished, and the inexorable tide of custom, embracing a loveless marriage and quantities of lands and titles, would close over his memory as something too unaccountably foreign to be worth holding on to.

He didn't mind that. The sop to pride, which in circumstances of this kind we administer by saying that it is the others, rather than we ourselves, who will most feel the loss, is only a temporary palliative. The truth was that he would miss them far more, and this was to be his punishment. Such time as was left to him, then, he would use in their service, if only they would love him afterwards.

In the synagogue, with his hat on, hearing them singing the psalm on Basevi's wedding day about the fruitful vine and the young olive branches, he shivered a little at the sudden thought that he had got himself into yet another scrape. They had planned the expedition, he and Mariclò, with immense care, invoking the aid of Cristina, glad to find some distraction from brooding over Guido, and of Aldegonda, who, though on principle she profoundly disapproved of a Rangoni attending a Jewish wedding service and thought it distinctly English and peculiar of Edward even to want to go himself, would at the last, as Mariclò somewhat ruthlessly assured him, do anything for a sister.

Discretion, finally, had fought with nature, and curiosity had overcome them both, so far as to make Aldegonda declare that she could not possibly allow Mariclò to go without a chaperone. And if Aldegonda came, then Cristina, in whose yellow britzka they were all to make the journey to Carpi, could not be left out. Edward was a little cross at having to presume so far on Basevi's good feeling towards him, but the request was taken as an honour rather than otherwise, and the secret grew less perilous for being shared by four people instead of two.

Their subterfuges were still elaborate. The adventure was something which, if ever discovered, could imperil the reputations of the three girls among their own people and brand Edward as a corrupting influence upon them all. If word of it ever reached Villafranca, they could only hope that such an escapade would be seen as a mere frolic, and that their position and character might somehow still protect them. Nothing, accordingly, was said to the household servants, and Cristina's coachman was placated with double wages. The Marchesa Rangoni and her mother were told that the four were going to spend an afternoon at the convent at Bastiglia: while Edward looked at the church, the girls would buy some of the pretty embroidered pillowcases for which the nuns were famous. They were to be home, it was promised, by dinner time, and Edward, to increase the air of preciseness in the engagement, carefully declined the Marchesa's invitation to an evening at cards, saying that he could not leave his aunt by herself for the whole day. As he knew she would, the Marchesa baulked at inviting the Countess to supper, but smiled benignly at her mother-in-law with that look which meant that she thoroughly approved of such a charming piety in a young man.

He trembled at the recollection, cravenly hoping he would be the other side of the Apennines and posting to Radicofani before the two ladies discovered him for a viper. There had been a little heart-stopping embarrassment when, seeing Cristina so gaily dressed and Mariclò wearing her cousin's present of an Indian shawl she had hitherto vowed to keep hidden until they returned to town, and Aldegonda in a bonnet rendered unrecognizable by swatches of lilac riband, the old Marchesa muttered something about fine feathers making fine birds and the immodesty of their appearing thus before nuns, but her daughter-in-law, satisfied, as always, that her family were making a show, waved it aside, saying that they were young and that if such things weren't to be worn in summer, then when, goodness gracious?

Once at Carpi, after a journey in which Edward had twice to stop the carriage so as to reassure Aldegonda that they were not being followed, they were set down at the entrance to the ghetto, while the coachman was bidden to drive on to Bastiglia with a present for the sisters and a letter to the reverend mother from the Marchesa, and to be at the cathedral steps by half past six.

The synagogue was an elegant, sober, well-lighted room up two pairs of stairs, with a handsome cupboard for the scrolls and a frieze with sacred texts in grisaille, but the atmosphere was as unlike that of a church as Edward could possibly have imagined. There was a good deal of gossip and chaffering among the men in their caps and shawls before the service began, and something volatile and raffish in the air of the place and the people that delighted him. Basevi's brother, fubsy, balding Abramo the musician, had taken his arm and found him a seat, and now acted as explicator, as though he were explaining the plot of a play.

'Now the two rabbis will read the marriage contract, and then

Daniele will take the oath and sign it. And then, you'll see, he'll stand under the canopy till the bride comes in. He has had a new coat and trousers made, and the waistcoat and gloves I brought him from Venice. Smart, no?'

There was no denying it. Basevi seemed deliberately to have put aside the cultivated anonymity which cloaked him as Count Castelvetro's steward and assumed, as a birthright, the true sophistication Edward always suspected him of concealing. For today at least he could be what he was, among his own folk. Tomorrow, with his characteristic niceness of perceived irony, he might shade into a domestic nothing again.

The bride entered, and they sang the Hebrew words which mean 'Blessed is the one that cometh in the name of the Lord'. Despite Abramo's friendly nudgings and whispers, Edward was scarcely following the service itself. The not unpleasant smell of best clothes and lavender water and scented hair-oil and pomade, the glitter of rings and jewelled studs and watch-seals, the sheen of the damask canopy, that strange sound, a sort of rich braying, made by the cantors, the faces so intensely knowing yet subdued with mournful amusement, all this made him feel his alienness. In themselves these Jews, in the upstairs room of a drab-fronted house in the ghetto of Carpi, were no more or less interesting to him than other people, their virtues no more remarkable, their manners no more attractive. His community with them lay in the one significant fact that he was a foreigner.

Certainly Basevi could not have chosen, for his Christian witness demanded by legal custom of the duchy, a more obvious Gentile than Edward. He was reminded of it when signing his name upon the register under the superscription 'Rivers, Mr Edward, presently domiciled at Villafranca, subject of Her Majesty the Queen of England'. It seemed to him as if the occasion were the culminating act of some process inexplicable to others, which might justify all the waiting and observing of which his life had hitherto consisted. He felt as though, having served an apprenticeship, he had just been presented with his freedom, the freedom simply to be what he was. It was perhaps only that he had sloughed off the last traces of shame or embarrassment at being, in perpetuity, the interloper, the visitor, the outsider. On these terms alone was his right to belong in Villafranca, the statutory foreigner, guaranteed. Without looking about him, he walked purposefully downstairs to meet the girls.

In the tailor's house there was such noise and feasting that the walls seemed ready to crack, and old Limentani's pontificating, which had silenced the table when Edward had visited the first time, was drowned with healths to the bride, the clatter of guests helping each other to this or that across the table, odd improvisatory bursts of music from the band, who seemed wanting them all to dance before they had sat down to the first course, and much ribbing and chaffing of the groom, in a taste more sincere than genteel. The stupid cousin from Leghorn was there with her husband, gloomily filling his glass as she emptied words into the air and shouted from time to time at Basevi's father, who grinned and nodded at Edward in a way which suggested that they knew she was a fool but there was no help for it. A woman in spectacles whom everyone called Lea kept attempting to rise from the table and leave and was made to sit down again, while Signora Limentani plied those on either side with the *maccheroni* and the rice and the boiled beef and the green dumplings, and the older girls and boys tripped up and down with the *vino pregiato*, a present from the pawnbroker Sacerdoti, so good, Abramo declared, that it must have been someone's unredeemed pledge.

He had busied himself with looking after the Rangoni and Cristina, all placed together with Edward at one end of the table to become the cynosure of the guests when they were not trying to catch the attention of Anna and Basevi. As there were other Gentiles at the feast, it looked as if the distinction, though kindly meant, had been made in deference to their rank, and, under cover of a great burst of applause and thumping of the board in deference to someone's joke, Mariclò, leaning close to Edward, murmured:–

'I wish they hadn't done this. It looks as if we wanted it, as though we thought ourselves an honour to them. It makes us look vulgar.'

Cristina, overhearing her, said:–

'They are going to dance afterwards. And we can't all dance with you, Edward. It does seem a pity if none of them will stand up with us because they're afraid.' Then, without a trace of haughtiness, she turned to Abramo, who was helping himself to figs and walnuts, and asked, so that Aldegonda could not hear:–

166

'Signor Abramo, will you be kind to my poor cousin over there and ask her to dance, when they're ready? Your brother tells me you're a capital dancer.'

Edward spluttered into his napkin. Abramo, blushing hotly, scratched at his neckcloth, which had suddenly grown too tight. Pressing upon him like a victorious commander, Cristina said:–

'Come now, do tell me you will. If you're shy, I'll ask her on your behalf.'

'I'm sure . . . I don't think the lady would want to dance with me,' mumbled Abramo, half sheepish yet half eager to seize the occasion. Aldegonda was no beauty, but her *tenue*, combined with the artful way in which she had dressed her hair and with her animated absorption in the liveliness of the scene, made her infinitely winning. Thus, when the triumphant Cristina conveyed her manufactured request for Abramo's sake, it was granted with a smile of condescension which might, Edward feared, have a little to do with the excellence of the wine. Abramo could not credit his luck. Cristina looked so decidedly roguish that Mariclò guffawed, but they could say nothing more, for it was time for grace to be said and the Seven Blessings to be recited.

Only when they all trooped into the adjacent rooms and the sweet wine and biscuits were handed round was he able to say anything to Basevi and Anna, till this moment, garlanded as they were with benediction, prayer and innuendo, more like lay-figures than people, tolerating everything with the sort of barely perceptible amusement which longs for solitude to indulge itself. Slowly they made the tour of the guests, somebody's uncle, somebody's weeping mother, Lea who really must go, the stupid cousin from Leghorn whose husband was singing gently to his bottle, Gioacchino who was only twelve years old, the rabbi who looked like an innkeeper and the innkeeper who looked like a rabbi, and Abramo glowing with embarrassed eagerness to dance. On any other occasion Basevi would have bowed to the girls in token of his position, but now he clasped them all cheerfully by the hand.

Anna, in any case, could never have curtseyed. Although that fierceness was laid aside which Edward had admired on the afternoon she had spoken up to her father in this same house, her slightly grim beauty, recalling the gallant women of Suli or the wife of Hasdrubal, endured beneath the artificial blandness of bridal attire. He saw her look at Cristina and Cristina look at her and caught the hint of a challenge immediately tempered by admiration. The moment held, very briefly, a kind of greatness. His parents would have abhorred its levelling implications, yet he realized it fulfilled something he had waited his entire life to behold.

'You're a fortunate fellow,' he said to Basevi, as Mariclò and Aldegonda began quizzing Anna as to lace and ribbons.

'I wish you may be as lucky,' rejoined Basevi, guiding him gently towards the embrasure of the window, 'it is what you deserve.'

He leant out and peered into the street, then, turning Edward slightly as if to point out the prospect, said:–

'They came to see your uncle again last night, Massimo, Sighinolfi and the rest. He told me about it. They accused him of being a friend to the Austrians, of being afraid he should lose his post at court, they even accused your aunt of influencing him . . .'

'That's not true, she knows nothing of it. If she suspects, it is something else entirely.'

'Anyway, they as good as threatened to denounce him. They could do it, how not? He has given them money, he has forged passes for their friends to Lombardy and Romagna, he even hid a cousin of Taccoli's for a month or two when there was a proclamation out for him. He has done enough to hang himself.'

'I suppose Guido . . .' Edward began, then stopped abruptly, remembering how he had failed in his errand of enlistment. Basevi, smiling sagely, shook his head.

'His intelligence frightens them, but they scorn his effeminacy. And he has refused to speak to your uncle. He says the matter is one of conscience. Perhaps when he knows more he will be less scrupulous.'

Basevi's countenance, where ordinarily merriment lurked somewhere within, had never seemed so dismal. For several moments he could not speak. From behind them came the suddenly oppressive noise of other people enjoying themselves.

'Our desires and intentions don't matter,' he finally said, almost in a whisper, 'it is what we do with them that counts. All very well to be quoting Tacitus, "*praecipua sub Domitiano*" and suchlike, to be vowing and swearing and scheming, but this . . . this vanity will destroy us in time.'

'What are they trying to do?'

'They are all wanting to dance,' came Anna's voice from over his shoulder, 'and you're looking as grave as a pair of judges.'

Basevi laughed. 'It won't do, will it, on my wedding day,' and muttered something which made her smile. She knew, Edward realized, what the matter was: once more there arose that immediacy of understanding between the pair which he remembered envying when he saw them first. Instinctively he drew close to Mariclò for reassurance. She hardly looked at him, but casually let fall her handkerchief and, as he returned it to her, contrived to press his fingers with her own. Laughing at the absurd subterfuge, they looked at each other, sighing and shrugging and laughing again. Then they heard Signora Limentani exclaim:–

'This is a fine wedding! We have dancers and no music. One of the fiddlers is drunk, the other has cut his finger and that idle ruffian who plays the clarinet has slipped off goodness knows where.'

'So my daughter has no dancing at her wedding!' exclaimed Limentani, almost joyful in anticipation of a storm.

There was universal clamour and a thousand suggestions were proffered at once. Somebody would run back and fetch their flute, somebody else would go and knock up the town trumpeter, everyone let out a groan when Abramo announced that his violin was locked inside the theatre seven miles off at Villafranca, where they had been rehearsing the *Foscari* for the opening of the season three weeks hence, and the cry went up for the piano at least to be opened.

'And who is to play it?' enquired Limentani with a resolute cynicism.

'Daniele is the bridgegroom and all the young people would be dancing if they could,' said his wife.

The stupid cousin knew a minuet if she could remember the tune, and Basevi's shrewd papa looked as if he were preparing to tempt her towards the instrument so that he could watch her make an idiot of herself, but Limentani, who wanted merely to be left alone to talk about the King of Sardinia and what Austria

169

would do if the Pope declared for a customs union, testily called out:–

'Come, an end to this, no music, no dancing.'

'So you'd disgrace your own daughter?' exclaimed his wife, histrionically flinging up her arms. 'Whoever heard of a wedding without dancing? We shall be the talk of Carpi.'

The tailor glared at her as if to say that they had already made sure of that. An unseasonable embarrassment was starting to creep across the company when all of a sudden Cristina stepped forward and, with that cool absoluteness which had characterized her earlier, announced:–

'Since there is nobody else, I shall play for you.'

Murmurs of delighted relief mingled with general surprise. Aldegonda could not contain herself from saying: 'Cristina, I really . . . I think . . .' but one glance from her cousin quelled opposition. Cristina, facing them all, might have told them to jump out of the window and they would have obeyed. With disarming sweetness, however, she moved towards the instrument.

'I'm not very good. And it is only waltzes, polkas and mazurkas, no quadrilles, I'm afraid. But they are this season's in Milan. I learn them as exercises, you know.'

Signora Limentani was speechless. The stupid cousin whispered 'an angel!' to the ceiling. The tailor merely grunted and sloped off to the cigar smoke in the next room. Edward watched, incredulous, as Cristina, shaking back her lace sleeves, settled the chair to her liking and tried a few chords. He wished Guido had been here to know her in all her consummate absence of the commonplace.

'Now we may touch each other lawfully,' he said to Mariclò, taking her hand to lead her to the floor, and they swung into the polka with the devoted concentration of those who know the stern limits of happiness.

Indefatigably Cristina played on, while the afternoon deepened into evening, the old aunts nodded in sleepy complacency, the smokers in the next room began an endless card game, Lea with the spectacles succeeded in leaving at last, and the couples changed partners in giddy, breathless desperation that it might not all end just now. But it was for Cristina to unmake what she had made, and with a little shout of mock-exhaustion she threw up her hands at the end of a set of waltzes, crying: 'There, I've done, that's all I know, I've forgotten the rest,' and springing from her chair she came into their midst to be kissed and applauded. Watching Anna greeting her as ardently as though she were a cause to be espoused, Edward shook his head in renewed amazement. Mariclò seized her cousin's hand, crying:–

'You are too splendid! None of us could have done that,' and it was true, they could not. Together thus they seemed like the embodiments of his own instinct. What he was told to admire or what he thought he ought to admire was the finished perfection of accomplishment; what in the end he truly cherished was something whose form was altogether less obvious in its definition. Cristina, at her most confidently superb, was to be paused in front of, poses were to be taken up before her, drawings to be made, descriptions to be penned. Mariclò, her untidy black hair clinging to her shiny forehead, a hole in her stocking, and an inch or two of petticoat having somehow managed to edge themselves out beneath the hem of her dress as she danced, would achieve none of this, but those armed with that heroic perversity of discrimination which would rather go its own way would catch a glimpse of something demanding more than mere reverence, which made them look within themselves, which gave for a moment some vague but essential understanding of proportion and order beneath its wildness and irregularity. The moment's tyranny bore down upon him.

'Come, we must see them away and then go home at once,' he said restlessly, as they followed Basevi and Anna downstairs.

'Six o'clock, good gracious, and the carriage will have been waiting,' cried Aldegonda, briefly, as it were, becoming herself again. However democratic and sans-culotte-ish they might have been upstairs, their protestations were useless against the deference of the other guests in falling back to allow them precedence in taking leave. As Edward and Basevi embraced, the latter half-whispered:–

'We are only going for a few days to Parma to visit my mother's family: we'll be back within the week. Watch everything for me at San Gaudenzio, you understand?'

'You may count on me for that.'

'We have counted on you for too much already,' said Anna,

kissing him in an elder-sisterly fashion he scarcely thought he should have tolerated from anyone else.

It was another quarter of an hour before they disengaged themselves from the family and got round the corner of the street to bolt towards the carriage which, somewhat to their surprise, stood by the church steps with Antonio on the box philosophically chewing at a piece of cheese. Eyeing them sceptically, he whipped up the horses almost before Edward had handed the girls inside, and they bounced off at a pace which suggested that there was better things to be doing than dawdling in Carpi on the pleasure of a parcel of girls.

'Well, that was a Jewish wedding,' announced Aldegonda, 'and very pretty and amusing I thought it was. And Abramo, you know, is a capital dancer, and told me no end of interesting things about the Jews, which you couldn't credit. It seems the groom always breaks a glass at the wedding, as we saw him do from the gallery. And I asked him about their eating pork, and he said it was to be a secret, but they eat – well, some of them – *zampone* and *salsiccia* like the rest of us, except on holy days. I should not have thought a Jew could be so much the gentleman.'

She rattled on, exhilarated, while Mariclò and Cristina, agreeably fatigued, were content to listen. As Edward heard her, it began to dawn on him that what the four of them had done was so utterly contrary to anything imaginable among the good families of Villafranca that once known it would never be forgotten. He was about to rally them all to swear complete silence when the carriage turned in at the sweep-gates of Scarabello, the door was opened and there, as they got down, stood Massimo.

No point in even beginning to pretend. His mouth, pouting in fury, looked like a baby's.

'Leave us,' he snapped at the coachman, who drove off to the stables with an air of work well done.

'How dare you do such a thing?' he thundered at his sisters, who, though flinching somewhat as the lash fell on them, still stood their ground. 'To lie to your mother is bad enough, but to go to the wedding of a Jew, and a servant, which is worse, with the riff-raff of Carpi all around you, to sit in the synagogue watching mummery and herding with tailors and fiddlers. Have you no sense of honour?'

'We thought . . .' Aldegonda began.

172

'Oh, you thought, you thought it would be a scrape, a prank, to go jaunting off among the Jews for the afternoon like a pair of kitchenmaids on a feast-day, you thought – you never thought of what we are, of the difficulty your mother, your grandmother and I have in maintaining our position in Villafranca. What will be said of us, did you think of that?'

'Yes,' said Mariclò defiantly, 'or at least I did. We were invited and it would have seemed churlish to refuse.'

'Invited! By Count Castelvetro's house steward!'

'He is a gentleman, Massimo,' said Cristina, with the implication that this was more than her cousin would ever be, 'and I'm pleased to have been able to wish him joy. We danced a little . . .'

'Cristina played waltzes and mazurkas to a miracle,' added Aldegonda enthusiastically.

'You did what? Go in at once, the pair of you! Your mother and grandmother are not yet returned from . . .'

'When they do, you will say nothing,' Cristina interrupted him, 'because there is nothing to be said. You will stop making a vulgar show of yourself this instant. None of us will say anything more about this. I have given a *douceur* to Antonio, and he knows he will lose his place if word gets out among the servants. That, Massimo, is enough.'

Models of outraged dignity, the three girls swept into the house. No sooner were they gone than Massimo, turning to Edward, said:–

'It's your doing, all of it, with your English liberty and Jacobin manners. Your influence is getting quite pernicious. You had better not . . .'

Edward took Massimo by the coat collar and said, very softly but precisely:–

'Cristina is right. There is no more to be said. Otherwise I shall do my duty and tell your mother about Tacitus and Domitian and all those comings and goings at San Gaudenzio. And we don't wish, do we, to alarm your grandmother? So why don't you simply drop the matter at once? It does you no credit.'

Massimo looked as if Edward had hit him in the stomach.

'How did you know?'

'That's my affair. It's enough that I do know. Now you will be a good fellow and walk in with me as if we were friends – which we are, no? – and you will guess no more about the Jew's wedding than if we had been in Madagascar. For that matter, who told you?'

'One of the men from the farm happened to be at Carpi and saw you going into the synagogue.'

Sullenly Massimo walked beside him up the steps into the house. Something, however, got the better of his anger, for as they went into the hall, he said, to Edward's huge enjoyment:–

'Those are nice gloves you have on. Are they French?'

'Yes. Try them, they might fit you. You shall have them as a present, to show I've no hard feelings.'

But oh, thought Edward, you are a dangerous oaf.

19

THE MESSAGE ARRIVED as evening came on. It read: 'The Count has named a rendezvous in the barn at the end of the field below the park at San Gaudenzio. I am to come there at midnight with my guardian, and I have asked that you be present, to which he has agreed. Basevi will accompany you. C.' Edward watched the messenger out of the house before sitting down with the piece of paper still in his hands and staring at it for a while impassively. Its brevity and abruptness unnerved him. Held in a paralysis of reverie he did not hear his aunt come into the room.

Her surprise was as great as his own. In the last light flooding the doorway she looked flustered and old, as if the object of whatever she was in search of had long ago been buried in the pursuit. Distractedly she put a hand up to her neck and turned a weak smile towards Edward. He had folded the paper and was keeping his hand over it.

'Did I tell you that the Marchesa Rangoni is taking me with her to visit the Corradini this evening, and that it may be we shall stay to supper? I call it very civil of her. I thought I'd go into the garden for a little until she arrives and walk on the terrace,' said the Countess, with an air of not having thought any such thing. 'There's a breeze which makes it less oppressive at this time of day. Shall you walk a little yourself?'

Together they went out onto the terrace. The light airs of early evening were up, ruffling the smooth surface of warmth which lay across the garden. He gave an arm to the Countess and the two began slowly to pace the paved walk flanked by bulky pots, each with its lemon tree, which ran the length of the colonnade on the western side of the house. As they moved, it felt as though she were exercising him, so firmly did she grip his arm, yet he was pained to be reminded at the same time of the invalids he had seen in the watering places visited with his parents. Never before had he felt so essential to her existence.

They talked, or rather the Countess spoke and Edward listened to her, in that desperate fashion which is really a means of saying what cannot be articulated. The canvassing of trivialities, the insistent formulation of questions whose answers inevitably go unheeded, the vanity of speech as a means of avoiding the responsibility of silence, become the paradigms of that terrible, soul-oppressing inner language of misery, grief and fear.

He knew this was how it was with his aunt, but what she wanted exactly to express was beyond his reach. There was something in it more intense than that inchoate mass of disappointed expectations she habitually carried about with her. Even if he had had the courage to ask her what it was, he could not then be sure that in doing so he was not opening some concealed wound. So, for a while, they moved up and down, treading out her sadness on the warm flagstones of the terrace until, able to bear it no longer, he burst out:–

'In a short while, aunt, you know I may go over to Scarabello. Is there any message you wish me to take?'

She looked at him almost angrily, as if he had woken her from a dream. 'None, save my usual wishes to the old Marchesa, who I don't expect will come with us. You go there mostly for Cristina's sake, I suppose.'

'Not necessarily,' said Edward in surprise. 'I believe they like me to go there.'

'And you like to go?'

'Yes, aunt.'

She paused, as though this were not the answer she had expected. 'Doubtless Cristina is always pleased to see you. I don't like her, you know. I never did care for her from the beginning. I think her very proud – pretending to know everything because she comes from Milan. And immodest too, good gracious! You will learn, Ned, if you have not done so already, that we have different ideas in England of what makes a lady. But then, among the Rangoni, what may we not expect?'

Edward, however amazed by her outburst, could only suffer her to continue. He was besides absorbed in the novelty of what she had to say, for it seemed to conceal that something which he had tried to unmask earlier.

'It is not that I disapprove of the association,' said the Countess, staring fixedly at a lizard in the act of climbing a flowerpot, as if she were addressing that rather than her nephew. 'Indeed I encouraged it from the beginning. It was I who . . . no, that's not strictly true, it was the old Marchesa who first suggested it. And Signora Lupo.' She paused, glaring even harder at the lizard. 'She, I fancy, has much to answer for. Not that she would. It is her pride which corrupts that girl.' Edward felt the tight grasp of her fingers upon his arm. 'Who sets her cap at everyone. Who . . .'

She froze as footsteps were heard along the path below. It was Matteo to tell her that the Marchesa had arrived and was waiting in her carriage. Edward was struck by the fact that, if the Marchesa were really as civil as his aunt supposed, she would have taken the trouble to come into the garden. One look at her gaunt face peering impatiently from the carriage window confirmed his suspicion. Her ruthlessness was of the sort which finds it tiresome to engage in elaborate deceptions of other people for the sake of sparing their feelings, and she went so far as to make a little gesture of peevishness at the Countess's innocent protestations of gratitude. When she gave Edward a knowing grimace, as if in pity for his kinship with an undoubted fool, he dismissed it with his own frosty contempt. There were times when it seemed as though Mariclò, in her abundance of honesty and warmth, had been created as an atonement for her predatory, calculating mother.

That the Countess was a victim of collusion designed to remove her from a scene in which her curiosity might prove inopportune became increasingly clear as Edward endured the rest of the evening until Basevi should appear. The hours followed one another with a dismal slowness, as he tried first one book, then a second, then a third, and then found himself falling back on the albums of drawings which some Castelvetro of the last century had brought together. Tacitus lay open, as formerly, on the table, and the fates of Massa Baebius, Helvidius and Senecio reproached, as before, the senate's general guilt, but Edward had seen the red-marked passage too often now either to fear or to doubt its implications. The angels and saints, Davids and Judiths, of Domenichino or Saraceni seemed nearer to what he was capable of imagining at this moment than a conspiracy meant, as it seemed, to beguile a dull hour among Italian nobles in the country. He shut his mind to it and was distracted by nothing more than a moth or two batting against the lamp-glass until Basevi's hand was upon his shoulder.

'It is time, then?' Edward looked up.

'Yes.' As he prepared to speak, Basevi put up a hand. 'You are going to ask me why, aren't you? And I don't know. It is as though he had never spoken the same language as the rest of us. Come, let's be off.'

As they crossed the terrace into the garden a shape moved out of the darkness and turned itself into Guido Tagliabosco. He contemplated Edward with the merest touch of nervousness, though it was the boy himself who felt the more culpable.

'Did you pass anybody on the road as you came over from Falconara?' Basevi bluntly enquired.

'Nobody,' Guido answered. 'In any case I can't think we shall be observed. I take it you know what he intends to do.'

'It's something concerning Cristina,' said Edward.

'Yes. She asked me to accompany you. I should feel honoured, I suppose.'

'Do you?'

'It's too hard to say what I feel, though no doubt you would say that was like me.'

'Shall we go then?' said Basevi anxiously, and in silence the three slipped away through the warm summer gloom into the depths of the park.

As they walked down the avenue Edward felt a ferocious exhilaration at the thought of a possible danger. It was thrilling not to know the object of this stealthy progress. Suddenly, as they neared the field gate, he saw Basevi's lank form ahead of them stop abruptly and motion to them to do the same. They watched him move forward and peer into the open country. Guido started on again, but a gesture from Basevi checked him sharply, before the latter opened the gate and walked a little way into the field.

'Do you think . . . ?' whispered Edward, but Guido, anticipating him, answered:–

'Don't be afraid.'

'I'm not.'

'Aren't you? I am. Once Castelvetro has made up his mind to something he cannot be brought to change it. He does what seems good to him. Like a god. I wish I were like that.'

Frogs croaked, and from a little coppice to their left Edward heard an owl call *kee-wik*, *kee-wik*, *kee-wik*. Basevi turned and summoned them onwards.

Ahead, as though it had suddenly wandered into the landscape out of the darkness, a barn, heavy, solid, imposing as a church, rose up on its brick columns.

'There's nobody here.'

'Please don't speak so loud, it frightens me.'

Basevi waved his hand to silence them. They stood like children in a game awaiting their leader's command. Edward wondered whether, if Basevi turned round again and caught him moving, he wouldn't have to go all the way back to the house and start afresh. He watched Basevi disappear under the pillars of the barn, then, re-emerging, beckon them to follow. They went after him up the steps and through a door opening into the loft.

There was nothing there save the long, bare space, its windows stuffed tightly with bundles of old hay and wads of sacking. A lantern, hanging from one of the beams, cast a strange warmth across the room, enabling the three who had entered to see Count Castelvetro awaiting them, together with Signora Lupo and Cristina.

She had the air of someone who has paused in the midst of a journey elsewhere. The black cloak she wore looked like a domino for a ball, an effect which both suited and was ludicrously at variance with an occasion which seemed to have been devised by the Count for the potency of its effects as much as for the solemnity to which they were evidently meant to contribute. After a perfunctory greeting the Count stepped forward and took her by the hand. Among much which was destined to remain unresolved in Edward's shadowy impressions of his uncle, this gesture retained a species of pathetic dignity.

'I could have wished this had all been more simple,' he said, sounding resonantly insincere, 'but these people are the only ones I can trust. You were not alone in wanting Edward here. He is a member of our family.'

The implied distinction in this was mystifying. Cristina looked faintly as if she thought so too, but she was plainly in a state of such nervousness that it was impossible to relate phenomena to their causes within her. She was as far now from frosty Milanese self-assurance as Edward had ever known. All her sophistication had ebbed, she was a young girl, and it was thus that the Count addressed her.

'It may be that what I have done is wrong, or selfish, or merely stupid. I can't tell if it is so. But we felt it right that you should know, and this way was the best.'

Her mouth opened as though to form a question, but she made no sound, only staring at him in her intense desire to be released from his obliquities. Edward had never known his uncle to come to the point: it must kill him if it were ever to happen. Like a benighted traveller the Count rambled on, in a maze of qualifications and half-finished sentences, talking about the law, the Austrians, the Duke's spies, the wretchedness of his own life, what it was he had needed to conceal, why only now it was to be disclosed, his estate, his hopes and disappointments, an incredible document of self-pity in which he sought mysteriously to enwrap Cristina. Little by little Edward began to lose the thread of all the *oppure*, *comunque* and *cioè*, and found himself falling into the habit he thought he had lost ages ago of hearing a mad sequence of English words forming out of the Italian.

'Trumpeter,' he heard the Count say, 'hippopotamus veracity antidote defer armadillo the every Paraguay barouche no tentative ogle baptismal the captain pilgrim island princess potato furnishing under feeble Saturday cucumbers too hospital sulphur bassoon.'

Just when he supposed that the next stage must be to impose rationality on this disorder, he saw his uncle pause to look at him, and realized, from the expression on Basevi's face, that he had yawned without knowing it.

'I have said what I can,' muttered the Count, 'there is someone who will tell you better than I why we brought you here.'

As if she had known all along that this was her moment,

Signora Lupo stepped forward. Her customary vatic omniscience had burgeoned under the moment's irresistible influence into something awesome and subduing, the very justification, as it appeared, of what she claimed to be. Her weariness cast briefly aside, she looked like the priestess of a cult, whose loyal tending of holy and concealed things was now to be rewarded. Silence with her was not, as in others, a simple matter of having nothing to say. The quiet absorption of her countenance drew wisdom into it and she spoke only when she must. The situation invited her to command it.

'We have talked many times, Cristina, of your mother, Rosa Rangoni, who was sentenced to perpetual imprisonment in the Convent of the Mantellate at Novellara by the last Duke of Villafranca for being found to have embroidered a patriotic flag. She was nineteen at the time, the harshness of the sentence was too much for her, and it was this which was thought to have killed her when she died some eight months later. But it was nothing like that.'

She halted oracularly. Edward had already realized what she was going to tell Cristina, had realized too, without any preternatural skill, what the Count had been preparing to disclose, and felt a spurt of intense, protective rage at both of them for insulting the girl with this bizarre ritual of public intimation. He saw Guido's face lengthen in amazement and knew instinctively that it was the same sort of surprise they both shared. That refinement of feeling and judgment he had often found himself despising in Guido seldom seemed more apposite. Cristina stared at her guardian as at a different woman altogether from the one she presumed to know.

'Before the events of that year,' the Signora went on serenely, 'she had been secretly married to a young man of good family. Her parents having intended her for somebody else, she had contracted herself to the man she loved in the hope, wild as it appears, that once it was revealed they would be forced to accept him as a son-in-law. The young man loved her too much to delay. But then, a month or so following their marriage, rebellion broke out in the city and the Duke fled to Ferrara.'

She stopped once more, daring any of them to remonstrate against the story or her telling of it.

'You were born in the convent, at ten o'clock in the forenoon, and your mother died in giving birth to you. It was understood that I, as her friend, and having the means to bring you up as her daughter, should take you away. Her own family had lost all, or nearly all, through taking part against the Duke in the revolt, and her husband's father made him promise not to see you until you had come of age or were preparing to marry.'

Edward caught Basevi's eye, and felt a wild urge to ask him whether he had not known it from the first, but his friend's countenance was clouded with something which might almost have been anger.

'It was not to be thought of,' said the Signora, 'that he should break his word, and he was too miserable to refuse any injunction laid on him with regard to his family's honour. So he resigned you utterly to me, already married, and you were named after your paternal grandmother, Maria Cristina Bentivoglio. He wishes now to make amends, to acknowledge you as his daughter, and to ask your forgiveness.'

The sadness which never altogether quitted Signora Lupo, even at her most animated, gave a sort of echo to her words which robbed them of absolute spontaneity. When at last, after, as it were, nerving herself to utter the words, she said:– 'Count Castelvetro is your father, Cristina,' it was admitting a certain kind of defeat.

Silent all this while, the Count, solemn in the lantern light, stepped forward as though to claim his daughter. But Cristina, with a moaning sound like a revolt against everything's sheer preposterousness, raised a hand to ward him off and tottered to the floor. And in that moment of baffled grace and reconciliation, with the girl lying, a prone bundle of dress, shawl and petticoat, weeping on the bare floor, Edward saw something happen whose truth he alone could perceive, an epiphany which passed beyond the faded histories of error and pride retailed by the Count and Signora Lupo. For, as the latter made towards Cristina to comfort her, Guido motioned her back with brusque authority. Falling to his knees, he looked down at the wretched girl, his habitual expression of childlike self-absorption replaced by a frankly involved curiosity. Some realization seemed to transfix him, prompted, as it might be, by her lying thus in her huddled misery.

Then, with a singular tenderness, envied by those who saw it, he contrived to raise her head slightly, so that his own was suddenly very close to hers, and they heard him murmur something to her. Slowly, painfully almost, she put her arms around his shoulders, he drew her upwards with him, and the two clumsily hung there, contained by whatever it was, in that instant, they mutually perceived. The others watched with the helpless calm which is born of knowing our own powerlessness to direct what we have set in motion. When the Count once more, with desperate foolhardiness, seemed to be trying to engage his daughter's attention, she turned angrily to face him.

'Oh, not you,' she cried, 'you have learnt nothing!' and, followed by Guido, she ran out into the dark.

20

T HE HEAT WAS the only thing which made that last week at San Gaudenzio at all memorable. In other years when Edward had sweated and gulped his way through the tyrannies of an Italian August there had come that benign interstice of a few grey days which by custom ushers in the memorable sweetness of September, whose first weeks in Venice or Florence or Genoa are like the valedictory caresses of a lover. This time there was nothing of that sort. The storm on the day of his fateful embassy to Guido had offered a single niggardly concession. Otherwise the hot weather thrust itself upon them with a renewed fierceness. Edward lurked about among the cool spots of the house, sitting in the darkness with a jug of lemonade and reading by the merest crack of sunlight let in through a chink of the shutter, or else lying naked on his bed under the weight of terrible afternoons when it grew so hot that the world seemed to have stopped moving.

There was no visiting at Scarabello, since the Marchesa had now taken away Mariclò and Aldegonda, dutiful but protesting, to one more of their inexhaustible supply of cousins. It was necessary, in any case, to leave Cristina alone to work out her fortunes. His single hasty interview with Mariclò on the morning of her departure, when he had hurriedly retailed the episode in the barn, made him little the wiser regarding Cristina's state of mind. All Mariclò was able to say was that she had either kept to her room or else gone out with Signora Lupo, who, no doubt considering that she had given away quite enough already, was not disposed to communicate anything further. The pair of them, ward and guardian, were now alone at Scarabello, Massimo having ridden back to town on pressing business.

Its nature was obvious to Basevi, who cursed when Edward told him of it. They sat together with Anna in the steward's house, which, in a few days, had become something of a refuge for Edward and where he had taken to calling almost every night after dinner.

'Damn the young monkey – and when all the others are lying low!'

'I fancy my uncle is not lying low. Lord knows he is restless, but since last week he has not sat still from one day to the next. I meet him from time to time, you know, walking about in the corridors and peering out of the windows.'

'He can't wait to get back to Villafranca, that's all.'

'With respect, I don't think so, if that makes you happier.'

'If that's your respect I shan't be happier,' said Basevi, 'but go on.'

'Well, it is something I thought the other night, when my uncle told Cristina that he was her father. I looked at him and I thought: "You don't care that she is your daughter. Any of the girls hereabouts would have done instead, actresses taking a role. The important thing is the disclosure itself." And I still think that was true.'

'Certainly he is made no happier by it. Perhaps you're right, and he has done it because it seemed acceptable to him. Maybe this business of Massimo, Sighinolfi and the others has set him going.'

'I rather supposed it was the other way round,' murmured Anna, not raising her head from her work. 'If Cristina looks like her poor mother to a marvel, might it not have stirred something in the Count? Thus, to join this conspiracy – if it's even that – is an act of piety.'

Basevi turned to look at his wife, and his face in the lamplight wore an expression of triumph. It was a satisfaction no more selfish than that of having gained the love of such a woman. Still Anna did not look at him, but her smile betrayed what she knew. Basevi filled his glass and slid the bottle across to Edward again.

'We shall know nothing more until we're at Villafranca,' he

said, 'and by then it may be too late. These Austrians at Ferrara have set everybody on edge. Who knows whether Massimo won't invoke it as a justification? Guido Tagliabosco could have stopped them all, I still believe that.'

'Ah, my fault there,' said Edward glumly.

'That's by the way. No doubt he'll marry Cristina at last, so something good has come out of this. These days they are never out of each other's company. And never in anybody else's.'

'Do you miss them, Edward?' Anna bluntly asked.

'Yes. Because they don't need me any more. Though when they did it used to make me cross.' He laughed. 'I speak as if it had happened years ago.'

'Yesterday they were in the garden at Falconara, when I was over there to see Malagoli about buying hay, and they looked as if they didn't recognize either of us. It wasn't that they had suddenly decided to put us in our places – Malagoli was Guido's father's bailiff and manages the estate like a Richelieu or a Mazarin – it was only that they didn't see us, we weren't there for them.'

'Who can tell what they see now?' said Edward, with a pang of sadness. 'It is another territory they inhabit altogether.'

Anna looked once at Basevi and once at him, and he knew, as one morbidly nervous of overstaying his welcome, that it was time to leave. At the door she gave him a kiss, saying: 'Come to us tomorrow night. We love to see you, you know.'

For the briefest of moments he looked back into the house, so different in its simplicity from anything with which he was familiar, and felt once more that stranger's desire to belong which never truly left him.

'Come on,' said Basevi, 'I'll walk up as far as the villa with you.'

As they moved on in the darkness, Edward said:–

'There are still two things you must tell me. Why did he never speak to her before? He knew where she was, and we must presume he paid for something at least, and that it wasn't all Signora Lupo's money. Yet it seems he never even saw her as a grown girl until she arrived here in April. Why?'

'You must ask the Lupo. And don't forget the promise he made to his father. All sorts of things were conditional upon that. What's the second question?'

'Why did he marry my aunt, if not to make her miserable? She knows something has been going on, you may depend on it. There was collusion between my uncle and the Marchesa to take her off to the hills.'

'She guesses that?'

'Daniele, she is as desperate, after her own fashion, as he is. If she could buy a love-philtre to put in his coffee she would do it, or any such fiddle-faddle.' Edward stood still for a moment. 'I used to think she was a nuisance, a mere copy of my mother, with all her crotchets and none of her wit and liveliness.'

'We're all very fond of the Countess,' said Basevi, 'I thought you knew that. We shouldn't . . . we'd be sorry if anything happened to her.'

'What will?'

Basevi chuckled cynically. 'Nothing. And that is the trouble, no?'

A light burned in the hall, indicating that the servants were still up.

'I suppose I could come in and start giving Matteo his orders for shutting up the house on Thursday, but better a lazy steward than a bad husband. It seems odd that we should be off so soon after Anna has made everything down there so snug and trim. Goodness knows how she'll take to the palace. Does she frighten you less these days?'

'You'll never believe I wasn't frightened by her, will you? She thinks I look sickly and need caring for. Mariclò, on the other hand, says I look too healthy and that if I were dying she would find me more interesting.'

'Well, you are not to die before Saturday night and the *Foscari*. Abramo says the tenor Fraschini is first rate, and the prima donna was recommended by the composer himself. It's a gala night, with a procession from the palace and that sort of thing, and your uncle will be dressed in his chamberlain's uniform, and the Duchess has asked your aunt to wait on her in the box during the performance. So you'll be alone the whole evening, unless you care to join Massimo and the swell mob in the pit. But I expect you'd rather be with a certain sister of his, in that seedy old box of theirs that hasn't been done up since the Catalani was warbling Cimarosa and folk were getting a bit windy about the news from Paris.'

'And you, where will you be?'

'Oh, me, I'm always somewhere,' said Basevi, and was off like a snake into the darkness.

It was too much to expect that the Count should accompany his wife and nephew back to Villafranca in his own carriage. Edward, on that Thursday morning of prolonged *emballage* and unmaking of beds and scattering of dustsheets and retrieving at the last minute of things thought lost or left behind and the horses and grooms getting restless while the Countess's maids fussed in and out with bandboxes and shawls, looked on sardonically as his uncle, bestowing perfunctory farewells upon the household, set off at a canter as though existence depended on it.

The Countess was slower in parting because, as Edward suspected, she was afraid to leave. She had kind words to say to the *fattore* and his wife and evoked a little chorus of blessings on herself when she presented a purse with gold pieces in it to the cook's sister, recently brought to the bed of a son. As he handed his aunt to the carriage, he heard one of the maids mutter '*Poverina!*' and turned to stare at her, irritated by her sincerity.

For the first quarter of an hour Edward and his aunt said nothing to each other, except now and then to remark on the occupants of the other carriages on the road, returning, like them, to Villafranca. He looked out of the window at the countryside, stripped for harvest, brown and draggletail under the rising heat. Its lineations, in the hard, firm bars and stripes of field and causeway, ditch and path, echoed in the verticals of the serried poplars, were what he had always seen before, no less resistant to the changes which the season or the farmer might have wrought upon their surface. Yet it was with a new animation that he now confronted the familiar prospect, the very landscape, as it were, of those experiences through which he had begun to know himself.

He had long ago acknowledged, though at first without giving it a name, a feeling for the land. Those unacquainted with this fellowship which the responsive imagination creates between existence and the places which nurture it cannot, like atheists in the love of God, credit its apprehensions in others. To those whom such things inspire, however, the details of a remembered country, fat cornlands, say, to the east and bald hills to the westward, with something less blatant in woods and orchards, are what endure as a perpetual form of truth amid the obsessive variety and alienation of cities.

Edward now felt this complete inseparability between his own nature and what he saw through the carriage window. He had learned, without the least encouragement or direction beyond the promptings of his own heart, to love this landscape because of the way in which it and he had both found one another out.

'Tell me something more about Staffordshire, aunt.'

The Countess laughed good-naturedly and said:–

'Dear Ned, your grandfather would have approved of you, I think. He always used to say, when Uttoxeter and your mother and I were little, that Staffordshire might well seem the dullest county in England, but that there were rewards in paradise for those who were fond of it. And I own we thought most of it very ugly in comparison with Derbyshire, which lay just across the river. But I fancy one doesn't give very much thought to that sort of thing as a child, and, if I saw dear Horninglow or Tutbury now, I should consider them handsome enough.'

As though at an awaited signal, she launched, with unwonted enthusiasm, into a memory of the southern borders of the county which she had known when a child, and from this it was a short step to a long, rambling account of the affair of the living of Stramshall, and Mr Millichamp the incumbent, who had run away to Matlock with a Mrs Fulljames the apothecary's widow from Rugeley and of how a Miss Parkin of Coventry had named him the father of her natural child.

'All of which,' said the Countess, ending her narrative as artlessly as she began it, 'goes to show, as your grandfather used to declare, that Cambridge men are not to be trusted.'

'And what happened to Mr Millichamp?'

'He was deprived, or the Bishop of Lichfield unfrocked him, I suppose, at papa's instigation. And the living was presented to a Mr Thurkettle from Christ Church, who was bald and had four daughters. When you go to England, Ned, I hope you will go to Oxford, but I wish you may not be a Papist. When your uncle Marchington, Lord Cannock that now is, was up, he said it had got very Papistical, and that all the young men at Oriel talked of nothing but rites and vestments and I don't know what else.'

Edward laughed. 'The Papists can whistle for me. I shall

189

remember our prayers together in the laundry room, and we'll have some more before I go, shall we not?'

His aunt stared musingly at him. He wondered what she knew or, rather, what she thought she knew.

'Dear Ned, will you write to your queer old aunt when you're gone?'

Embarrassed by the appeal she seemed to be making, he looked out of the window and felt the day's tiredness beginning to spread itself upon the fields as if they too were to be put away till next season. The idea came to him that Basevi was right, that nothing would ever happen to his aunt, and because of this he felt sorry for her with a sympathy it baffled him to express. He did not answer her question until they had passed the customs post at the Porta San Francesco.

The city crowded strangely upon him, a place recognized solely for having once given him a home but otherwise as foreign as ever before. As the carriage bowled along and he caught glimpses of other families emptying themselves and their belongings back inside their palaces, Edward felt the first inroads of care over the thought, never till now taken seriously, that he was bound to leave everything which the relish of possession had taught him to enjoy. Tonight he would go to the Rangoni, as a hundred times previously, but the resumption of a hallowed custom would be darkened by the knowledge that in a matter of a fortnight or so he must break with it, and by the suddenly looming question of the terms in which he was to speak of it with Mariclò.

His longing for her, that continuing experience of incompleteness which her absence created, was mixed now with a fear of wasting the time that remained between them on useless regrets. He did not want sadness to be ordained, if only because he acknowledged the grim possibility that either it would be a long time before he came back, or else that he might never return at all. Tonight he was to find out whether Mariclò also had understood this. He must simply try, he thought, not to enter that ultimate state of infirmity in which each minutest action is seen in terms of never being performed again. But it was hard to shake off the sense, as he got down from the carriage, that the journey from San Gaudenzio to Villafranca would never be repeated, and that the movement of stepping down into the

190

courtyard of the Palazzo Castelvetro was in itself an act of renunciation.

While his aunt gave directions to her maid and the footmen unstrapped the trunks, Edward glanced up for a moment to the windows at the further end of the courtyard and saw above them, as if newly placed there, the marble medallion of Evaristo Castelvetro, the curls of his periwig frothing like sea-foam, the field-marshal's baton and the folds of his lace stock looking as though they would bear him away, and an air of contemptuous roguishness in the everlasting gaze of his horse-nosed face. Evaristo Castelvetro, the son of Count Flaminio Castelvetro, nicknamed Sprecasoldi because he had frittered away his patrimony in cards and wagers, Evaristo Castelvetro, who had ridden with Morosini into the Peloponnese against the Turks and been made governor of the island of Santa Maura at the age of twenty-four, and who commanded a wing of the Austrian army at Prince Eugene's daring attack upon Cremona, who had been his master the Duke of Villafranca's plenipotentiary to the Most Serene Republic of Venice, where his picture had been drawn by Trevisani in martial costume with a background of fleeing Janissaries and he had married the noble lady Chiara Foscarini, daughter of the Provveditore of Sebenico, and returned to Villafranca to build his family's palace anew and set a fine façade of the best Istrian stone on the church of the Servites, Evaristo Castelvetro who corresponded with the Abbate Conti and the learned Scipione Maffei and to whom the poet Paolo Rolli of Todi had dedicated an epistle 'Chi della tromba bellica il suono &c', who had been admitted a member of the Roman Arcadia under the pseudonym of Leocadio Eleutheropolitano, who had presented bundles of brown Greek manuscripts from the monasteries of the Morea to the Collegio di San Carlo, who had composed *Torrismondo Re dei Gepidi* and *Il Magnanimo Disfatto*, lyric dramas put into music by the ingenious maestro Antonio Lotti of Saint Mark's in Venice and given with great applause at the San Fantin theatre during the carnival season, and who had himself written six sonatas for the transverse flute with a bass, which Edward had found in a heap of oblong folios in a musty corner of the library – this Evaristo Castelvetro was someone he felt suddenly ready to emulate or even to become, and at whom, in the desperation of the minute, he looked steadfastly, as if the pair of them had just challenged each other to combat.

He looked at Evaristo again that evening, when, after supper, he was setting forth for the Rangoni. The Countess, to his relief, pleaded a headache, and he could walk, as he had wished, alone through the streets to the Piani d'Ungheria. When, in taking his plate away at table, Annibale had asked him whether he wanted the carriage and he had said no, a look had come into the man's face whose implications Edward appreciated at once. It meant that, whereas in anyone else such a refusal would have been considered an undignified eccentricity, in Edward it merited respect.

The square of night revealed above the rooftops of the palace still had that polish on it which the declining summer insistently left behind. Even at this hour the servants were busy carrying things here and there within the house, and, according to custom on the first evening of the family's return to the city, they had placed lighted tapers in all the windows as an earnest of the life renewed. Edward, having guessed nothing of this, stood entranced by the beauty of the effect, as the tiny points of flame sparkled and quivered against the darkened bulk of the palace. As he stood, he felt someone near him, and saw his uncle looking at him from the shadow of the gateway. The Count came closer, like a dog for company.

'Do you like this?' he said. 'It reminds me of when I was a child. I never cared to go into the country even then. I remember what a waste of time I thought it; I think it so still. The one source of pleasure for me was to come back and see the palace lit up with *moccoli* as it is now. It always seemed to justify the *villeggiatura* as nothing else did, and I'm glad we keep up the custom. I hope you . . . I mean to say, would you keep it up if you lived in Villafranca?'

'Yes, of course, uncle. How did it begin?'

'You are a fine boy, Edward,' said the Count, ignoring his question. 'I wonder, did my disclosure to Cristina alarm you? I would not have alarmed you for all the world.'

'You were wrong to tell her,' answered Edward fearlessly. In the gleam of a torch stuck in a bracket on the wall, his uncle's face looked grey and moribund, as though all resource had exhausted itself. He longed to ask the reason for everything that had happened in the barn, but knew that the Count would probably not give him the answer.

'I think certain things become clear, don't you? It is a question, simply, of telling others what we know.' The Count, in saying this, turned and, placing his hands on Edward's shoulders, gave him a little cold kiss on the forehead. In the degree of embarrassment which overcame him, Edward was forcibly reminded of his aunt, feeling that she would have done exactly the same, and was not altogether surprised by the resemblance. Puzzled, nevertheless, by the gesture's implications, he said:–

'Shall you go to the Rangoni tonight, uncle?'

'No,' the Count replied wearily, 'there is always too much music there, and I seldom was very fond of it, you know. Though I shall have to keep awake at the opera.'

Withdrawing once more into himself, he stood back and looked at Edward as though he had created him. Then, with something like a sigh of contentment, he walked off into the house.

Casting the encounter from his mind, Edward set out on his solitary ramble towards the Piani d'Ungheria. The town was as he remembered it at such a time, almost void of life until the noise and glitter of the Via Emilia, loud with the clash of carriages, its arcades choked with evening strollers. Up and down the streets were other taper-lit palaces, where, through the open windows of the upper floors, floated the sound of those glad to have shaken off the *villeggiatura* for another year and got back again to the companionable huddle of the city.

When he came into the Piani d'Ungheria he paused, with an instinctive piety towards earlier associations. It was here that he had stood, months ago, alien and afraid, gazing up at where he supposed Cristina sat watching him, and hoping always that she might come to the window at last. The great oval lay empty, hollow and grim as ever, the Plains of Hungary, named for a sister of King Matthias Corvinus who had come all the way from Buda to marry one of the Dukes, but said to be much older and to have eaten up within its ragged girdle of houses the masonry of a Roman amphitheatre, whose four gates still marked its entrances.

He looked towards the theatre at its eastern end, where the sounds of the band rehearsing could be clearly heard and where a party of workmen was busy, even at this late hour, manoeuvring the pasteboard arches of mediaeval Venice through the doors which gave onto the stage. Facing it, though apparently at an immeasurable distance, stood the Rangoni palace, its gaunt loftiness sporting illumination like a grudging smile. All the windows onto the square had been flung open, and the noise of the company, interwoven with the sounds of someone singing Donizetti to the harp, drifted from the balconies. Above everything, Edward caught the gusty laughter of the Rangoni, edged with its invariable defiance. Stepping into the middle of the paved plain upon which he was now the only thing that moved, he felt the sweetness of the night wind against his face. He stared up again towards the palace and said softly to himself:–

'Italy.'

21

THEY HAD TALKED of little else but Guido and Cristina. Watching them both moving, with a laborious separateness, among the crush of guests, Edward found it easy enough to accept Mariclò's theory that this mutual distance was merely a ruse to suggest that their position still lay unaltered. He believed her when she told him that Cristina had twice refused to see the Count, on his calling at Scarabello, and that it was with a kind of sullen penitence that Signora Lupo, in those last days in the country, accompanied Cristina to Falconara, but, if the servants' tales were true, spent most of her time there alone.

Something, surely, had changed. The vague, detached quality of their response to those around them was patently a polite rebuttal of any attempt to follow them into the territory they had sequestered for themselves. They were to be left alone, enfolded within that novelty of understanding to which the crisis of the moment had introduced them. What was more, their practice of deception, even to those who guessed at it, was to be acknowledged as something graceful and appropriate. Perhaps Edward and Mariclò envied them, but only because such new dispensations of feeling were so incalculable.

'They'll marry soon enough now, I suppose,' Edward said, looking sidelong at Mariclò, who was staring out of the window and swinging her foot to and fro against her chair.

'Can you believe it?' She turned a disingenuous glance upon him. 'With Massimo to give her away, and some exquisite old lace in her veil from Signora Lupo, and half a dozen pomaded exquisites from Bologna as Guido's groomsmen, and a trousseau from the Count?'

Edward laughed. 'You're right, it doesn't seem possible.'

She put her hands under her chin and looked so comically herself, glum, shrewd, quizzical, affronting him with her directness, that he shook his head, crying:–

'It's too bad, so it is, Mariclò.'

'What is too bad?'

'You know.'

'Isn't that what your uncle must have said to my poor aunt Rosa?'

'Maybe. I wonder if Guido ever says it to Cristina. Or whether the language they speak is something else, a sort of Hottentot or Esquimaux of the heart.'

'You're fanciful tonight.'

'It's this place which makes me so. Like one of those caves in the wilds of Scotland in the time of Ossian, where the bards sat alone in the darkness to gain the gift of prophecy.'

Thus it had been on the evening he first came here and met Cristina for the second time: the same play of light on the frescoed walls, the same crush of people, many of whom would be roundly abusing the Rangoni even as they drank their wine, and much the same kind of music, a scene of itself nothing, merely another token of that world of banter and trifling from which his apprehensions increasingly turned him away, yet also one of those sublime commonplaces to which the retrospective imagination loves to cling. He felt the weight of eventual sorrow ready to fall, and knew, by the way in which she greeted Aldegonda, who now came to sit by them, that Mariclò sensed it also.

Something of the same spirit permeated the next day, when a letter from his mother served to plunge him into further despondency. He was hardly surprised to find that, owing to some freak of his father's, they had given up all intention of remaining at Naples for the autumn and returned precipitately to Florence, 'where,' wrote Lady Augusta, 'I shall receive *le monde* as of former times, if it chooses to visit so tired a thing as I now am after our summer retreat. You will find your father much improved, but myself a little *jaded*, though there is nothing like

Florence for a *restorative*. We expect to see you within a fortnight, & you will write to us *à propos* yr journey. Yr father has asked Brini, in V. Rondinelli, to write to yr uncle Castelvetro to say that he may draw on them for such expenses as he thinks fit. We were v. pleased, *qu'on se le dise*, that everything was dealt with so fairly *à l'égard de ces choses-là*. Due, we gathered, to yr uncle's man of business (a Jew but trustworthy). Yr aunt has been v. pleased with you all summer & says she will miss you, whch we took as a gt *çompliment*. Yr suggestion that she might wish to visit us in the winter was v. well received by yr papa. *Mes adieux* &c as I am being whisked off in a trice to the Cascine. Yr always affec. mamma.'

The one consoling reflection in all this was that he would shortly go to England. Irked at missing Naples, he had no special longing for the cold finishes and decorous suavities of Tuscany. In the shadow cast by the absoluteness of his mother's letter, he wandered through the palace, doing precisely what he had determined not to do by thinking perpetually of his last moments within it. He stroked the tops of tables abstractedly, sat down on chairs as if they would fly away and looked mournfully at the portraits of his uncle's family in search of some influence to save him from exile. And, when in the library he found still open on the reading desk the volume of Muratori through which he had been browsing when, some three months ago, they had told him the carriages were ready to leave for San Gaudenzio, he felt a shudder of grief go through him. Outside in the garden the leaves had not turned and the sun still blazed on the fountain, but the library suddenly had a smell of withering and extinction which frightened him with his own solitariness.

Guido, with his customary alertness to these things, must have guessed at what he now felt, for that evening as they addressed themselves to a cold supper at Bertocchi before the opera, he was solicitous in a fashion entirely free of those dubious hopes of advantage which had so often clouded his conduct towards Edward in the past. He had seldom seemed thus charming, and his unforced affability, as he tasted this and that and commended the wine, grew warm on the theme of Verdi's music and eagerly listened to Edward's account of hearing the *Lombardi* given in French at Paris, gave him unfamiliar dimensions of purpose and resolve.

Perhaps it was only because, amid the blaze and glitter of the café, its hubbub louder with the excitement of the opera in view, he appeared endued to the element, a favourite with the young waiters, who relaxed their haughty insouciance on his behalf, and with the tables of habitués, who kept summoning him to keep them from each other's throats over Barbieri Nini's *fil di voce* or whether Malibran had ever sung at Parma.

To Edward's eye, however willing to apprehend it, there was something else. It was the first time he had been alone with Guido since the fateful afternoon at Falconara, and he had no difficulty in realizing how the other's feelings for him must be unaltered. What had changed was the way in which he chose to show them, though it was ironical that such friendliness should make itself felt when so little time remained for Edward to improve their association. Cristina's connexion with all this was not to be doubted, yet he could not believe that Guido's new discretion owed anything to her direct prompting.

'Did you see Basevi before he left?' asked Edward.

'Yes. It's a disgrace that a man like that should be a mere steward. Anywhere else a fellow of his qualities would be chief minister of state. As it is he is having to hang about with a bunch of lackeys at the theatre in his gala livery, to open the boxes.'

'Perhaps he prefers it thus,' said Edward thoughtlessly. Guido pounced on the remark.

'Galley slaves prefer their oars, no doubt, yes?'

'I've never heard you so pronouncedly democratic. Not about your own steward, anyway.'

'Malagoli will do very well, but he is hardly of the *genus* Basevi. Your uncle's got a diamond there.' Without noticeably lowering his voice, in the justifiable assumption that the tinta-marre of crowded tables and clatter from the kitchen made it impossible to overhear any but the loudest conversation, Guido suddenly announced:–

'I spoke to him last night. Your uncle. It must have been just after you left for the Rangoni. I'd hoped to take you up on my way, but I wanted to see him too.' He emptied some more wine into Edward's glass. 'I think he is probably quite mad at last. Cristina thinks so definitely. He has frightened her very much, and that's not easily forgiven. Who cares if he is her father? Does anyone? Do you?'

'Yes,' acknowledged Edward, 'but only because of my aunt. I wish I could carry her to Florence and convince her of being happy there without him, but it won't answer.'

'We'll take care of your aunt. She was kind to me once, you know, when I was sad a year or two back and had nobody to talk to. I never told you that. You know, by the by, that they have persuaded him to join them. I tried to warn him, begged him at least to see how matters lay with the new Pope and the King of Sardinia. He was good enough to say that my arguments might have worked with him a month ago, but his feelings had now undergone such a change as to render such warnings useless. But he thanked me for my patriotic advice.' Guido's eyebrows lifted ironically as he sipped his wine. 'I wasn't quite so obtuse as to ask him what they intended to do. Nandino Taccoli is sitting over there with his brother – perhaps I could ask them.'

'Guido, you . . .'

'What's the point of keeping silent? Why do you think I can speak of it now without lowering my voice? There's nothing left for us to do: it's a game they've decided to play among themselves. Let's be off.'

As they crossed the square, Guido slipped an arm through Edward's. It was done with no superadded assumption, though he could not but feel that the gesture was designed to test something.

'The cathedral,' said Guido as they passed it, 'which Cristina won't go into any more, because she says it makes her afraid. I think . . .'

He stared at Edward with an expression of exultant confidence.

'What do you think, Guido?'

'I think I am going to try to persuade Cristina not to be afraid. Has anybody told you what excellent Italian you speak?'

'Italians are such dreadful liars that I never believe that sort of thing.'

'Each of us believes that our own nation is the only one with any sincerity. I'll tell you one thing you must understand, Edward.' The great black points of Guido's eyes shone with that barely suppressed excitement which now seemed the principal source of his animation. Disengaging his arm, he said:–

'She has told me I must forgive you.'

They had talked about it then. Edward was staggered. That he had never supposed there was anything to forgive was beside the point. What arrested him was the proof thus offered of their community of understanding.

'So there, I forgive you. Absolutely. But that doesn't mean you won't always be, in whatever sense, the dearest thing in the world to me.'

Edward looked at him narrowly. 'She understands that?'

'Let's say . . . oh . . . that she knew it from the first.'

The crowds were gathered along the streets where the Duke's procession was to pass, and the Piani d'Ungheria, by the time they reached it, had seldom been so lively. That good-humoured patience which prevails on such occasions meant that each new carriage arriving before the theatre steps was greeted by the throng with a burst of indulgent enthusiasm, implying that, though it wasn't the equipage they desired, it was welcome nonetheless for swelling the scene so agreeably. Guido having parted from him to conduct the Rangoni from the palace, Edward was left to enter the theatre on his own and to wander about exploring corridors and staircases in that state of limited solitude which he most enjoyed.

There was that feeling everywhere of inhabited, familiar opulence and triumphant sociability which Italian theatres, by their very nature, so incomparably convey. The faces of those roaming in search of word-books or lost companions bore a general expression of intentness on enjoyment which lightened Edward's spirits even more. The smell of candle-grease and the acrid reek of the dusty silk upholstery of his uncle's box, the apotheosized flight of Music and Poetry across the ceiling and the sight of the orchestra's tapers being lit as they shuffled in and began tuning, made him still further determined to like what he heard without regard to its quality.

He wasn't remotely bored. There were the ushers to watch, bustling about with chairs and cushions in the ducal *loge*, whose mirrors and gilding and white and blue festoons made it like a grotto beneath the ocean, and the Austrian officers in the pit, strolling up and down and vulnerably tweaking their moustachioes, and the faces peering from the gallery rail of those who, as Basevi said, understood the lyric drama best and so must be packed out of everybody's reach.

It was Basevi himself who now came into the box, clad in knee breeches and a resplendent dress coat in the Castelvetro livery of green with gold facings.

'Thanks,' he said, on receiving Edward's compliment, 'my father-in-law made it, as you may suppose. But I don't think I like so many people to see my calves.'

'You haven't got any to speak of, so there is nothing to look at.'

'Anna said I should stuff them with rags, as flunkeys do. Or rather, she said it was just like me not to have done so. Shall you be happy here on your own?'

'Just at present I am not unhappy. It flatters my vanity to be looked at as the solitary tenant. When does the Duke arrive?'

'After he has had his supper and signed a few more death warrants and gaol sentences. They say he likes doing that best after dinner. The *maschere* will go about and ring the bells to clear the staircases and that is the sign that he is expected. Then you wait in your box and stand up when he enters.'

'And shall you hear any of the music?'

'Yes, but your uncle has given me leave to come to the next performance so that Anna may hear it besides.'

'Is he always so considerate?'

'There's generally some reason behind it. Tonight, however, I am to wait on you.'

Edward, protesting, told him what Guido had said earlier.

'Well, you and he had better relish the irony. He is in high glee this evening, isn't he? He said I looked like an ostrich when I saw him just now. And look, *à propos*, he has brought her and Lupo into his box. Now all Villafranca knows they are to marry. And there, for the love of God, are the Rangoni, like the Amazons drawn up for battle!'

Edward stood up, placed his hands on the velvet coping of the box and leaned forward to eye the spectacle. Others too must have been arrested by it, for a sort of hush ran through the gathering audience as the four Rangoni, squired by Massimo, held themselves for a moment upright and motionless before sinking very slowly onto their chairs. Each was dressed with a grandly tragic simplicity, furiously at odds with the carefully studied *tenues* around them. Even Cristina and Signora Lupo, three boxes along, were put in the shade by such a masterstroke, which gave an unwonted loftiness to the old Marchesa's frail,

201

sickly figure, lent to her daughter the grim dignity of Pasta or Rachel, and made Aldegonda and Maria Clotilde into things numinous and incontestable.

A noise like a barely audible sigh ran among the boxes. Everyone knew the Rangoni hadn't a penny to their name, that music and politics had ruined them concurrently, some must have guessed that Cristina's munificence had paid for their dresses, and a few that Massimo was once again bent upon compromising the safety of his family, if not their honour. Yet, in such a moment of declaration, they might have commanded anything and been obeyed.

'I doubt we shall see better than that this evening,' said Basevi. 'Listen, there are the bells going. I'll leave you now. Watch Massimo if you've time – he'll be down in the pit with his friends, talking about waistcoat buttons – and tell me who he's with. That's if you are not watching the stage. Oh, and there isn't a ballet, because the Duke and Duchess don't like it.'

He bowed and was gone before Edward had time to exclaim. Of a sudden the entire audience rose to its feet as the ducal family entered the mirrored grotto, accompanied by a shoal of courtiers and ladies-in-waiting, among whom were the Count and Countess Castelvetro. There was a pause, during which the Duke received the polite applause of the house, without, as it seemed, very much satisfaction. Perhaps he understood how much of his arrival's effectiveness had been improperly but successfully appropriated by the earlier appearance of the Rangoni. In the general atmosphere of gelid good manners, he sat down, and after a word or two to the Count, standing at his right shoulder, he gestured for the performance to begin.

Whether it was the Duke's presence or simply because the singers' artistry was so consistently to be admired, the audience showed a greater deference to the stage than is often the case on such occasions, and little by little the force of the music succeeded in taking hold, in all its noisy, brazen-faced impatience. At the end of the duet between Lucrezia and the Doge, Edward wanted to clap, but custom ordained silence throughout, even if some hardy soul in the gallery should bawl a '*bravi!*' The last time anyone had clapped on a gala evening, so Guido told him, was in 1831 at a performance of the *Italiana in Algeri* at the patriotic chorus of 'Pronti abbiamo e ferri e mani', and everybody knew what had happened then. The drop-curtain fell and he was about to go round to the Rangoni when the door opened and Guido and Cristina came in.

His surprise was not so much at the swiftness of their arrival as at the way in which the pair of them seemed as if wanting him to understand something without their having to articulate it for themselves. He saw it in their complicity, that infinite mutual knowingness which their eyes, lips and hands expressed, and in a sort of mildly patronizing benevolence which they assumed towards him.

'We have come to take you to see the Marchesa,' announced Cristina, after a few moments of chat between them on the matter of historical truth in the scenes and costumes. It struck Edward somehow that they had come with no such purpose, but the really important thing they meant him to know still eluded him. As he followed them from the box into the corridor, he noticed a little glance, as though of expectation, pass between them, and felt suddenly vulnerable to the novelty of their closeness to one another.

There was no possibility, in any case, of doing more than mouthing a few commonplaces to the Rangoni, enthroned amid a press of visitors, over whose shoulders he managed to exchange a look of amused hopelessness with Mariclò. Yet the image of Guido and Cristina must inevitably return during the prison scene which followed. The strains of 'Speranza dolce ancora' were those which dated an epoch of his existence. He was a different being in the moment he had first heard those notes at Villafranca, and he wondered whether he were not about to be changed yet again on hearing it now. As the desperate joy of husband and wife surged up once more, banishing the vulgar noise of the revellers across the lagoon, he felt the music's physical influence upon him, endowing him with a greatness beyond himself. Shortly he would know Guido and Cristina's secret, even if by then it were too late.

So utterly preoccupied was he with the scene of Jacopo's banishment that when it ended he did not hear Basevi come in.

'Edward, your uncle is waiting for you,' he said, and ushered him hurriedly out to where the Count, in his chamberlain's scarlet, stood pacing fretfully up and down the corridor.

'His Highness has asked to see you. You are to come at once to his box.'

'Me, uncle?'

'He had the kindness to ask what you were doing alone, and the Duchess remembered you from the Congedo. It is a great honour, we must not keep them waiting.'

Through a little door which Basevi opened, they went down the private staircase to the lobby of the ducal box. This, unlike Cristina's odd invitation, was plainly authentic, and Edward started to feel embarrassed at the thought of what he should find to say to the Duke and Duchess beyond those trifling exchanges they had made previously. Matters were not improved by the mob of courtiers cramming the lobby, who all turned to stare at him with a decided air of making him feel his own unworthiness as he was ushered into the presence.

The Duke and Duchess and their children sat at one end of the hot little room, beside a table laid with *friandises* and glasses of wine. They looked no different now than when he had seen them last. The Duchess was a touch more gristly about the neck, the two princesses were still sad and unhusbanded, and the youngest prince retained that sensual podginess Edward had noticed earlier. As for the older boy, his eyes were as unseeing as ever, but his countenance had contracted that familiar quality of scornful discontent which is born of examining the world on its capacity for fulfilling ideals beyond all power of achievement. He was of the sort which knows everybody's family quarterings, complains endlessly of *mésalliances*, talks of little else but ancestry and whose devotions are such as to embarrass the Pope. He stared at Edward resentfully as the latter advanced to make his bow.

'Ah, yes,' said the Duchess, 'this is the boy, we remember him.'

'Indeed, hmmm, a good boy. And loyal to his family, we hear – rare enough in these times, what?' said the Duke. He was in a good humour at last. 'Do you understand Latin?'

Edward replied that he did, whereupon, for no very obvious reason, the Duke and Duchess burst out laughing and there was a sycophantic titter among the courtiers.

'He will be telling us next that he reads the Bible in Greek, like a true heretic!' spluttered the Duke and, still shaking with laughter, he pointed a plump finger at Edward. 'We shall have to get Stappler to . . . what is it he calls it? . . . ask after you,' at which the courtiers rocked. Then, taking a tiny strip of paper from under one of the glasses on the table, he waved it at him.

'They threw this, you know, through the carriage window at me in the Piazza d'Armi. Can't make head or tail of it. Forgotten most of the Latin I ever knew. Stappler doesn't know either.'

'And your uncle couldn't make it out,' said the Duchess with a reproachful toss of the head. 'We asked him.'

'So we sent for you. Your aunt says you're a scholar.'

Edward glanced at the Countess, quailing beside the buffet as if she had betrayed him, and wished more than ever that she were coming with him to Florence. Then the Duke handed him the note. His bowels turned to water, for he knew at once what it was. There was a silence while he pretended to con it over and dared not look at his uncle.

'It's something about . . . about a Roman emperor – Domitian – and a blush. But I can't tell you exactly. Some of the words are hard to translate. I think it means that he had a red face. And that they were afraid.'

The boy with the sad eyes gazed at him in relentless incredulity, ready, no doubt, to add him to the vast catalogue of human inadequacy his experience had already compiled. The Duke laughed again, not unkindly.

'Well, well, we shall spare you this once. But it's not good for a young man to spend so much time in libraries. Reading, on the whole, is to be discouraged. A bad influence, hey?' He nodded to the Count, as a signal that the interview was at an end, and Edward bowed once more. As they left the lobby, he caught a glimpse of his aunt looking anxiously after him, as though she had not wanted him to go. It was how he would always remember her.

No words passed between him and the Count as to the quotation from Tacitus. Since its significance was plain, discussion seemed pointless. Nevertheless Edward sat through the closing act of the opera in a subdued restlessness, only half enjoying the tenor's scene of farewell and old Foscari's final annihilation under the weight of Loredano's vengeance, and distracted even more when, raking the pit with his glance, he found that Massimo was nowhere to be seen.

The Countess had warned him of what was supposed to happen when the piece came to an end. 'A little applause is permitted, you know, in charity to the singers. Nobody may leave the theatre before the Duke and Duchess, but it is expected that as many as possible will go down and be ready to acclaim them as they leave. Sometimes they have a kind word or two to say to people as they pass through the crowd. And then, when they have been seen off, the carriages are called and everybody goes home.'

It had already been decided that Edward was to take Mariclò and Aldegonda back across the square, but he was resolved first of all to find out what had happened to Massimo. Edging his way past those already crowding onto the staircases, he managed to insinuate himself into the doorway of the box as the Rangoni's moth-eaten steward, the Caleb Balderstone of Villafranca, tottered out backwards, bowing to the Marchesa. The latter, still feasting upon her triumph, smiled affably at Edward, to whom her mother-in-law gave an indulgent nod.

'Massimo is not here then?' he asked abruptly.

Aldegonda threw back her head crossly. 'Massimo went off a century ago, with Leopoldo Sighinolfi and the rest. He said he thought Barbieri Nini sang like a frog and the tenor was like a butcher.'

'And that the band was coarse,' added Mariclò, 'which was simply an excuse for them all to adjourn to Bertocchi for cards.'

The Marchesa, looking decidedly as though she had kept her own council on the matter, gave him a sybilline smile. 'So you may take the girls with you, Edward, and we shall come down when there is room on the stairs.'

Which means, thought he, that you're deuced if you'll deign to come down and honour the Duke. Still anxious as to Massimo's intentions, Edward contrived to let Aldegonda pass in front of him so that he could whisper with Mariclò. As they moved out onto the staircase landing, he muttered:–

'And did your brother really go to Bertocchi?'

'Massimo?'

'Yes.'

'What else would he have done? They all go off and drink toasts to the singers and quarrel and swear and protest eternal friendship and make holes in each other's purses. And tomorrow

206

Massimo will be in a foul temper all day and shouting at mamma.'

'It would hardly be the first time he wasn't telling the truth, Mariclò,' insisted Edward.

'I can't think why it should be so important to you.'

'It isn't,' he answered peevishly, 'I just want to know where he is, that is all.'

She bit her lip and drew away, frowning, to talk to Aldegonda as they turned the bend of the stair.

Still angry and nervous, he followed them under the arch into the oval foyer, itself like a theatre, where the ushers were already pressing back the crowd. As the three obediently assumed a station near the doors onto the square, before which the Duke's carriage was drawn up with the mounted escort of the bodyguard beside it, Guido and Cristina walked together into the open space across which the Serene Highnesses were soon to pass. Their appearance at this juncture was as telling as the Rangoni's had been formerly, and, since there was already much curiosity as to their suddenly aroused enthusiasm for one another, the same momentary stillness held everyone as the pair moved through the throng.

To Edward it was a brief hallucination. That sense of abandoning the narrow sensual limits of the immediate world, which had so strongly pervaded their encounter in the barn at San Gaudenzio, was sharpened here by a sudden effulgence playing about them both. For a second or two they seemed not to tread the earth. Then, as if it had been a mere afterthought, they turned at the entrance to the porch and stood facing Edward and the girls.

At that moment a hubbub on the stairs proclaimed the Duke's approach. The ushers threw back their arms, contriving simultaneously to bow as the party came forward beneath the arch, pausing to acknowledge the *evviva*'s and handclapping. It had been, after all, a happy evening and the Duke's glistening, lacteal countenance wore a contented smile, and, as the people in the square outside began to cheer in anticipation, even the Duchess's mouth became expressive of pleasure.

Edward could not remember afterwards how it was that Count Castelvetro had somehow managed to get himself in front of the ducal family so as to confront them in their progress towards the

207

porch. But he would not forget the expression of horrified amazement in the Countess's face as she saw what her husband was preparing to do.

For it was the operation of a moment for him to draw, from inside his dress coat, a pistol and to level it before him. In the instant's hesitation which paralysed the onlookers, Edward saw his aunt hurl herself towards the Count, and in that same instant he heard the pistol go off. As though someone had cut the ropes which sustained her, the Countess staggered and fell. Elbowing the usher aside, Edward ran to where she lay. The ball had pierced her neck and she was dead.

In an agony of fear and astonishment, he turned to face his uncle. The Count stood muttering and shaking his head, unresisting of those who now pinioned him and took away his pistol. Edward looked again at his murdered aunt on the checkered marble of the floor, with the blood on her gala dress, and felt Mariclò's arms come round him as he shook with soundless misery.

The Duke's face had resumed its air of satisfaction. He looked about him with an extraordinary certainty. He was alive, and the blow intended for him had gone wild. Those who cared to notice the face of the elder of the two princes must have perceived its unwonted animation. It was the liveliness, not of joy or even of sheer relief, but of a withering contempt for failure.

22

THE COUNT WAS never brought to trial. As they carried him away from the theatre, he drew a phial of poison from his pocket and drank it off. Presumably he had intended to kill himself after murdering the Duke, and his guards made no particular effort to prevent him from doing so now.

Custom, ironical to the last, ordained that he and the Countess be buried side by side in the vault of the Servite oratory adjoining the palace. Horrible as the idea must have seemed to Edward, he made no attempt to interfere, but the disposition of the ceremony was left to Basevi, who, at Guido's insistence, took charge of everything. There was, accordingly, a chilly little funeral, attended by members of the household and those bold enough to proclaim their friendship for the Count and Countess, in which the priest's evident eagerness to get to the end as quickly as possible seemed wholly pardonable to Edward.

The Countess's heretical practices having been known only to her husband, she was buried as a Roman Catholic; it was her nephew who made sure that she quitted the world as a Protestant. An hour or so before the coffin was sealed, Edward, having given orders that he was to be left alone with his aunt's body, began, with a terrible doggedness, to read over the burial service from his prayer book. Now and then, as he read, he looked down at her, youthful and composed in death, and a furious determination swept over him that the Papists should not have her. Yet the enactment of such a rite was not simply the

209

operation of a remorseful piety: what counted was what had always counted between them both, the secrecy in the doing of it, so that when he finished at last with the 'amen' it was with something approaching disappointment, as though the essence of this final act lay in the arrival of an intruder. For a single moment, recalling that afternoon in the laundry room at San Gaudenzio, he missed his uncle.

Villafranca, having ostentatiously stayed away from the Count's funeral, was nevertheless officious in condoling with Edward on the loss of the Countess. It was discovered, as invariably succeeds, that she had been much loved and sincerely mourned, and all sorts of virtues were suddenly attributed to her. A long train of carriages appeared in the Corso Canalchiaro, from whose occupants Edward passively accepted the tokens of regret. He could honestly do no more, since their praises made her a stranger to him, but he wondered, even as he listened, whether his acquiescence, however unavoidable, were not a breach of faith.

If anything, the task of sorting through her effects was easier. Without either talent or originality of impulse, she had left nothing by which she might be remembered. The few poor treasures of her courtship, a bundle of letters from the Count and his portrait in miniature, were to be set aside, but little else remained to act as a memorial to the febrile longings which had governed her existence. It was a matter of a mere two hours to accomplish the business, in the little sitting room where she used to drink tea, and when he had received the keys of her jewel boxes and given charge of her bonnets and gowns to her maid and ordered her cluster of novels and annuals to be put in the library, there was not much else to do beyond inspecting, without surprise, what the escritoire and bureau contained.

After that there was nothing left for him to attend to, apart from arranging with Basevi which of her things were to be returned to his parents. He had written to Florence the briefest possible account of her death, taking care to inform his parents of the exact date and time of the funeral, but sending it late enough for them to be absolved of any sense that they might have been present had they wished. His father, feeling well enough to write, chided him gently for the delay, but urged him to see everything settled and to bring away any necessary papers.

Something characteristic in this amused Edward. There was not, it seemed, much difference between him and Basevi now. He was yet again the steward, the executor, the intermediary, charged with powers that others were too idle or scrupulous to exercise for themselves and rewarded for his gravity and tact with extraordinary burdens of expectation. Surprised as he was, pleased even, by the sudden confidence placed in him by his parents, he saw it in the end as nothing more than the repetition of a design he had already begun to take for granted.

Thus when, some three or four days before his departure, Basevi came dressed as usual in his mourning livery to see him, it felt to Edward, for the briefest of moments, as though he saw his own reflection. In the steward's eyes there was a momentous heaviness. He paused in the doorway, gazing at Edward as if to confirm some already formed impression, then advanced half-way across the room, apparently determined to keep a respectful distance between them. When Edward tried to rise, he said in an almost offended tone:–

'Please be seated. I have something important to tell you.'

'What? What's happened?'

'It's better that you know now. Then if you like you can refuse. You don't have to choose at once, but they told me I might inform you of it. They'll write, of course.'

'Who?'

'Well, the lawyers. Your uncle's will was read yesterday, by the notary Ceccarini, with Guido Tagliabosco and old Count Molza, who is everyone's trustee because he is so famously incorruptible.'

Some sort of pleasure lit Basevi's face as he halted momentarily, the pleasure deriving from the power of doing good which invests all bearers of fortunate news.

'There is a portion for Cristina, naturally, and provision was made for your poor aunt, but it is the law that a nobleman must name a male heir. Therefore you are the Count's sole inheritor. Everything here, at San Gaundenzio and elsewhere, belongs to you.'

'But you said yourself that the estates were forfeit through my uncle's guilt.'

'The Duke has declined to claim them.' Basevi laughed. 'It

211

seems you impressed him besides. Anyway, you can't have them till you are of age, they are in my keeping for the moment.'

'And if I don't want them?'

'But you must, there's nobody else, it has not even been thought of.'

As Edward nervelessly sat there, affronted by the truth of his unsolicited destiny, Basevi solemnly knelt down, took his hand and said: 'Now I must be loyal to you, as formerly to him,' but Edward, drawing back, cried:–

'No, no, I can't bear this, it's preposterous and insulting, leave off at once, Daniele, don't mock me like this!'

Suddenly Basevi fell back on his elbows on the floor and started laughing. Edward began to laugh as well in the infection of a hopeless amusement.

'You're right, it's funny, ah, dear God, it's funny. He was a humorist to the end, was my uncle. But must I, truly?'

Basevi picked himself up. 'You are afraid to take what he has given you, aren't you?'

'Yes.'

'Why?'

'Because of the Count. He still frightens me, even after death. And because of my aunt. There are practical considerations too.'

'Ah, hang practical considerations, Edward, burn them! I never thought to hear you talk so! Practical considerations are for those who do not trust to the truth of their own feelings, a hypocrisy of the worst kind. Now it's you who insult me.'

'Forgive me, Daniele, I meant only . . .'

Basevi shook his head inexorably. 'You meant none of those things.'

There was a silence between them. Edward felt a sudden spurt of anger at his friend for contriving, with his invariable success, to force a confession from him.

'What is it that you want me to admit?' he asked coldly.

'That it is neither a dead uncle nor a dead aunt who frightens you, but we who are alive in Villafranca, Anna and I, Mariclò Rangoni, Cristina Bentivoglio, Guido Tagliabosco and everyone else from the courtiers in the Duke's antechamber to the boy who sweeps the stableyard at San Gaudenzio, we are the ones you truly fear, isn't it so?'

'No!'

'Don't lie to me! You are made the heir to the finest estates between Bologna and Parma, with a town house, a villa, two castles in the mountains and revenues fat enough to make Baron Rothschild envious, the way is cleared for you to take up your inheritance, yet you spurn it with some fatuous put-off or other. Why?'

Edward faced him, silent and furious in his vulnerability, shaken besides at seeing Basevi so passionate.

'Because you had much rather we didn't love you, that Villafranca were not disposed to take you to itself, that you should bowl off to smart, smug Florence and forget about – what is it your guides call it? you told me once – ah yes, "a sombre city", "a place of little account". That's it, in the end, no?'

The square of carpet on which they stood was like a plain where they had drawn up for combat. Edward shrugged, vanquished as he knew he must be by Basevi's sheer assiduity, and the two embraced one another.

'You know it's true, what's the point of pursuing it?'

'To get you to acknowledge it, you fool. Take Villafranca, it's the best thing you have.'

Edward, still moored to Basevi's arms, muttered:–

'Maybe. I don't know. I have to go away from it for a while. I mean, from Italy altogether. Otherwise, if you can understand, I should never come back.'

'You may trust me to keep everything as it should be until you return. I am your steward now.'

'No you're not, let us have none of that, unless it be for form's sake.' Edward drew away and stood for some time staring into the courtyard below. Then he asked:–

'Would you think me calculating if I begged the privilege of not choosing just now?'

'You are not forced by any means. All this will be here for you if you wish to take it. We shall wait for you like a prince in exile.'

Edward went on looking into the courtyard. 'What if the exile should last for ever?'

'That is not for me to answer, is it?' rejoined Basevi. 'Now I've to ride out to San Gaudenzio with Guido Tagliabosco and put everything in order there.'

Turning to face him as he stood at the door, Edward, laughing, said:–

'You have that abstracted look which means that you are not going to tell me precisely what is required to be put in order, for the present at least.'

'Don't say that you blame me for that.'

'No, I love your dishonesties, because of the way they always seem calculated to save other people from themselves. Go, go to Guido and do whatever it is you have to do, then come back and tell me about it.'

Once more Basevi stared at him and nodded in some sort of private satisfaction.

'Do you recall,' he asked, 'when we first spoke together, we were both enthusiastic for *The Bride of Lammermoor*? Well, you know, I am Caleb Balderstone after all.'

So far from being lost upon Edward, the irony of his position grew yet more obvious. That wish he had never frankly acknowledged, while knowing it always to be there, the longing to be a part of all he saw and felt in Villafranca, was now granted with an unctuous, superabundant completeness. When he looked up again at Evaristo Castelvetro, the stone portrait seemed almost to mock him. 'You wanted this: now you shall get it, by the cartload.' Thus he was afraid, as Basevi had rightly guessed, not so much of future vicissitudes which might stop him legitimately claiming what was his to take, as of the responsibility of confronting his own suppressed desire. Indulgence appeared, as he felt sure it would not have done to anyone else, a wickedness, or, if not that, a source of misery rather than pleasure.

He was not sure, what was more, that the way of life he had witnessed during these summer months especially attracted him. Until now he had been tied, of necessity, to his parents' quest for diversion and society, yet his shrewdness had already made him alert, not merely to the endless possibilities of boredom preying upon such an existence, but to its essential springs besides. He had witnessed, until he needed no further enlightening as to its consequences, the corrosive operation of idleness upon the ungoverned impulse, the nourishment it afforded to egoism, licentiousness and cruelty and the grotesque sanctification it proposed of the most trifling ceremonies and exercises as a counter to the emptiness which it embraced, like some sinister dead lake filling the cup of a volcano.

Thinking of what he now knew of matters astir in Italy,

Edward had begun, in his more jaundiced flashes of appraisal, to wonder whether much of what was supposed to be happening were not owing, in some part, to a crude wish to supplant the vacancy with action. The plot against the Duke which had destroyed his aunt was perhaps, as he had early suspected, no more or less than this, the subversion of an overwhelming dullness and boredom whose hold upon Villafranca was stronger than any legitimate sovereign with a Croat garrison and the assurances of Metternich to stiffen resolve.

In the end he was no better than Massimo Rangoni, as young and certainly richer, even without the dubious advantage of his uncle's gift. If this did not mean that Massimo was the less despised, the causes of what he had so rashly and zealously set on foot were more readily perceived. Edward imagined that his condescension, in the light of this, must seem suitably galling, but felt no qualms where Massimo was concerned.

It was to the Rangoni, indeed, that he went next day, determined, in justice to Mariclò's regard for him, to tell her honestly of what had happened. Beside what she had to announce, however, his new fortunes appeared singularly commonplace.

Having led him to the gallery and shut the door, she came towards him with the air of somebody whose desire to shake off the burden of a secret is qualified with a fear of the dangers intrinsic to its revelation.

'Edward,' she said, 'you mustn't be angry, with me or with them. Cristina and Guido.'

He laughed. 'I'm not. In fact at present they rather please me.'

She smiled and he took her hands. 'You see, they went into the country early this morning. At least Cristina did. Guido, I think, went last night. Not that it matters.'

'And she married him,' said Edward banteringly.

'Yes . . . I . . . how did you know?'

Her question staggered him. 'She has married Guido? Cristina?'

'This morning. In the church at Falconara. She left a letter for my mother and one for Aldegonda and me.'

'What!'

'They left at once for Bologna, it seems. Guido has a house there.' She touched his face consolingly. 'Yes, there's a letter also for you, with something from Guido in it, Cristina says. I

215

suppose no one will forgive them at first – it's like an elopement, isn't it? – but then they'll come back and be welcomed as if the Pope himself had married them and not the poor *parrocco* of Falconara with his snuff and his stammer, and all because Guido is so rich. You're not angry with them, are you?'

'No, not angry,' answered Edward truthfully. 'A little crest-fallen, even humbled, perhaps. I'd hoped, you see, to be there.'

'Ah, we'd all hoped for that. To see something we never believed would come to pass. Mamma and grandmamma, of course, are furious and vow they will never exchange one word with Signora Lupo again. It seems she and Daniele Basevi were to be the only others present at the wedding.'

Edward smiled grimly. 'Yes, he told me yesterday that he had some business to settle. This, I imagine, was it. As for Guido and Cristina, we can scarcely reproach them, can we? It's what we wanted to bring about. Yet it seems . . .'

He paused, but Mariclò caught eagerly at his meaning. 'I know what you were going to say, that it seems like a rebuke to us, as though a real wedding, with flowers and a banquet and aunts who cry and children who make themselves sick on sugared almonds, would have been a capitulation they were too proud to make.' Then she said, without the least touch of malice, but very deliberately: 'There is a great deal of pride and selfishness in both of them.'

' "Never apologize, never explain" – the creed of selfish people who are afraid to be hurt. It's as though they had conspired against us,' said Edward. 'Yes, by God, I am angry. Hurt, too, why not? Yet it's arrogance in me to imagine I deserved any better.'

'You'll forgive them.'

He laughed. 'Why? Because you think it's romantic to be flouting custom like this? Yes, yes, I'll forgive them, I love them both so.' He kissed her and felt, in the empty vastness of the gallery, peopled only with bad Rangoni portraits, the containing impermanence against which the pair of them must strive. When she said sardonically: 'Well, Guido won't lack for money at any rate,' he knew it was time to tell her.

She listened without interrupting, her long, solemn countenance unmoved, as if she had guessed what would happen.

'You refused it, I supposed.'

216

'Why?'

'Because it is what you would do. It is what I would do, for that matter. We are both too afraid of good fortune, however it should arrive.'

She turned from him, as though in sudden, acute embarrassment, squeezing her hands together. There was a silence between them which inexorably demanded him to break it.

'Do you think I ought to accept it at once?'

Mariclò did not turn. Her arms and shoulders shook with emotion.

'Don't force me to answer that,' she said. 'I can't tell you. I am afraid of losing you.'

He came and put his arms around her, pillowing his head against hers, yet even as he did so he felt dishonest, as if, with such a tenderness, he were trying to stifle her justified fears. So that she would turn to him he drew back.

'I will . . .' She halted. Her voice fell almost to a whisper. 'I will wait until you return.'

'Oh, don't promise such things, Mariclò!' he cried. 'That terrible patience of women, that is what killed my aunt, not love in the end but waiting. Don't kill yourself with constance . . .' He could not go on. Angry at the feelings he was no longer able to mask with a factitious manliness, he cried:–

'Do you think I am not afraid of losing you? I must go. Out of Italy, for a year or two.'

Seeing her there, the only absolute thing in the vaulted gloom, he did not believe hc could love anybody else.

'Where will you go?' she asked.

'To England,' said Edward.

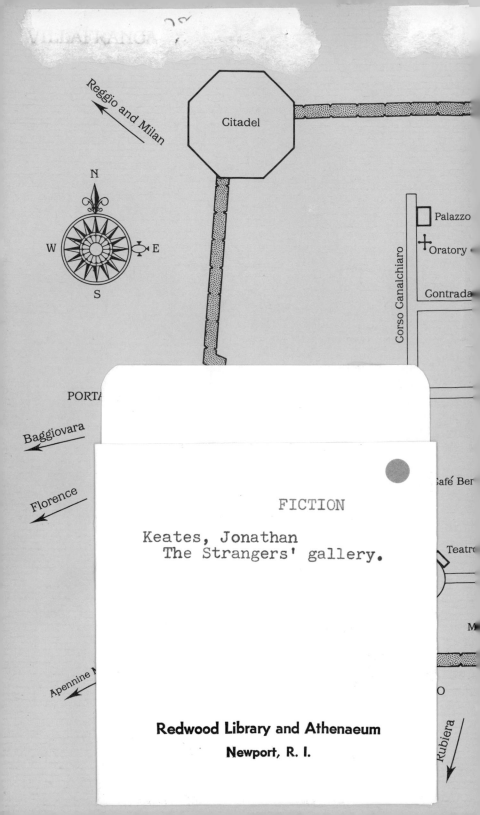